HARRY'S OUR MAN

A Novel

By

Jay O'Callahan

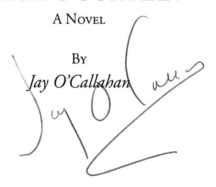

Artana Productions

For more information visit: ocallahan.com
Cover Art & Production: Tara Law
Text layout & Production: Robert B. Smyth

PUBLISHED BY:
Artana Productions
P. O. Box 1054, Marshfield, MA 02050

DEDICATION

To my parents,
Edward J. and Helen Gately O'Callahan,
who had all the style in the world.

<u>*CHAPTER 1*</u>

May 1950

H arry had an erection. "Ah, dear Holly Bush," Harry said aloud. That's what he secretly called his wife, Jillian, who slept in her own bedroom. When Harry said he had needs, Jillian said, "Grow up, Harry. We're past that." *Past that, I'm forty-one. She's forty-two.* He sat in his tiny office at Northeastern University and went back to his journal: *Semester almost over, question for next year: How can I get my students to pay attention? I mention the name George Washington and they're asleep. Next year try talking about the birth canal. This country came down a long birth canal. Maybe that will convey the struggle and get attention.* He stopped writing; it was time to go. He walked down the stairs thinking about the decision he'd made early that morning. *Could he really do it? It was impossible.* He hurried across Huntington Avenue where the traffic was heavy and saw that block away people were streaming out of the Friday afternoon Boston Symphony concert which always earned the orchestra a standing evacuation.

"Professor Hutchinson! Want a ride?" Ernie Marion called. Ernie was in his wheelchair on the other side of the street. "No thanks, Ernie."

Ernie's driver was about to push him up the ramp into the van. The back seat had been removed.

"Come on, Professor Hutchinson," Ernie called. He didn't take no for an answer. Thinking, God, Ernie is a pain, Harry crossed the street.

"Thank you Ernest."

"Ernie. Call me, Ernie, Professor. Good class today. But Washington was a creep."

Harry got in. The driver was a husky man of about forty with powerful shoulders but nothing like Ernie's whose shoulders were huge. Ernie's head was big, and he had thick eyebrows set on a prominent forehead which made his black eyes look threatening.

Ernie Marion stood out in Harry's class both because he was in a wheelchair and he looked like a gangster; he was twenty-six, a veteran, smart and tough, and the other students were afraid of him. He asked good questions and shelled peanuts during lectures.

Harry sat in the front seat of the van. "Why don't you like Washington?" Harry asked.

"He's not human," Ernie said, lighting a cigarette.

"I'll give you a piece by Alexander Hamilton. Hamilton was critical of everybody and had little respect for the Revolutionary Army."

"So?"

"In just a few sentences Hamilton describes Washington rallying the army from what could have been a disaster to beating the British. You can almost smell the battle and see Washington everywhere directing it. No one else could have won that battle. You saw plenty of action in the war. Don't you admire a good general?"

"He's unreal."

"Babe Ruth's unreal. The power of myth." Harry changed the subject. "So Ernie, you live down the Farm?"

"Yeah. We're the pigs at the bottom of Pill Hill."

"Why do you say that?"

"Because that's the way Hill people see us. Maybe not you but the richies on Pill Hill."

"Ernie, you're too smart for that kind of generalization."

"It's true."

Harry knew it was but wouldn't say so. His great decision made at dawn that morning seemed absurd. They rode in silence down Huntington Avenue, and Harry wished he'd taken the trolley; he would have gotten off at the Museum of Fine Arts and wandered in silence in the Egyptian section. He'd like to be a mummy. Silent. His morning brainstorm was madness.

When they arrived at the tenement section called the Farm, Ernie surprised Harry by inviting him in.

"I didn't sleep last night, Ernie. Another time."

"Come on, Professor. See how the other half lives."

"All right. Five minutes."

The street was lined with triple-deckers, most of them run-down; Ernie's gray triple-decker was halfway down Pearl Street, which Harry thought was no pearl of a street; there wouldn't be a real pearl in any of these flats. There were a few shiny Fords and Chevrolets parked on both sides of the street, and he wondered why they didn't buy houses instead of cars. The mailboxes were nailed to the front of the houses; two of the mailboxes were rusted and had no tops. There was no number on Ernie's front door.

"Eight-fifteen," Ernie said to the driver who hadn't said a word.

Ernie wheeled himself up the ramp into a narrow dark hall that smelled of cigarette smoke, cooked cabbage and turpentine. There was a bicycle at the back of the dark hall, and Harry wondered if it had once been Ernie's.

Ernie unlocked a door leading straight into a living room with a pale orange rug, a table filled with magazines and books, and a

3

small, chipped upright piano. The couch was green and sagging, the curtains white and clean. There was a small vase of lily of the valley on the windowsill.

"Come on in the kitchen."

The late afternoon sun lit up the kitchen table, which was covered with a red and black checkered oilcloth. The kitchen was uncluttered so Ernie could wheel himself around. Ernie reheated the morning coffee and poured a cup for Harry. There was a paperback of Stendhal's, *The Red and the Black*, on the kitchen table.

"Are you reading Stendhal, Ernie?"

"My mother is," Ernie said. There was an edge to his voice. "Straight A's in high school. She dropped out senior year to marry my old man. A drunk. Died when I was two."

"She must be very smart," Harry said.

"Yeah. She was going to go to college. Teach French some day. My grandmother's French Canadian. Now my mother's working in a fucking donut shop. Milk or sugar?" Ernie asked.

"Black." Harry sat at the table. "Ernie, I can understand Washington's not being real to you, but you dislike him. How come?"

Ernie wheeled to the refrigerator and got some evaporated milk. He wheeled back saying, "Washington was an asshole. He was a fucking snob like the Pill Hill assholes. We're trash to them. Catholic trash."

"Are you Catholic, Ernie?"

"I'm not a fucking Catholic. I'm not a fucking anything. I'm just your run of the mill legless bastard." Harry was silent. Ernie went on. "It's all right to get your fucking legs cut off for your country, but if you're a fucking Catholic from the fucking Farm, you're nothing. Washington was an asshole."

"You have to admit he had courage. And brains."

"I'll admit he had slaves. Perfect father of the country."

4

Harry was glad when Ernie's mother came in. Her hair was brown and cut short, her eyes gray-blue; she was attractive and at ease. Harry was feeling awkward; his woodenness was coming over him.

"This is my history professor, Mom, Professor Hutchinson."

"What a surprise Professor Hutchinson! Let me get you some cake." She pronounced cake with a hard "A." A working class "A." Amelia Adams on Pill Hill would almost sing the word cake; it would pass through Amelia's nose and come out as a cake that the Queen of England might enjoy.

"I will not protest," Harry said, feeling like an ass. I will not protest. What about thank you? Why can't I just relax?

"I'll be right back," Ernie said and wheeled himself off. Good, Harry thought, maybe he'll get locked in the bathroom for a year or two.

"Ernie is wild about your course," she said. "Call me Meg, by the way."

"What do you mean wild?"

"He loves it, Professor Hutchinson."

"Call me Harry."

"He won't say it, but your course is what's kept him at Northeastern."

"I never would have guessed. This cake is delicious."

"Have more."

"Thank you, I will. Your kitchen reminds me of my aunt's kitchen in Wyoming." Harry cut a big piece of the Boston cream pie; it was the best he'd had in years. He was tired of being polite and he might even take the last piece. Meg got Harry a glass of milk, and Harry surprised himself by going on about his aunt.

"She had a big cabin in a little town in Wyoming," Harry said. "Her kitchen was full of sunlight and very simple, a table and a few chairs. When I'd visit, we'd have coffee and cake and she'd tell stories. When I was a teenager, she encouraged me to do whatever I wanted. This kitchen has the same feel." As long as

Ernie isn't here, he could have added. He was surprised by Meg's intelligence and annoyed to realize he'd expected a gum-chewing woman like Gladys, the ten-cent store cashier in the village.

Ernie came back into the kitchen as Harry was saying, "I was thinking of my aunt this morning."

"Any special reason?" Meg asked. She was sharp.

Harry reddened and said he'd better be going. "You can have the last piece of cake if you tell us," Meg said.

"I was thinking about running for Congress," Harry said reddening still more. "My aunt would have liked it because it's nuts. No money, no track record, no organization, I'm forty-one and I'm pretty much what's called a socialist."

"Believe it or not," Ernie said, "we know what a socialist is, but thanks for enlightening us."

"It would be exciting," Meg said. She looked as if she could hit Ernie over the head.

"I wouldn't have a chance," Harry said.

"Then why run?" Ernie asked.

Harry was ready to explode but ate cake instead. He drank all the milk, wiped his mouth and continued. "To say things that won't be said by anybody else because they'd lose if they said them. We're too frightened of the Communists. We're mesmerized by the atomic bomb. We're not paying attention to anything at home. Ernie, you lost both legs. That's incredibly awful, but if your skin were another color it would be worse. When we don't pay attention to our own people it makes the whole country a fraud."

Harry was so wound up his fist came down on the table. His cake bounced. Chagrined, he said, "You see why I wouldn't win."

"They'd run you off Pill Hill," Ernie said.

"They may," Harry said realizing the conversation was getting out of hand; he was sounding as if he would run.

6

"No one will vote for you down here," Ernie said. "They'll think you're what's called a Commie. You know what a Commie is don't you?"

"I better get going."

"No," Meg said. "Ernie, will you shut up!" She turned to Harry. "I want to hear more about your aunt."

"She escaped from the family," Harry said. Harry seldom talked about his family but he liked Meg. "She hated the narrowness of Boston. She left college after four months and went out West with almost no money. My grandfather was furious and wouldn't give her a penny. She cooked at a ranch for years, then got her own small ranch."

When Harry left, Meg walked him out to the sidewalk.

"If you run, I'll be glad to stuff envelopes or whatever. I'm sure Ernie will too."

"Thanks for your encouragement," Harry said.

"Ernie's got a chip on his shoulder as big as this house, but he admires you. You've changed his life. He's a good worker. I'm sure he'd help."

CHAPTER 2

"I hope you run," Meg called after Harry. He turned, waved and walked on angry he'd told them; angry his aunt was dead; angry at Ernie. I'd make a fool of myself. Who'd vote for me? Jillian wouldn't. It was the truth and made him laugh. He walked along River Avenue, the river was hidden by tall green reeds, as a shiny red Chevrolet drove by, its chrome gleaming; its dual exhausts roared then quieted as it turned into the Farm. Save your money, Harry thought, and buy a house instead of a new car. I'm such a snob. Buy a house. I've got a house, a museum, and I'm a museum piece. Why not get a shiny car? These guys down in the Farm were all in the war. They come back and they're cops and firemen; they buy a shiny car and I'm upset. The armchair socialist. Some platform. Don't buy shiny cars, take elocution lessons, buy a house and put the peanut butter away.

He thought of Aunt Harriet everyday. He asked her once how she escaped. "Well, I just had to," she said smiling. He could see her in dungarees, work shirt and cowboy boots; small, strong as a wire, her hair pulled back in a bun, her face wrinkled and tanned, and a red bandana around her neck. She loved horses and taught Harry to ride. "Sometimes you have to leave to arrive," she said, laughing one day. "I sing a lot now," she said. "I had to leave Boston to sing." She thought that was hilarious.

When he'd go on tirades about religion, politics and anything else, she'd listen carefully and then say, "Now sing me another song. You don't want to get too stuck on the same tune." Harry crossed the street and sat on a bench looking at the reeds; he saw a black boot lying upside down and he shuddered and remembered standing in the vast rubble of Hiroshima two months after the bomb had been dropped.

He'd stayed in Hiroshima for three weeks writing articles for the armed forces newspaper, *Stars and Stripes*, and there was one moment he'd never forget. Harry had gone to a clinic to see what survivors looked like. A young Japanese woman had stumbled, and Harry had instinctively touched her shoulder to steady her, and the woman began to bleed; they couldn't stop the bleeding. The bomb had changed something inside her and thousands of others, and they couldn't be touched; thousands and thousands were bleeding to death; he remembered families sitting around waiting to die. Seventy thousand had died in the blast, but it was a slow death for many who lived. "Slow Death", he called an article. The army killed all of the articles and made him sign a release that he wouldn't publish them. When he returned home, he told Aunt Harriet about Hiroshima and didn't talk of it again.

He walked up Forceps Avenue, so called because of the women's hospital at the bottom of the hill. "Hi Reggie," Harry said to a skinny ten-year-old boy.

"Hi, Professor," Reggie said.

"Reggie," Reggie's father, the General, said appearing at the doorway. "Your room is untidy!"

The boy quivered but had the spunk to say to Harry, "The four o'clock inspection."

"I mean now, Mister," the General barked. Harry knew Reggie was allergic to everything imaginable and wondered if allergies came from childhood trauma.

When he reached the tennis court, Florence Beam was whaling the hell out of the ball. Florence and Edie Lawrence were playing, a rare event. Mutt and Jeff. Edie Lawrence, slim as a willow tree; Florence Beam, round as a Russian bear and twice as loud. Edie swung gracefully and missed the ball by several feet.

"My game," Florence boomed. "Harry! What have you taught the bus drivers' children today?"

"Florence, you're just mad the British lost the revolution."

"Edie tells me you're writing a book on Washington."

"I am indeed."

"Don't make him a socialist, Harry. Edie, don't stand there like an egret. Serve the ball."

Harry walked on. Old John of the Tennis Court was in the barn next to the court putting away the roller. John, referred to in the neighborhood as Old John of the Tennis Court, was of an indeterminate age, maybe in his fifties or sixties. He looked as if he'd been thrown against a wall as a baby and had grown up mangled. His mouth was where his cheek should be, his face was a mass of scars and grafted skin, and his ears were small as shriveled apricots; his nose was mashed and his eyebrows gone. He had a sprinkle of dark hair on his head; a purple scar ran from his forehead straight back as if parting his skull. He wore rumpled gray work trousers and a shirt of the same color.

Three years ago in the Boylston Street subway station in Boston, Harry had heard a primal sound; it was a deformed man trying to tell Harry that a book had fallen from his briefcase. Harry thanked the man and they got talking because Harry had the patience to try to understand his speech. It was quickly clear the man's mind was all right and his name was John. They'd sat on a bench and let a slew of subway cars go by. Harry asked John if he'd been in the war.

"Wa wa on," John repeated several times. John had been in World War I. He and several men in his unit had been trapped in a burning house in a French village. A German tank had come right through the wall; the floor had partly given way, and John was trapped between the tank and burning timbers. His shoulders and arms had been very badly burned; his hands and chest had been crushed and his face torn apart.

Maybe it was because of the woman in Hiroshima, but before they parted that day, Harry mentioned that the tennis court in his neighborhood was looking for a caretaker. John got the job, and now during the spring, summer and early fall when Harry strolled the neighborhood he'd go by and say hello.

"Greetings, John," Harry said, going into the clean, cool, dark barn which still smelled of horses that had been stabled there years ago. The barn had been used as a garage until five years back when the Pill Hill neighborhood tennis court association bought it. John got two wooden chairs and put them down on the stone floor.

"Thanks, John."

The trunk of his body was twisted and John limped when he walked.

"I think I'll run for Congress, John."

"Unnnn."

"I have no money and no chance, but I think I could get on the ballot. It would be a chance to say what I think."

"Goo."

"You've been through a hell of a lot, John. You inspire me."

Old John grunted a laugh.

"I think I could get my daughter involved. And my wife, Jillian, knows everybody."

John nodded and Harry stood up. "I'm kidding myself, John. It's crazy."

"Nooooo," John said. It was an awful sound. "You wan raaa. Raa. Ah help. Ah fo enva lops."

"Thanks, John, but I'd better stick to teaching."

John stood up and Harry shook his hand, which meant two fingers. The others were curled and looked useless.

CHAPTER 3

Ten-year-old Oak McCormick, big eared, skinny, wearing thick tortoise shell glasses, was sitting on a branch up in the maple tree on the sidewalk opposite the Hutchinsons' house. Oak had run home through the village, up Pill Hill, dropped his books at home, got a peanut butter sandwich, stuffed it in his pocket and run out to climb the tree. The bark was hard; it scratched and didn't yield. No wonder no one climbed it. The first branch was fifteen or twenty feet up so it was a long, slow shinny. Shinny. He liked the word. Shinny. He wondered if it was in the dictionary. Oak's mother loved language which Oak thought absurd except for some words like shinny. There were other words he liked: Bolster Bar. O Henry's candy bar. Cheerios. Kemosabe. Silver bullet. Relevo. "Get off your feet," which his father said when he thought a request was ridiculous. His mother said her father's favorite was, "It's all made of wax." Grandfather thought life was all made of wax. "In the beginning was the Word." What did that mean? The nuns had some favorites. "You're a bold, bold boy." They didn't like anyone being bold. Adam and Eve and the tree. It was good there were trees in the Garden of Eden. Adam and Eve probably shinnied up the trees. It would be hard to shinny naked. Imagine just being born grown up. They could speak right away. They had no parents. What did they do all day? Sat in trees and talked. Halfway up Oak rested and inspected the scratches on the inside of his arms. At any one time he had at least eight scratches, bruises, cuts and bumps.

On his Sitting Branch he felt like a sailor in the mast watching the narrow black waters of Hillage Avenue. His peanut butter sandwich was mashed, but it didn't matter; it was dry but tasted good. His mother refused to buy Peter Pan peanut butter, saying she wouldn't pay more for advertising, so they bought peanut butter which came in heavy cardboard containers and glued his mouth together. A sloop was coming! Old Miss Hatcher, sullen, forbidding in her black coat, came sailing down with her pug dog in tow. The pug's nose was too occupied to smell Oak's scent and Miss Hatcher sailed under Oak's mast unaware she was being spied on by Oak, the pirate.

Professor Hutchinson came around the corner from Pill Hill and tipped his hat to the elderly Miss Hatcher who gave a frozen nod and passed on by. Slender Professor Hutchinson held a fat brown briefcase in his right hand.

"Oak," Professor Hutchinson called up to Oak when he'd reached the tree. "What did you study today?"

"Benedict Arnold."

"Sad story."

"Yes," Oak said. "He was a traitor."

"The saddest part," Harry said, "was that Arnold didn't tell his wife. She was left to face the music alone. He never even told her he was thinking of going over to the British."

Oak felt bad for Benedict Arnold. He imagined Arnold sitting in England with his children saying to his daughters, "When you girls get married you'll be rid of my name. You boys will have to change yours." But he'd left his wife and family. Oak imagined Benedict Arnold standing alone in heaven or maybe hell.

"Arnold entertained a lot, Oak. Got into money troubles. But the crucial thing was he felt he wasn't getting the proper respect, so he made a big mistake. It's one of the things I want to write about, Oak."

"Making a mistake?" Oak asked.

"Yes. Making a mistake so big you can't recover."

The thought upset Oak. He let it fly on by, but it circled around and sat inside him. Although just ten, the idea of making a mistake that ruined life frightened Oak. His friend Chickie, who lived down on the Farm, bought a pint of whiskey last year when he was in the fourth grade and got so drunk out in back of the Five and Ten he couldn't even crawl. Maybe Chickie's life was going to be ruined.

Professor Hutchinson took out his Chesterfield cigarettes, lit one and put the match in his pocket.

"Someday Oak, I'd like to write about mistakes whole countries make but that would be a book so big I don't know if I could do it. Germany made a terrible mistake. Horrible. Japan too. Italy. We did too. We built the country with slave labor, and we stole the land from the Indians. Oops, I'm off on my tirade."

"I like it," Oak said still thinking that if he made some awful mistake his life would be ruined. What would the mistake be? Some terrible sin like murder or stealing? Then he'd go to jail and everyone would be ashamed of him.

"We work too hard, Oak. That's a mistake. It's in the cultural genes. I'd like to take the time to climb a tree but I don't. I'll tell you a secret but keep it under your hat. I'm thinking of running for Congress."

"Whoa!"

"I haven't any chance of getting beyond the primary but it might be fun. I'd run on the Do Less ticket but dress it up in fancy terms. My theory is if we weren't so busy we'd take better care of one another."

"I'll work for you."

"You might be the only one."

"Mom thinks I might be governor."

"Would you want to?"

"Maybe."

"One more secret, Oak. Please keep this to yourself."

"I will."

"When I was little, I mean about four, my dad would send me to the closet. I'd sit there for hours and hours. We lived in Cambridge in a house as big as yours. My dad would get mad because I'd break something or spill something. The closet was on the first floor and they'd forget about me. I made friends with the coats and boots and the dark. That's like history, Oak. I made a mistake by breaking a glass. Then my dad made a mistake forgetting I was in the closet. Then I'd get mad and break something else and he'd get mad and on and on. That's history. The question is, can we ever break the cycle? This must sound like nonsense."

Oak shook his head. He was hot and startled because he too had been put in a closet, and the memory came back like fire. The memory caused him to have a vague, uncomfortable sense that something was wrong with him. The woman who took care of them, while his mother was teaching, put him there. Oak had shut the door on the memory, and Professor Hutchinson opened it.

"Mum's the word, Oak. I'll decide for sure next week."

"I won't tell."

Professor Hutchinson winked and walked across the street.

CHAPTER 4

Harry changed into old clothes and went out to the back-yard where he put a log on the sawhorse and began to work. He waved hello to Oak who was still up in the tree. The rhythm of sawing freed him to think about his decision to run. It would be the wildest thing he'd ever done, and he could still back out.

Last night around six he'd gone for his usual walk around the neighborhood, a neighborhood of big old Victorian houses built close together called Pill Hill because it was filled with doctors who practiced in nearby Boston hospitals. The curved, sloping, sprawling streets resembled the arms of a sleeping octopus.

"Professor Hutchinson! I have news!" It was Lydia Cobb, now a junior at Wilmont Academy. Harry crossed the street to say hello as Lydia came leaping down her lawn, spun in the air then bowed low so her long, red hair fell over her head.

"Bravo!" Harry said. "My favorite dancer. Where have you been hiding lately?"

"Playing piano," Lydia laughed, placing the back of her hand on her forehead in a mock dramatic gesture. She was tall for a dancer, broad shouldered and unable to keep still, but he could see the graceful woman she'd become. Her brown eyes shone; her face was not beautiful but it was striking.

In the eighth grade Lydia had danced in a school play and announced to her family she'd be a dancer. Her father Dan Cobb, an eye surgeon, thought dancing frivolous, and instead of just letting it be he laid down the law: Lydia was to give up dancing, take up the piano, get good grades, go to Wellesley, marry well and have children.

"I have the lead in the school play!" she said to Harry as her hands danced in the air. "And," she said lowering her voice like Marlene Dietrich, "I dance." Then she squealed, jumped up and began twirling before him. She spread out her arms and he applauded.

"That's great, Lydia. I'll come if I may."

"In May it is," she laughed. "The sixteenth of May, the very month of May, so you may."

"May I?"

"You may take two giant steps."

"And," Harry said, "may I say it's great your father has relented." He had put his foot in it. Lydia's body changed. She hunched over, her shoulders curved inwards and her eyes were full of fear.

"No! Daddy doesn't know. He's going to be in Chicago. Please don't tell him. Please!" She looked like a terrified little girl.

"Of course I won't," Harry said. "You'll be great."

Lydia recovered enough to say, "I will reserve a seat for you. Front row. I'll put a rose on it." She ran up the lawn, her long red hair trailing behind her.

Harry continued on, rounding the corner and walking up to The Green, a tear shaped public green around which big old houses sat. He stopped to say hello to an old friend, Amelia Adams, who was watering her tulips. "Harry," she said turning, "how's your book on Washington?" She was a small woman of precise gestures; her nose and mouth were well shaped, her eyes were warm, her voice so nasal her words had an underwater sound. "My publisher's putting the pressure on," Harry said, "he's given me six months."

"You'll do it, Harry. What was Washington really like?"

"He was like me, brave and fearless."

"Amelia! Amelia!" Eliot Adams, her husband, was standing behind the screen door calling in his high, angry voice. It sounded as if he were calling the dog.

"I'd better run," she said. Yes, Harry thought, run or he'll put you in the kennel for a month. Why did she marry that son of a bitch? Harry and Eliot had been at odds since they were at Exeter together. Eliot, two years ahead of Harry, had been tennis team captain, and when Harry tried to get on the team, Eliot blacklisted him for no apparent reason. But it was only two years ago they had become real enemies. At a meeting of the Pill Hill Association, Eliot, balding, red bearded and attractive in tweed jacket and pipe, had made a little speech. He'd contracted tuberculosis during the war, and it had made his voice sound high and strained. "I've discovered," Eliot began, "that a Doctor Levenson is looking at the old Curtis house at the end of Hillage Avenue. I suggest that the Association buy the house and sell it to someone of our own class." Harry had jumped up, but Val McCormick was quicker. Val, an unusually handsome man with black hair, a red mustache, and a square, rugged, intelligent face, had a rich voice and spoke with authority. "If there's any more of this kind of nonsense, I will put my house up for sale in the morning." Harry followed saying, "I was the one who told Sol Levenson about the Curtis house and will do all I can to help him." The Levensons had moved in and Eliot Adams had not spoken to Harry since.

After his aborted talk with Amelia Adams, Harry went home and settled for tuna in a can for supper. If he left so much as a crumb on the table Jillian had a fit, and he didn't want to fight tonight. He corrected papers until eight when the phone rang. It was Edie Lawrence who lived around the corner.

"Harry, Lydia Cobb has been sent to the hospital. She slit her wrists."

"What happened? I talked to her only a couple of hours ago. She was all excited about dancing in a play."

"Evidently Dan came home furious because he'd heard she was in the play. He told Lydia she would not be in it. Can you come over?"

"Of course." Harry hurried down Hillage Avenue, took a right on Pill Hill, walked by the McCormicks' great house and crossed the street to the Lawrences. Lydia Cobb babysat for the Lawrences and was very close to Edie Lawrence. Their sausage dog, Bones, yapped as Harry went up the path. Edie was in the kitchen with her daughters, Carrie and Monica, who were both in grade school. "Finish your homework," Edie said, "and I'll come up." She poured two S.S. Pierce bourbons, and she and Harry went into the living room, a comfortable room of old stuffed chairs, a single couch and a great red rug; its one exotic touch was a five-foot arrow above the fireplace. Edie Lawrence was angular, her hair long, her face sculptured and her voice low. She had been Summa Cum Laude in Ancient Greek at Wellesley and was incapable of uttering a cliché.

"All is misery," she said sitting on the chair by the couch. "One feels helpless," she said. "Lydia is so full of life, and I have seen it draining out of her. She bends over that piano year after year, and I know she hates it."

The phone rang; when Edie went out into the hall to get it, Bones wiggled his bottom and leaped up onto the couch, sitting in Harry's lap. Harry got up so Bones flopped to the floor. Edie returned saying, "That was Craig." Edie's husband, though only forty-three, was in charge of the Canton Hospital in the Jamaica Plain section of Boston. "He says Lydia will be fine, but Dan Cobb is there saying he's going to send Lydia to Creighton Mental Hospital."

"God Damn!" Harry said his fist slamming into the pillow. "Why the hell can't he just let her dance? Jesus Christ!"

"Why are the young unhappy?" Edie said. Three of the children on Pill Hill had tried to take their lives. Harry and Edie talked for an hour. Harry left feeling guilty because he was no one to judge Dan Cobb. Four years ago Harry's daughter, Ophelia, had swallowed a bottle of sleeping pills; luckily Harry had found her in time. Now Ophelia was a junior at Vassar and may well have been on the moon for all they saw her.

Harry walked down to the village; he crossed the broad street and went into a working class bar that smelled of stale peanuts. It was dark and had a long bar with only a few men sitting on the stools. "Bourbon and water," Harry said to the bartender.

"Professor Hutchinson?" Harry turned and saw Ernie Marion in his wheelchair. Ernie was drunk. "Slumming, Professor? Buy you a drink?"

Harry sat down at Ernie's table. The cigarette smoke reminded Harry of a bar he'd been in in Paris at the end of the war.

"You're a good fuckin' professor," Ernie said. Drunk and sloppy. What the hell am I doing here, Harry thought.

"This is Professor Hutchinson," Ernie announced to the air. "He knows more about George fuckin' Washington than any man alive."

Harry drank half his bourbon. "I hope you're studying for the exam, Ernie."

"Fuckin' A. You're the only fuckin' reason I'm staying in that fuckin' college. If it weren't for you, all I'd do is drink and get laid. I can still get laid." The bartender came around and said, "Ernie, you've had enough."

"Get me a boilermaker, asshole."

"I'm gonna throw your ass out of here," the bartender said.

"Ernie," Harry said. "Do me a favor, I need some air. Let's take a walk."

"Walk? I'm not Jesus fucking Christ. I've got no fucking legs."
Ernie finished his drink and slammed the glass down. "Let's get
the fuck out of here." It was dark now. Ernie and Harry crossed
the wide street to the firehouse where several firemen stood outside talking.

"Hi, Ernie," one of the firemen yelled. Ernie wheeled himself
toward the tenement section and Harry walked along side into
the Farm's series of three-story wooden tenements.

"I got a pint," Ernie said. "I'm goin' down to the river and get
drunk with Hi Ho." He wheeled on leaving Harry in the darkness.

Harry couldn't sleep. At four-thirty, he dressed, crept down
the stairs of the museum, which he called his house, made a cup
of tea and sat on the porch stairs. He was glad he'd put a sweater
on because the May night had a touch of fall about it; the moon
was white and round and he caught the scent of lily of the valley. The old fashioned street lanterns were electrified but looked
like gas lights; they softened the night and revealed the greenness
of the new maple leaves on the tree Oak climbed. All these kids
growing up in a new world. Why are they trying to kill themselves? Ophelia, Lydia, Johnny Green.

Harry had the urge to go up and get into bed with Jillian. He
felt he'd made the same mistake as Washington; he failed to marry the woman he loved. Sophomore year at Boston University
Harry had fallen in love with eighteen-year old Betsy McNabb
who worked in the cafeteria. She was peppery, daring and bright.
Harry's mother told him that Betsy would be unhappy with him.
"It's just not fair to her, Harry. If you feel deeply about her, let
her marry someone of her own class." Harry continued to date
Betsy, but she grew distant and broke off the relationship. Last
year, at a family gathering when his mother drank too much, he
found out that his mother had gone to Betsy and told her insanity ran in the family. She had given Betsy some money to help
her get over her grief.

Harry walked down to the bottom of Pill Hill, crossed the wide street and went into the White Tower, an all night breakfast and hamburg spot which had a gleaming white plastic facade. The tower part looked like a square white chimney.

There was light in the sky. The clock on the wall read five. A new day. "Black coffee and eggs over easy with toast," Harry said. It was very small. Three booths. Eight stools at the counter.

A skinny boy with black hair was eating breakfast at the counter and two policemen were drinking coffee and reading the newspaper at the end of the counter. "Hey, Chickie," one of the policemen said to the boy. "Doin' your paper route?"

"Two," Chickie said. The boy looked about ten and although he had a nice smile he seemed old.

The cops went back to their coffee. The cook, a skinny man with a white shirt under his stained white apron, said, "Williams hit a home run last night in the seventh."

"He's a crybaby," one of the cops said. "Can't even tip his hat."

"Yeah?" the cook said. "He fought in the war didn't he? Lost his best years in the war. If he hits home runs, that's enough. Fuck tippin' his hat." It was said in a cheerful spirit.

Harry's eggs were done just right, a light white film over the yoke. The coffee revived him. He started thinking of Washington's unsuccessful suit for Sally Fairfax. Had Washington been passionately in love? When he'd told Jillian he was writing a chapter about their relationship, Jillian had said, "Don't put the father of the country in bed with a tart."

"She was not a tart," Harry had said. "She was a very respectable widow."

"Harry, Washington is Washington. Keep him in the dining room with Martha."

The cook picked up the Record American newspaper, "Some congressman says we otta' drop the A bomb on Russia and China. Wipe 'em out and start over. He's right."

"Kill millions of civilians?" Harry asked.

The cook looked at Harry more closely. "Commies want to take over the world. If we wait, it's gonna' be millions of us."

Harry shook his head. "Russia was bled dry during the war. Stalin won't start anything."

"My brother was a boxer," the cook said. "He always said, if you have a punch use it."

"Wouldn't that be like Pearl Harbor?"

"I don't trust Stalin," the cook said. Several men came in, and the cook got busy.

When Harry left the White Tower, the sky was filling with pink orange light; he crossed the street and sat for over an hour on the bench by the side of the fire station thinking about Lydia and Ophelia and Jillian and the bomb, and when the fire station tower clock rang six, he said, "I'm going to run for Congress." He laughed because he was startled to hear himself say it, let alone think it. "I'm going to run for Congress."

He knew the idea was absurd. He'd never run for anything in his life and knew himself well enough to know that he was a good lecturer but an awkward public speaker. Not only was he not chummy, he was exactly what he rebelled against; he was a stiff man from an old New England family. He didn't have the common touch but he could speak his mind, and it would be a perfect way to get his family together. Jillian could run the campaign; Ophelia might come home for the summer and help.

People will ask why I'm running. I don't know. I'm running because Lydia's bending over her piano and slitting her wrists because she's terrified of her father. We're terrified of Stalin. Maybe he's our father. Our Father who art in Russia. We don't talk about the bomb. It's the golden calf. Who am I? Moses? He laughed.

He was elated walking up Pill Hill. His father would be furious with him but his father always was. When Harry was eighteen he told his father he didn't believe in God.

"You're a fool, Harry." They were in his father's study, his inner sanctum. "This is a phase and you'll outgrow it, but you may never outgrow being a fool."

Harry had stood there staring at his father. He, eighteen, wanting his father to talk to him as a fellow human being, was suddenly burning with an anger he'd never known before. Red faced and shaking, Harry had said to his father, "I've decided not to go to Harvard. I'm going to Boston University."

"Harvard has accepted you, and you will go. If you don't, you'll pay your own way through college."

Harry went to Boston University and worked as a waiter to pay his tuition. His father didn't speak to Harry until his senior year when Harry got engaged to Jillian and then it was only to say, "Marrying Jillian is the first intelligent thing you've ever done." Harry's father expected Harry to go into banking, but he got a PhD in American History at Boston University and began to teach at Northeastern.

"I'm running for Congress," Harry said to himself as he strode over Pill Hill. Harry went home, showered, dressed and had tea in the immaculate kitchen. Jillian came down looking brisk. "I'm going riding this morning, Harry. Oh, I'm having supper with the Collingworths."

"I have some news, Jillian."

"I'm afraid I have to run. Can it wait?"

"No, this is important."

"Well, go ahead. What is this earth shaking event?"

"I'm running for Congress."

"You're not serious."

"I am."

"Harry, finish your book and don't be absurd."

"It would be great if you could run the campaign or just give me some advice. Maybe Ophelia will help. Someone needs to talk about where we're headed as a nation."

"Harry, I've got to run."

"For Congress?"

"Harry, the truth is you'd make a terrible candidate. We'll talk about it later. Don't tell anyone about it until we've talked," she said and left.

Harry was sweating. He'd been sawing logs for an hour. He wiped the sweat away and saw Oak was still in the tree across the street. "Oak," Harry called, "it's not a secret anymore. I'm running for Congress."

CHAPTER 5

While Harry was eyeing the large bottle of Wildroot Cream oil on the glass shelf by the mirror, Louis the barber was cutting his sparse hair. The Wildroot label, which showed a picture of a man with thick black hair, reminded Harry of his father's being exasperated when he was a boy. "God, Harry, you haven't got my brains or drive. You haven't even got my hair. What have you got?"

The radio was turned low but Louis turned it up when Bobby Doerr hit a double; then he turned it low again.

"The Red Sox are opera," Louis said clipping away. "The Yankees are not opera. They always win. The Sox are tragedy. That's what you need for opera."

"You should write it," Harry said, looking in the mirror at Louis's sleek black hair and long face. He looked Italian but his features were so distinct, his nose, chin and narrow head, that Louis looked as if he were a race of his own.

"I'll retire and write it," Louis grinned. "Problem is there are no women. Who wants an opera without women?"

"The heroine could cause the tragedy," Harry said. "She gets the whole team drunk before the playoff with the Yankees. Maybe that's what really happens. Sing me a little Verdi."

Louis sang the Slave Chorus from *Nabucco* until Hi Ho, the bum came in. "What do you want, Hi Ho?"

"Barbour said he'd be here at five for his haircut," Hi Ho said. Barbour was the fruit man across the street. Hi Ho wore his filthy dungarees with a dungaree jacket. Hi Ho, all six feet four of him, spent his days standing on the sidewalk outside Barbour's Fruit Market.

This was the first time Harry had heard Hi Ho speak. He had a hoarse voice ruined by drink, cigarettes and sickness but nevertheless it was a low, scratchy, pleasing voice.

"Thanks, Hi Ho," Louis said, and Hi Ho left.

"Hi Ho could have made a living singing," Louis said. "About twenty-five years ago I had a barbershop quartet, and I got Hi Ho to join. He was good."

"How old was he then?"

"Maybe twenty-five. He'd been in prison. He was going to college. His father thought Hi Ho was getting above himself, so his old man told Hi Ho he had a friend in the high school office who said Hi Ho's IQ was so low he wouldn't last a quarter in college. So Hi Ho went to work for the town. Somehow Hi Ho found out his father made the whole story up, and he went down to Denny's bar, pulled his father out onto the sidewalk and knocked the shit out of him. His father brought charges and Hi Ho spent five years in jail."

"My God. What did he do when he got out of jail?"

"Went to work in Springfield, I think. He's got a green thumb. Then he came back here and started drinking. He stayed in the barbershop quartet about two months. He could sing."

"How does he live?"

"Barbour gives him a buck if he stays sober during the day, so he stands there like a God damn totem pole. He buys a bottle of Thunderbird and gets drunk every night. Sleeps where he can. His wife lives down the Farm. She threw him out maybe fifteen years ago."

"What college was he going to go to?"

"Cornell. Least that's the story. Might have been BC, but I heard it was Cornell."

Harry and Louis grew silent. Harry sat in the chair looking across the street at the hulk of Hi Ho standing in front of Barbour's Fruit Market. It struck him that that was Hi Ho's whole life; he could have gone to Cornell.

Louis turned up the radio. Billy Goodman hit a single driving in the winning run for the Red Sox.

"They beat the Yankees," Louis said.

"Louis," Harry said, getting out of the chair. "I'm running for Congress and I want a headquarters here in the village. I haven't got much money. Any suggestions?"

"Congress. Start at the top. What about the place next door? Old Sam Wolper's hat shop. He died last month."

"I didn't know him."

"He was one of the last hat makers around. He always said if you wanted a hat, hurry because he was eight-eight." Louis showed his bright teeth. "If you don't mind the train goin' by, it might be the place. You want to look? I have the key."

"Hi, Chickie," Louis said to the black haired boy Harry had seen at the White Tower. "Get in the chair. Here's the key, Professor. You take a look."

Harry stood on the sidewalk. It was a simple storefront space with a wood-framed glass door and a storefront window looking onto the street.

Harry put the small key in but it didn't turn. Louis came out saying, "I forgot to tell you, jiggle the key to the right."

The key was worn down. Old Sam must have turned this key thousands of times. The brass doorknob was dull, the door hinges were loose and the door sagged when Harry pushed it open. He switched on the light. Three ceiling bulbs. He'd need lamps. It was a long empty room that smelled of cloth, mystery and hats. The wooden floor had give. There was a rear door leading to a bathroom and a small room. Harry liked the place. It was right in the village and it had the feel he wanted. It looked across the street to Barbour's Fruit Market and Hi Ho the Bum.

Harry closed the door, jiggled the key and went next door.

"What's the rent, Louis?"

"Sixty bucks a month."

"Too steep."

"Fifty for you. I own it."

"Forty."

"Forty-five."

"It's a deal. I'll write you a check."

Harry walked up Pill Hill feeling elated. The door had opened to his campaign. He had never done anything as wild before. Bold. I am Washington on the Delaware.

Harry Hutchinson he thought; pale, dutiful, forty-one, assistant professor is running for Congress. He walked as if he had his hinges oiled. His briefcase swung up. "This is absurd," he laughed. Frightening. Thrilling. Not too late to back out.

He walked by the Lawrences' house lost in his campaign plans not seeing Edie Lawrence digging in her garden. She called out, "One is contemplating George Washington." Bones, her sausage dog, ran to the fence yapping at Harry.

"He thinks I'm Benedict Arnold," Harry laughed. "Edie, believe it or not, I've decided to run for Congress. I've just rented a storefront for my campaign headquarters."

"One is Hephaestus, hammering one's vision into shape," she said and shook her head.

"It's clear I'm not a god," he laughed.

"One is Odysseus, setting out on a voyage."

Harry bowed. "My campaign headquarters is right beside Louis's barbershop. Even if I get four votes, it's already been worth it. I feel like a kid out of school."

"Can one help?"

"I'd love it."

Harry laughed and waved good-bye. I am Odysseus. He walked up Hillage where Oak was in his tree.

"Oak," Harry said, "I've got a campaign headquarters. Right beside Louis's barbershop."

"The old hat shop."

"Want to help?"

"Sure."

"I'll get through graduation and we're off and running."

———

Jillian got home at eleven that night and went into the dark kitchen to make sure all was neat. She snapped on the light and Harry stood and saluted.

"Sergeant Hutchinson presenting the kitchen for your inspection, ma'am!"

"Harry," she said, "you scared the life out of me. What are you doing?"

"Waiting for you. I've rented my campaign headquarters. Small but just right. I'm as excited as a kid. A very grand headquarters."

"The hotel?"

"I was joking, Jillian. Let's take a drive and I'll show you."

"Harry, I'm exhausted and I have a meeting at eight-thirty."

"I rented the space beside Louis's barbershop."

Jillian stood still a moment then said, "You're not serious?"

"It's perfect. In the village. Everyone goes by."

"Harry, you're not running for town clerk. You're running for Congress and the idiots who walk by probably don't vote. They live in the tenement section. They're drunks and truck drivers. Tell whomever you rented it from that you made a mistake. I'll make some calls in the morning and get something suitable but that's all I can do. You need money, and no one with money will take you seriously if you have a dump like that."

"Jillian, it's the right place. You'll love it once you see it."

"Harry, I'm very tired. My suggestion is the same as this morning. Drop the whole thing. Write your book. Turn the light off and go to bed."

Harry went outside, turned right and walked down Hillage Avenue to simmer down. He stopped to look at the moon and was amazed it could look so orange. The beauty of it calmed him down. Jillian can be helpful if I can bring her around. She's so dammed arrogant. Cold. God, she's cold. She could raise a lot of money for me. I've got to be patient.

He went down to the little traffic circle at the end of Hillage Avenue and sat on the bench under what Oak called the Jump Tree because he jumped from the bench to a branch.

Harry heard the peepers warbling as a car pulled into the Levensons' driveway. "Hello, Harry," Sol Levenson said getting out of the car. "How's life?"

"Unsettled. I just rented Old Sam's hat shop for my campaign headquarters."

"What are you running for?" Sol, compact and brisk, was a surgeon and had been on his feet all day.

"Congress. And no lectures on how foolish I am, Sol."

"Why run?"

Jillian had put him in a bad mood and he felt defensive. "Because I'm living in a ghost country. We don't talk about things. The bomb for instance. Why the hell are we turning out more and more atomic bombs? Or are we? We don't know. Why can't the public see the film footage the Japanese took of Hiroshima? Because we're children. And race. We don't talk about it. If you're a Negro in this country you're going to get a lousy education. In the South if you're a Negro, you go to ramshackle Negro schools. What are we doing about that? Nothing. And class. We scorn the people at the bottom of the hill."

"You got my vote, Harry."

"You think I can get the Jewish vote?"

"I'll bet you're the most liberal one running. Any Jews running?"

"No. Ten in the primary so far."

"Who's got the best chance?"

"Don Nestor."

"He's a dope."

"Good war record," Harry said. "Dartmouth. Money. Beautiful wife. He'll say the right things. More bombs. More planes. Everybody hide."

"What chance do you have?"

"None. I won't get beyond the primary. But I'll be able to speak and maybe get a debate going."

"You sure you want to do this?"

"No, but I'm doing it."

"You're running as a Democrat?"

"Yes. I'm a socialist but I'm running as a Democrat."

"What if you won?" Sol asked.

"Then I'll bring Louis down to be my barber."

"I better get in," Sol said. "I know Sid Gold at the *Globe*. I'll give him a call. Maybe he'll do an article."

When Sol left, Harry lit a cigarette and saw someone had turned a light on in the second floor of the Hatcher's house. Two old sisters in their late seventies; only one of the Hatcher sisters ever came out. Miss Hatcher, ever straight-backed, always with her dog, always frosty. I'll ask *her* to be my campaign manager. Miss Hatcher's white tulips were closed up. Asleep I suppose. Me too. To sleep.

<u>*CHAPTER 6*</u>

"Harry, go to Maine," Jillian said the following evening. "You always take a few days in Maine after graduation. This whole thing is just because you're exhausted. You're on the verge of a nervous breakdown."

"Don't start that Jillian. Let's talk in the kitchen."

They were in the living room which Harry felt was as comfortable as one of the roped-off rooms in museums. He wanted a drink. The sky was darkening early. It started to rain. There was a crackle of thunder.

"I prefer the living room. Harry, I'm worried about you. You know what happened to your uncle."

"Uncle Fred went nuts. Lots of people go nuts. I'm not going nuts. I'm running for Congress."

"Which is full of nuts," Jillian laughed.

"Jillian, if you were my campaign manager it could be fun and maybe Ophelia will help. She loves drama. Politics is drama. Imagine the three of us working together."

"I almost forgot," Jillian said. "Ophelia called me at work today. She's very excited. She's been awarded a yearlong scholarship to the University of London to study Shakespeare and theater. It's just come through. It starts June fifth."

"That's absurd," Harry said. "They're giving her a little over a week's notice?"

"Ophelia was second in the audition. The girl who won has mononucleosis. I'm bringing her things up, and she'll be off after her exams. So Ophelia won't be here, and I'm too busy to help you, so forget the whole thing, Harry. Go to Maine, then come home and write your book. That way you'll get tenure, and you can relax. Now I've got to get going."

"Jillian, let's go out to supper. Call whomever it is and say you can't go. This is important."

"Harry, I'm running the United Way campaign for the state. These local meetings are our bread and butter."

"The hell with the local meeting," Harry said standing. His right hand flew out and hit a small glass vase which fell and shattered.

"My father gave me that," Jillian said.

Harry restrained himself from saying, why didn't you marry your father? Jillian was far closer to her father than she'd ever been to Harry. She'd fought with her father for years and years and they still fought, but they had a bond Harry envied.

"We'll talk it over tomorrow, Harry. Try to look at it dispassionately. You haven't any money and I'm certainly not going to contribute to a campaign I think is a waste of time. You don't like small talk. You don't like glad-handing. You're no good at organizing and you're just not built for the rough and tumble of politics."

"I want to talk about things like the bomb. I want to talk about how frightened we're becoming as a country."

"Then talk to your friends but don't run for Congress. No one wants to hear some professor pontificate about the bomb. I've got to run. Sweep up the vase and make sure you leave the kitchen clean."

Harry was too angry to clean up the vase. He went out and stood on the small front porch. It was rainy and windy and the lightning crackled far away. He grabbed his raincoat and hat and stormed down the stairs. What the hell could be more sane than deciding to run for public office? No, it's evidence I'm losing my mind like Uncle Fred.

Harry always felt he understood Uncle Fred. Fred was the oldest of four, thirteen years older than Harry's father. Fred loved to paint, and he had had talent. Dutifully he went to Harvard Law School, married well and lived properly for most of his life. He hated being a lawyer so he drank a lot, and one night he snapped. A policeman walking the night beat on Washington Street in Boston had looked in the Jordan Marsh display window and seen a man in bed with a woman and they were not sleeping. It was all hushed up. Fred was sent to Creighton Mental Hospital where he died four years later. Looking back, there had been warning signs all along the way but no one had paid attention.

Harry walked along Hillage Avenue by the long, low stone wall of the McCormicks' house. He could see Val McCormick playing the piano. Val, handsome, powerful, dignified, would make a good candidate. Jillian would make a good candidate. Jillian wouldn't talk about the bomb. Neither would Val. Hell, Jillian's right. I'd make a lousy candidate. Course if I ever won the primary I'd be in. So I'm a lousy candidate. Who cares? Jesus, we're all frozen with fear.

He turned the corner onto Pill Hill. The rain felt good on his face. The McCormicks' magnificent house looked like some great ocean liner about to steam over Pill Hill. He caught sight of Oak McCormick and his sisters running around the piano room.

The scent of the storm buoyed him. The sky blackened and the rain came hard as Harry walked down to the tennis court on Forceps Avenue. The lightning was closer and thunder exploded as rain pelted the clay court. Only ghosts played tennis in the rain.

CHAPTER 7

Harry spent the next week correcting exams, grading papers and advising four doctoral students. He worked in his small office that looked out on Huntington Avenue with its trolleys and traffic. He enjoyed the city sounds.

Wednesday he took the trolley to Park Street, walked up Beacon Hill and went into the State House to get his nomination papers. He'd need twelve hundred signatures to get on the ballot. Jillian had asked him how he'd get them, and Harry said he'd go door to door. She just shook her head.

Harry saw Don Nestor standing alone in the Hall of Flags, a vast, circular, marble floored ceremonial room with flags at the edge of the room where the air was always musty and the place felt dead. Nestor, who would almost certainly win the congressional race Harry was entering, looked like a lifeguard in a suit.

"Mr. Nestor, I'm Harry Hutchinson."

"Glad to meet you," Nestor said. He had good teeth, a tan, strong handshake, brown eyes, a dark suit and a beautiful wife who hurried towards him. Nestor looked over Harry's shoulder. Harry sensed the man's impatience.

"I'm in the congressional primary with you," Harry said.

Nestor's face altered just slightly; he took Harry in and spat him out.

"This is my wife," Nestor said. "Julie, this is Mr. Hashman. Well, we've got to run. Good luck, Henley."

The next morning at seven-thirty as Harry was in his head-quarters alone, Meg Marion came by on her way to work.

"Hello, Professor Hutchinson."

"Meg, come in. You're my first visitor. Haven't even got chairs and tables yet. I've been correcting all week."

"You're beginning today then?"

"No, actually I have business at Northeastern today and all weekend. We end the year with meetings and Sunday is gradua-tion. Monday I'll start getting signatures." Harry picked up the long sheets that lay on the kitchen chair he had brought from home. "These are the nomination papers. I need twelve hundred signatures."

"Twelve hundred. Just to get on the ballot?"

"Afraid so."

"I'm going to be late. I work at Honey Dew Donuts. Good luck, Professor."

Harry stood in the empty storefront. Not even a chair to sit down on. Louis the Barber came in.

"How's the campaign, Professor?"

"As you can see Louis, it's booming."

"I'll talk you up," Louis said. "You got any posters?"

"Nothing so far."

"You need signatures? Gimme the papers. I'll get some for you."

On the trolley Harry tried to put his thoughts in order for Dean John Whitton who met at the end of the year with each assistant professor for a review session. A young woman sitting opposite Harry on the trolley distracted him. He wanted to see her naked. For the thousandth time he wondered if his desire was just part of being male or if he was perverse or over-sexed. Over-sexed? There is no sex in my life. I'm running for Congress and am enamored of you and your green dress. Could we go somewhere so you can take it off?

Whitton's office was on the second floor. Whitton's secretary's office was three times larger than Harry's. The secretary, Mrs. Petin, a hearty, short, broad-shouldered woman, smelled of soap and had a voice that carried. "Is the Dean expecting you?"

Yes, you dimwit. Look at your book. And keep your clothes on.

"Yes, nine o'clock."

"Ah yes, Professor Hutchinson. Dean Whitton is just a little behind schedule." Every year it was the same. The Great Man is behind schedule. President Truman is here to see you, Dean Whitton. Tell him I'm in conference with Stalin and Churchill. We're working Europe out.

Fifteen minutes later Harry was told to go in. Whitton's large office had a period couch with red fabric. Harry had no idea what period. The three chairs looked French. The walls were a light green and there was a portrait of some grim-looking man dominating the room.

Whitton, small, compact, and impeccably dressed in a dark blue Brooks Brothers suit, sat behind a handsome, neat desk. Every hair in place. Dandruff banished before birth, Harry mused. The man was shiny as a new baby.

"Harry, nice to see you."

"You too, Dean Whitton."

"Please sit down. Can I get you some coffee?"

"No, thank you." Harry took the chair in front of the Dean's desk.

"Well another year coming to a close, Harry. I'm sure you've got all your grades in."

"Yes."

"I'm sorry you were offended by my remarks a few weeks ago. I sat in on your class because as I've told you I've had complaints that your history lectures were slanted towards socialism."

"And I as I said, Dean Whitton, I welcome you to any of my classes."

"Harry, we don't see eye to eye on political issues. If any professor is slanting things I want to know about it."

"Speaking of politics, Dean, I want you to know I'm entering the Democratic primary for Congress."

The Dean's face reminded him of Miss Hatcher's bulldog. He thought Whitton was going to growl but he just looked at Harry, folded his hands and drummed his thumbs.

"It's not wise, Harry. I suggest you reconsider."

"The primary is September ninth. I won't win so it won't interfere with my teaching schedule."

"I thought you were writing a book on Washington."

"It can wait."

Whitton was in control but his breathing was shorter. He had angry eyes. Now his thumbs were at war with one another.

"Harry, let me be blunt. Your politics are out of step with the times. You'll be saying things which could reflect badly on the university."

"What I'll be saying is that we need to talk about the future."

"I suppose you're for disarmament."

"I agree with President Truman that disarmament is a good idea if we can have verifiable inspections."

"I'm not going to debate issues, Harry. You're interested in tenure of course. Your book could help. Please make sure your classes are free of indoctrination. I suggest you write this summer." Whitton stood up and nodded his dismissal.

Harry was so angry he went next door to the YMCA, swam in the pool and hit the punching bag so hard he hurt his hand. The next three days were consumed with meetings, social gatherings and an outdoor graduation that Harry enjoyed because of a sudden rainstorm that came while Dean Whitton was speaking.

Monday morning Harry tried to slip out of the house before Jillian got up. He almost made it.

"Are you going out, Harry?" She called from the top of the stairs. She was dressed in a skirt and bra. He couldn't remember when he'd last seen her in a bra. She was very good looking.

"Yes, I'm going down to the headquarters."

Jillian let out a sigh. "I thought you dropped that. You'll never get twelve hundred signatures. You're exhausted. Go up to Maine for a few days and think about it."

"I have thought."

"You always take a few days in Maine after graduation."

"I'll take them after the primary."

"Who's going to help you campaign?"

"Edie Lawrence and Oak have volunteered. And Meg Marion, a woman who lives in the Farm. And Old John said he'd help."

"Old John of the Tennis Court? My God," she said shaking her head. She turned and went into her bedroom saying, "God, he never learns."

———

Jillian was glad Harry was gone. Harry was a daily astonishment. How could she have married him? It's true, she admitted, he's a good lecturer but he has no style. He chews gum and puts it behind his ear. That's what he is, she thought, a gum chewing idiot.

She finished dressing and went down for breakfast. She took out the Grape Nuts and poured the gritty little grains into a white bowl. The slight ringing sound of the grains infuriated her because for some reason it brought Harry's congressional campaign to mind. His workers. His nuts.

"A circus," she said to the Grape Nuts. She could imagine his campaign headquarters. Edie Lawrence, who thinks life is a Greek tragedy, folding flyers and stuffing envelopes with horrible Old John of the tennis court and a ten-year-old boy. The thought of the campaign was too much this morning. Jillian put the elastic back on the Grape Nuts box, poured the Grape

Nuts into the garbage can, washed, dried and put away the bowl. There were several drops of water in the sink. She dried them with the dishtowel, folded the towel and put it neatly on the dishtowel rack.

Jillian amused herself thinking of living life without a body. A body is a pest but she loved horseback riding so she would put up with a body. Harry may have been more successful in life if he hadn't a body. The idea of making love to him ever again was so ludicrous she laughed. Harry naked was hysterical.

"Why don't you divorce him?" her father asked at least once a week.

"I know what I'm doing," Jillian would say and change the subject. The night before she married Harry her father had said to Jillian, "I give the marriage three years at best." If he'd kept his mouth shut, Jillian would have divorced Harry years ago.

———

Edie Lawrence was in her yard. "Morning Edie," Harry said. "What are you up to?"

"I was talking to Bones. He is very wise. Is one finished teaching the young?"

"Yes, thank God. I'm going down to my campaign headquarters. By tonight I'll have phones. Nothing else mind you, but phones."

"One can then call for help," she laughed. She laughed like a thin tree might laugh. She shook.

"How's Lydia?" Harry asked.

"She's definitely being sent to Creighton Mental Hospital."

"My God," Harry said, "the poor kid. Jillian thinks I belong there."

"She is not in favor of your running?"

"No."

"Monica and Carrie are home. How can we help?"

"You could get signatures so I can get on the ballot."

Harry walked down to the village, got coffee at the White Tower then headed to the headquarters where he saw Hi Ho at his station in front of Barbour's Fruit Market across the street. He keeps regular office hours, Harry thought.

Louis flashed his scissors as Harry walked by. Harry's headquarters door was open and Ernie was in his wheelchair directing several young men who were setting up long tables and folding chairs. There was a map of the district on the wall. The phone rang and Ernie picked it up.

"Hutchinson headquarters," Ernie said as he wrote figures on a pad, thanked the caller and hung up.

"What's going on, Ernie?" Harry said.

"I got you some tables from the Veterans' Hall. Buddy of mine lent them to me. I hurried the phones up. They put 'em in Friday afternoon. I got printing costs here when you want to go over them."

The young men finished setting up, said good-bye and left.

"I'm amazed, Ernie. How did you get in?"

"Louis let me in. Have a donut, Professor."

Harry sat at a long table. "I don't know what to say."

"Let's make a list of what you need," Ernie said. "Cards, posters, publicity, money, a list of places the candidates are invited to speak at: Lion's Club, Rotary, all that of kind thing. Money, volunteers, money, money, money. And you gotta get moving. It's June fifth already."

"Well the first thing is to get on the ballot. I need twelve hundred signatures. That's a challenge."

"We got nine hundred over the weekend."

"You did!"

"Yeah, My mother and some of her friends went down to the Flower Show in Boston all day Saturday and Sunday, and I was at the Sattler at the Massachusetts Veterans convention. I got five hundred."

"This is fantastic. Are they good signatures? I mean are they registered voters in my district?"

"Most will be. You need fifteen hundred in case. Louis got forty. Mr. Paine got about thirty. You know Mr. Paine? Paine's Stationery store."

"Mr. Paine? He's a wonderful man, but he's an ancient Republican. How did you get him?"

"Same as everybody. I put on my uniform and my medals and show up in my wheelchair. By tonight you'll have a thousand."

"This is wonderful, Ernie."

"I'd be gettin' drunk if I wasn't doing this."

"Your exam was good. You'll get your grades in the mail. I gave you an A minus."

"Minus? I'm takin' the tables back."

"I'm inspired, Ernie. Let me use the phone." He got Edie on the eighth ring.

"Edie, it's Harry. Listen I've got nine hundred signatures. I may get another hundred or two in the village alone. Could you possibly get Monica and Carrie to go around the neighborhood and get signatures? I'm excited."

Edie called back in half an hour. "The girls are coming down now to get the papers from you. This is reunion weekend at Wellesley. I'll go and see if I can get you some signatures."

"You hate that kind of thing."

"If Odysseus can face the Cyclops, I can face reunion."

Oak came by after school and asked if he could help.

"You know the housing project?" Ernie asked.

"Yes, it's on the way to the pond."

"Go door to door and say Professor Hutchinson is running for Congress. Tell 'em you need signatures to get him on the ballot. See if you can get thirty today and thirty tomorrow. When does school vacation start?"

"Wednesday."

"You want to do more?"

"Sure."

"Good. There's plenty to do. Get going."

By Friday afternoon Harry had fourteen hundred signatures. And that was without Edie Lawrence's forty-five she got at the reunion. Harry was officially in the primary.

CHAPTER 8

On the morning of June eighteenth Harry stood in the silent headquarters amazed the campaign was taking shape. Volunteers came in the afternoon and evening: veterans, Northeastern students, Meg Marion's friends, Edie Lawrence, Oak and a few Pill Hill neighbors. With Ernie's help Harry had set up three storefront headquarters in different cities in his district. Harry was alone this morning because Ernie was having a checkup at the Veterans' Hospital. Harry had a League of Women Voters' luncheon at The Towers at noon.

The door opened and Amelia Adams came in looking behind her as if she feared she might be seen.

"I was just passing, Harry. I think you're so brave to run for Congress."

"Not brave, Amelia. Maybe foolish. How's Eliot?" He shouldn't have mentioned Eliot. Amelia looked out onto the street.

"He's sleeping late."

She wrung her hands. He liked her voice or perhaps it was her tone. She had a robin's voice, an orange-breasted voice. Its rhythms were the rhythms of nursery rhymes, full of little hills and valleys.

"I hope I can help in some small way, Harry. "

"If you ever have a moment we have a lot of mailings you could help with."

The door creaked open. Hi Ho came in and stood silent as a tree.

"Mr. Clancy," Amelia said as if Hi Ho were perfectly respectable, "My tulips are better than they've ever been. You are the master of the green thumb."

Hi Ho nodded.

"Please," Harry said to Hi Ho, "have some coffee and donuts."

Hi Ho took two donuts and poured a cup of black coffee. His right hand was caked with mud and what might have been blood, and his shoelace was untied so that he might trip and fall at any moment. Hi Ho stuffed the donuts into the pocket of his dungaree jacket and left.

"He is magic in the garden," Amelia said. They were both watching Hi Ho cross the busy street to Barbour's Fruit Market when Amelia drew in her breath. "That's Eliot," she said looking for a place to hide. Eliot Adams honked his horn at Hi Ho and pulled into a parking place just beyond Barbour's.

"Oh, Lord," she said. "Is there a back way out?"

"Amelia, just say you dropped in to say hello."

"No, Harry. He can't see me here. He's furious you're running for Congress. That's why he was up late last night. He started drinking. Oh, thank God, he's going into the bank. I've got to run, Harry."

For three years Harry had been making his Pill Hill walks and his chats with Amelia had become a part of his daily life. Harry realized now she probably paid a price for those talks. If Eliot saw her in his headquarters she would probably be confined to the house.

Harry sat at the table and began the task he hated most, raising money. He had a list of colleagues, veterans and banks. There were several professors at Northeastern with whom he was friendly. Mike Beard taught Greek and had a good sense of humor so he started there.

"Mike? Harry Hutchinson. I'm fine. You off to Greece soon? Yes, well, listen, I'm running for Congress. Yes. I'm serious. I really am. No, on the Democratic ticket. I'm looking for donations to keep the ship afloat. If you could? Sure. Sure. Thanks, Mike. Enjoy Greece. Give my best to Lani."

By noon Harry was wrung out. Six people had promised to send something, but not a single bank offered to contribute.

Harry was glad to step out onto the sidewalk. It was cold and didn't feel like June, but it was just what he needed to blow away three hours on the phone. He crossed Muddy River Avenue and started down Station Street catching a whiff of sweetness when a customer walked into the Station Florist Shop.

The Towers was a ten-story hotel that looked as if it belonged beside an English park. It always seemed unreal to Harry. The wealthy old residents walked about the halls with benign smiles and spoke in tones so low Harry thought they might be ghosts. Republican ghosts. Florence Beam waited in the lobby. "I'm glad you finally made it," she said. He was four minutes late. She was made of gristle, fat and disapproval. She was no ghost.

"We're in the Dickinson Dining Room. There are about fifty of us." The Dickinson Room was a long, narrow room with yellow wallpaper and round tables. A portrait of Emily Dickinson hung above a fireplace. After lunch Florence strode to the front of the room.

"It is my pleasure to introduce our speaker. Professor Hutchinson is a neighbor but of course that will not sway my vote. I want the most qualified candidate. Professor Hutchinson."

The applause was polite. Harry could feel the strange wood-enness take possession of him. Idiot waiter still pouring coffee. Where are my notes? Damn. Is my fly open? Damned waiter serving dessert now. Clink. Clink.

"Thank you, Florence and thank you all for having me. I hope I am as good as your dessert." A flutter of laughter. "This is a turning point in our history as a nation. The war is behind us. Where do we go from here? I think having a history professor in Congress is a good idea because we don't want to repeat the mistakes of the past." Clink. Clink. A waiter hovered over an old woman who was not happy with her pie. She shook her head and he took it away.

The applause at the end of his twenty minutes was slightly louder than the clinks. Florence stood and asked if there were questions. A hand went up. Harry pointed to an elderly woman whose voice was strong.

"We were talking before you came, Professor, and someone said you are a socialist. Is that true?"

"I am running as a Democrat," Harry said. "I think we should have a more equitable society. It seems to me that if we can win a world war we can find a way to relieve some of the poverty in the country. The G. I. Bill is an inspiration. I want to see more of that kind of thinking in Congress."

The same woman's bold trumpet voice filled the room. "Are you against private enterprise?"

"Not at all. Right now I'm more interested in thinking about where we are headed as a country. Russia is exhausted. It will take a quarter century for the Russians to get back on their feet so we don't need to be quite so afraid."

Florence Beam shot a question. "Churchill said we're in a cold war. I think we need strong men in Congress, not puff cakes. Do you agree, Professor Hutchinson?"

"Mrs. Beam, if I were President I might make you my Secretary of Defense. That would leave the Russians quaking. Thank you all."

By late June the headquarters picked up steam. Oak came every night as did Edie Lawrence, and Meg Marion brought five or six women from the Farm. Veteran friends of Harry and Ernie came, as well as Northeastern students. Ernie gave them maps and sent them out knocking on doors.

Old John of the Tennis court came in one night. He was like some terrible apparition, twisted, bent and misshapen. His eyes were somehow terrible. For a moment the headquarters fell silent.

"John," Edie Lawrence said, "one is kind to come. We are desperate for help." Meg brought John coffee. Ernie stared at John, and muttering an angry *Jesus*, wheeled forward. Meg put her hand on Ernie's shoulder saying, "This is my son, Ernie."

"Gla ta ma ya," John said.

"Sit down," Ernie ordered. "We're puttin' out a mailin'."

Conversation picked up and John sealed envelopes. A man came in asking for literature about Harry. The man stared at John and left without taking anything. Three other people came in that night and they saw only John.

By ten-thirty everyone had gone but Ernie. He always waited for Harry. Harry came in looking chipper. "How'd it go Ernie?"

"Good except we had a guy in here helpin' who belongs in the freak show. You gotta tell him not to come back. Oak said he's the caretaker of the tennis court on Pill Hill."

"Old John. He's a wonderful man."

"He scares people. I don't want him here."

Harry sat down. "John was burned and most of his bones broken in World War One," Harry said. "He went from being a good-looking nineteen-year old kid to being a monster, and his life has been a nightmare. His army records got lost twenty years ago so the government pays him nothing. He will work here any time he wants and I don't give a God damn if he loses me every vote."

"If that's the way you want it."

"That's the way I want it. And I want you to manage my campaign."

"Jesus, Professor. I'm only twenty-six."

"And I'm forty-one. Fifty dollars a week."

"That's too much."

"Not at all. It's settled."

CHAPTER 9

The following afternoon Harry went by the tennis court. John was in the barn in the small room to the right repairing the tennis court net. He barely acknowledged Harry's presence.

"Is something wrong, John?"

"Na."

"I wanted to thank you for helping out last night."

Harry was aware that although two of John's fingers were fused together his other fingers worked fluidly repairing the net. Harry was tempted to go but wanted to find out if John had been offended by something someone had said at the headquarters. He couldn't get John to say anything so Harry finally said, "I'm sorry if somebody was rude last night at the headquarters."

"Na," John said and then the story came out. John told Harry that after working at the headquarters last night he had taken the bus to Kenmore Square, then got on the subway car which was jammed because the Red Sox game had just let out. Some teenage boys in the back of the car were drunk and causing a ruckus and John, who had heard that laughter so many times, sensed it was at his expense.

A boy of about eighteen, wearing a brown leather jacket, bumped several passengers as he made his way towards John.

The rumble of the subway car didn't drown out the laughter of the boys in the back.

One of them shouted, "Ask him if he's Frankenstein." People froze.

"Hey," the boy said standing above John. "Is that your mouth or what? Jesus, are you Frankenstein's kid? Hey, look at me when I'm talking to you."

John grabbed the boy's shirt with his left hand, pulled him down, and with his right hand he took the boy's hand and twisted it so hard and fast that the boy screamed as the car pulled into Park Street. The driver slid open the window and shouted to a cop in the station. When the cop got on the driver said, "Those kids in the back are drunk. They're causing trouble."

Harry listened and just nodded and John said, "Happa ba fa."

"What happened before, John?"

John said that he'd been in hospitals for five years after the war, and when he'd gotten back to Boston he had taken a room in Charlestown. He was in a bar just over the bridge from Charlestown having a beer one night when six or seven guys started to make fun of him. When John left, they followed him out, cornered him and telling him they didn't want a freak in their bar they started to push him and punch him. John's rage erupted, and he hit one guy so hard the guy fell, hit his head on a stone stair and died. John was tried for murder, but his lawyer, a public defender, got him off on a plea of insanity and he was sent to the Massachusetts Mental Institution.

CHAPTER 10

At five-thirty in the morning, Old John looked in the mirror and shook his head. He rarely looked in the mirror, but he did that morning because of what had happened two nights before with the drunken kids on the subway. No wonder they laughed.

By quarter to six he'd said good-bye to his cat and, lunch pail in hand, was on his way to Pill Hill. At this time of morning the subway wasn't crowded and lots of passengers knew him by sight. His goal was to get to Pill Hill and sit in the caretaker's barn and have coffee before working on the tennis court. He walked all the way to Park Street. John held the banister going down the long flight of stairs into the Park Street subway station. Five minutes later the Huntington subway car was squealing into the station. He liked the cars painted orange and wondered who had decided the color. That would be a job he'd like; sitting in an office thinking about ways to make the subways better. It saddened him that kids cut the seats with knives.

John got on the rear door and sat in a double seat. There were only a dozen passengers. When the car squealed by the Museum of Fine Arts, John thought someday he'd like to go into the museum, but he knew he wouldn't because he upset and frightened people.

When he got off the trolley at the Muddy River stop, the air was still cool. The sun was going to be hot but the next hour would be the best of the day. He loved the early morning. He walked under the WPA bridge then along Muddy River and saw Hi Ho still asleep on the grass, an empty bottle of wine beside him.

John started up Forceps Avenue thinking about the people of Pill Hill getting up and looking in bathroom mirrors at themselves. He passed the tennis court and unlocked the barn where he kept his tools. It was cool, almost cold. He set his pail down, opened it and took out his thermos, poured black coffee, sat in the near dark in one of the old horse stalls and contemplated the day. He'd brought one sandwich for lunch and one for supper. He'd go down to Professor Hutchinson's headquarters at six tonight and he wouldn't leave until nine or ten, which meant there might be drunks on the subway again, but he liked working at the headquarters and he'd just have to take the chance.

———————————

John got to the headquarters at six that night; Ernie was alone.

"How ya doin', John?"

"Goo. La to wor ba off." John pointed to the back.

"Back off? Back office? You want to be in the back?"

John grunted and hobbled past Ernie and waved for Ernie to follow him. John opened the door of the small back office saying, "I wok he."

"I don't think Professor H would like that, John."

"Ya I tol him."

"You told him?"

"Ya."

"All right, John, I'll set you up. I appreciate it. People come in and they see me in a fuckin' wheelchair and then they see you lookin' like you got dropped from a plane and somehow they don't want to stay."

John grunted his laugh as Oak came in.

"Oak," Ernie said. "John's gonna work here. It's your job to check and see what he needs. Envelopes, fliers . . . give him whatever he needs. I'm hungry. Go to the deli and get me a hot pastrami on rye. What do you want, John?"

"Na."

"Yeah, yeah, yeah, you gotta eat, John. Get him a big chicken noodle soup. Here's five bucks."

Harry came in that night a little before ten. "John didn't come in tonight?" Harry asked.

"He's in the back office."

"What?" Harry said.

"He said he told you that he was going to work in the back office."

John opened the rear door and came in. "John," Harry said, "you didn't tell me you wanted to work in the back."

"Na?" John said. "Ma ta fo go."

"All right," Harry said, "then here's the deal. If you work for me I'm going to send you home in a cab."

"Na."

"Yes," Harry said. "It's settled. Ernie, do you know any cab drivers? Maybe we could get the same one every night."

"Richy McIntosh drives for Red Cab. I'll call him," Ernie said.

CHAPTER 11

Today Oak's job was to hand out Professor Hutchinson's campaign cards in the Farm. Oak walked by the fire station, past the car wash with the long red wall, and continued down the sidewalk into the Farm, a foreign world of about forty triple-deckers. Route Nine was only fifty feet away, but he had passed some invisible line and the noise of the highway was different here. The triple-deckers knew he didn't belong and so did the dust and the pigeons on the telephone wires. They clucked at him.

Oak went up the wooden stairs of the first triple-decker. The front door was open so Oak went into the foyer where it was cool and dark. He knocked on the first door which needed painting. A woman in a housecoat opened the door holding a baby in her arms. The baby's mouth was smeared with what was probably squash.

"Yes?" the woman said politely. Oak expected the people to be mean and have bad teeth.

"I hope you'll vote for Professor Hutchinson in the primary," Oak said, handing her the card. "He's running for Congress."

"Thank you," she said smiling. The baby's eyes were huge. "Ernie Marion told me about him."

"Does Ernie live here?"

"No. He's the next block over."

The first visit was a success. In the next two hours Oak got glimpses into the apartments where people had couches and chairs just like ordinary people. He was hoping Gail Mullen, who was in his fifth grade class, would open the door. Gail of the straight A's and tired gray face had circles under her eyes. Gail was ten but looked as if she'd been around hundreds of years.

On the third floor of one of the buildings, a man in a t-shirt with straps opened the door holding a can of beer. He had a big belly and his face was unshaven and splotched. The man smiled showing brown teeth which looked as if they had little caves in them. Oak gave him the card and asked him to vote for Professor Hutchinson.

"What's he for?"

"For Congress."

"I mean what's he stand for?"

"He wants people to have a chance."

"He the guy that's against the bomb?"

"He says the bomb is a knock on the door."

"It's a knock on Joe Stalin's door and without it we'd be up to our neck in Ruskies. You know what a pinko is?"

"No." Oak knew it was not good.

"A pinko is a man thinks the Commies are just like everybody else. He wants to give the store away. This is the best store in the world and any asshole who wants to give it all to Stalin and the Commies is a double asshole."

The man was getting wound up. Oak wanted to get away. The man shook his empty beer can and turned, saying he'd be back but Oak said he better get going. Oak admired the man being so informal.

When Oak got down to the sidewalk an older boy of seventeen or eighteen was standing there; his skin was the color of olive oil, his hair black and neatly combed.

"Who the fuck are you?" the boy asked. His teeth were white and accusing. He wore a blue shirt and clean dungarees with a garrison belt for fighting. The set of his mouth was like a fist in the face.

"I'm handing out cards for Professor Hutchinson. He's running for Congress."

"You're gettin' your ass outta here. Where the fuck do you live?"

"Pill Hill."

"Pill fuckin' Hill."

"Hey, Eddie," Chickie called. "What are you doin'?" At school Oak was called Eddie since his name was Edward.

"Handing out campaign cards."

"You know Pill fuckin Hill?" the boy asked Chickie.

Chickie grinned. "Eddie's ok."

"He's a shithead," the boy said and turned away.

The scene came back to mind that night when Oak was at the headquarters. The conversation got lively and he forgot about it, but it woke him in the middle of the night. Oak wanted to smash the boy. He wanted to smash and smash and smash. Smash all that arrogance. He wanted to smash all the people who wanted to smash him.

CHAPTER 12

Louis the barber was smoking a cigarette on the sidewalk, and Ernie wheeled himself out to say hello. They'd been campaigning a month. The sky was blue and the clouds looked lazy as frogs. Hi Ho was across the street standing outside Barbour's Fruit Market. The traffic was light for ten in the morning.

"How's business, Louis?"

"Good. And how's things with you Ernie?"

"Good. Going good."

"They're putting in traffic meters," Louis said. "Not good for my business," but he didn't look worried. His black hair was swept back as smooth as a seal's. He was a man in charge of his ship.

"How about a haircut, Louis?"

"Come on."

"Oak," Ernie called into the headquarters. "Watch the shop." Ernie's wheelchair bumped over the threshold of the barbershop which smelled of shaving lotion, hair oil and some mystery element that was in no other barbershop. Ernie pulled himself up into the barber chair, and Louis put the striped linen barber sheet over Ernie's chest. "So how's the campaign, Ernie?"

"You won't believe it, Louis. I'm campaign manager now."

"I believe it. I always said you'd go places. He got a chance?"

"You got the *Globe*?"

Louis gave it to Ernie. "Listen to this. 'Army captain, Harry Hutchinson, assigned to write for *Stars and Stripes*, the Armed Forces newspaper, was covering the battle between the Germans and the American Fourth Armored Division in Carbini, Southern Italy. The battle, waged over three days, became a fierce street fight. Private Edward Keefe was wounded and lay in the street when, amidst intense firing, Captain Hutchinson ran out onto the street and dragged Private Keefe to safety.'"

"That's what Kennedy ran on four years ago," Louis said.

"Yeah. PT boat wasn't it?"

"Yes. His boat was sunk and Kennedy saved some of his guys. His old man's Joe Kennedy. He's loaded. Spent three hundred thousand to get Kennedy elected. How much has Professor Hutchinson got?"

"He borrowed three grand. I bet we can raise ten grand. This *Globe* article's worth ten grand. We'll quote it in every mailing. War hero history professor."

A train rumbled by, shaking the Wildroot Cream Oil on the little glass shelf.

"When I retire," Louis said, "I won't miss that train."

"I hear you singing when you're alone here, Louis. Professor H says you should be in opera. Oak says when Professor H is in the car with him he sings opera."

Louis smiled. He had even, almost perfect teeth.

"Verdi?"

"Sure," Ernie said, wondering what Verdi was. When Ernie wheeled himself out, he was pleased. *The Globe* had put Professor H on the map. Louis's customers would eat it up. Everybody would. When Ernie came back into the headquarters Florence Beam was talking to Oak.

"Harry Hutchinson hasn't got a chance, Oak," Florence said. Every word she said had the vigor of a tuba note.

"I think he'll win," Oak said. "Mrs. Beam, this is Ernie Marion. He's the campaign manager."

"You're a little young aren't you?" Florence said, looking down at Ernie.

"Battle tested," Ernie said. "Would you like to make a contribution?" Ernie asked.

"I'm a Republican," Florence said. "Harry Hutchinson is a socialist. I support democracy, not Harry Hutchinson."

"Then contribute for democracy," Ernie said. Florence opened her pocket book and gave Ernie a dime. She left like a mighty tide.

Hi Ho came in for his free coffee and donuts. Hi Ho stood there in the headquarters eating a donut, his eyes were bloodshot, his hands caked with blood and mud, his face a grainy, bumpy, florid map.

"Sox won," Hi Ho said. His voice was a low monotone today. He was like an old building that made you wonder what it looked like when it had been new and all painted up. He smelled slightly of urine. His shoes were cracked.

"The Sox will fold," Ernie said.

Hi Ho had lost interest. He finished his coffee and returned to his post at Barbour's Fruit Market.

,

CHAPTER 13

Feeling lighter after his haircut, Ernie Marion sat in the head-quarters looking at *The Globe* article on Harry's heroism. The train sounded like a lion. Meg Marion brought in a big bag of day old donuts.

"Big piece on Professor H in the *Globe*," Ernie said.

"Good?" Meg asked.

"Fantastic. Professor H ran out in the street in the middle of battle, and rescued a soldier. Purple Heart. Bronze Star. This thing is gold."

"Great. I can't stay, Ernie. I'll be back tonight and bring Judy Murphy and Joan Connor to help out."

Ernie struggled with depression, but the newspaper article got him over the hump this morning and he started calling banks.

"I'm Ernest Marion. I'm working for Professor Harry Hutchinson. He's running for Congress. He's behind the banking legislation. If you read today's *Globe*, you know he's got a good chance."

Ernie struck out with his first three calls, but then he landed a one hundred dollar contribution. By noon, he had raised four hundred dollars. Later that morning, old Mrs. McCormick, Oak's grandmother, came in. She had a strong face with long wrinkles, pale blue eyes, a square chin, nice, even false teeth, and she smelled of toilet water. She usually worked in the headquarters in the mornings putting stamps and addressing envelopes with good, clear handwriting.

"Hello, Ernie."

"Sit down, Mrs. McCormick. Have a donut."

"I shouldn't."

"Then have two."

"You're a terror, Ernie. Where's Oak?"

"I got him knocking on doors in the village. Excuse me, Mrs. McCormick. The phone's been ringin' off the hook this morning." She got to work.

By six that night Ernie was tired but wound up; it had been the best day of the campaign. At seven Oak came back from supper, and he was followed by Meg and three other women from the Farm. The Tauntons, a Pill Hill couple, came to help, and Ernie thought Dr. Taunton looked like a British major; his mustache looked like frozen anchovies, his black shoes shone, his hair parted perfectly and, although it was hot, he wore a navy blue suit. Jesus, Ernie thought, all he needs is a walking stick. "Call me Betty," Mrs. Taunton announced as if she were doing them a favor. She looked like she was wearing a blue orange sleeping bag. Too many jelly donuts.

Betty Taunton gave a little speech, "We read the article in the *Globe*. We knew Harry was the kind of man we liked, but didn't realize how accomplished he was. And this headquarters is so *democratic*. Right by a barbershop with a train practically running through it. What can we do to help?"

You can shut up, Ernie thought, but what he said was, "We've got to get out twenty thousand pieces of mail in the next three weeks. And we need to raise five thousand dollars. You can lick envelopes, or better still, get on the phone and call anyone you know. We need money."

Dr. Taunton sat down at one of the tables with the women from the Farm. He was a renowned eye surgeon, a reserved man, but Meg set him at ease. Betty got on the phone. She talked so long and so fast that her first caller gave her fifty dollars.

"Fifty dollars," Betty said, "and the first call."

"That's great," Ernie said, "you're cookin'." Betty didn't tell them that she had called her aunt.

"Do you get good town services down at the Farm?" Dr. Taunton asked Meg.

"We don't," she said, "but we will if Professor Hutchinson wins." When Meg smiled she looked twenty years younger. Dr. Taunton looked as if he felt Meg's electricity.

So many nights it had been just the faithful five. Old John, Ernie, Meg, Oak and Mrs. Lawrence. Tonight by the time Mrs. Lawrence arrived with her daughters, Monica and Carrie, it was so crowded they took the last three seats.

Betty Taunton kept going to the bathroom, and each time she came out she looked more regal. She was short but with each bathroom trip she stood taller, held her head higher until Ernie thought she'd fall over backwards. "She's loaded," Ernie whispered to Oak. "She's got a bottle in her pocketbook."

As the evening progressed, Betty sounded more and more English. She bellowed into the phone, "Edgar, it's Betty Taunton. I'm fine, thank you." Her voice poured out like hot pudding. "Yes," she went on. "I'm down at Harry Hutchinson's headquarters in the Village. It's democracy in action. We have some of the people from the tenement section working side by side with my husband and Edie Lawrence. Harvard Medical School beside Muddy River High. This is democracy. Democracy costs money. Edgar, you can do better than that. Good for you, Edgar."

By nine Mrs. Taunton sounded so English she couldn't be understood, so Dr. Taunton took her home and everyone burst out laughing when they'd gone.

Ernie said, "She raised three hundred bucks."

———

At nine-thirty Harry went into a phone booth at the Kenmore Hotel on Commonwealth Avenue in Boston. He was in high spirits. "Jillian. I'm so glad you're home."

"Where are you, Harry?"

"As a matter of fact I'm in the lobby of the Kenmore Hotel. I'm flying. I went to a wake and Senator Saltonstall was there. We had quite a talk. You know he's an old family friend. And I just finished having coffee with Paul Dever."

"The governor?" For once Jillian sounded impressed.

"Yes. Dever thinks I might beat Nestor in the primary. That means I'd win, Jillian. I'm high as a kite. I could be home in fifteen minutes. I'd love it if you'd come down to the headquarters and just say hello to people."

"Dever thinks you have a chance?"

"That's what he said. Saltonstall said the same thing. Dever knows Nestor. He doesn't like him, said he's sneaky smart. How about it? We'll go down to the headquarters and then go out for a drink. Just the two of us."

"All right, I'll go down and say hello. But I won't stay."

Twenty minutes later Jillian and Harry drove down to the village. They parked by Goldman's Drug store and walked the block down to the headquarters. They stood on the dark sidewalk looking into the headquarters. Most people had left. Ernie was on the phone, Edie Lawrence was smoking a cigarette, Hi Ho had a broom in hand, Oak and was stuffing envelopes and Old John appeared from the back office.

"Children, cripples and drunks," Jillian said.

"Democracy," Harry laughed.

"It's a freak show. Take me home."

"You're not serious?" Harry said.

"If the governor had seen this he would have laughed in your face. God! Will you never grow up?"

Harry was so mad he just grunted. When they got to the car he flung her door open and slammed it when she got in.

"You're running for Congress," Jillian shouted. "Not zookeeper. And Edie Lawrence. My God!"

"What the hell is wrong with Edie Lawrence?"

"She lives in another world. That's what's wrong."

"Summa Cum Laude at Wellesley. She's brilliant."

"Then why have her stuffing envelopes? I'll tell you why. Edie Lawrence can't operate in the real world. Neither can you."

"Jillian," Harry said stepping on the accelerator so his old car roared up the hill, "*You* haven't the slightest idea of what the real world is. If you had gone into my headquarters you might have caught a whiff of it."

Harry screeched to a stop in front of the house. Jillian went in and he walked around Pill Hill to cool off. Thinking about *The Globe* article and about what Governor Dever had said about Nestor slowly restored his good spirits. When he got back to the headquarters at ten-thirty, everyone had left except Ernie and Oak. John had taken a taxi home.

"What a day, Professor H," Ernie said wheeling toward Harry. "We raised nine hundred bucks."

"No!"

"It's true. the *Globe* article was great. You're a war hero. And your book on James Otis won an award."

"A minor award and it's out of print. I talked to Senator Saltonstall at a wake tonight. He thinks I have a chance and so does Governor Dever. I had coffee with him."

"Fanfuckintastic," Ernie, said. "We got a chance. We have a real fucking chance."

Harry looked at the stack of envelopes. "Who stuffed all these?"

"This place was cookin'," Ernie said. "The nutcake Tauntons from Pill Hill were here. She got crocked but raised three hundred bucks. Mrs. Lawrence and her kids were here. Oak's been here all day. A couple of veteran buddies of mine showed up from the Farm, and one of them's going to run your headquarters in Brighton. My mother was here with friends and she'll bring more tomorrow. The Farm is taking over your campaign, Professor H."

"I'll take you home in a minute, Oak," Harry said. Harry was too excited to stay still. He took one of the stale donuts and pointed to Ernie. "We're in the ball game. A long shot, but we have a chance."

"Jesus," Ernie, said, "I feel so good, I could touch my toes." It was the first time Ernie had joked about his missing legs. Harry was unsure if he should say anything but went ahead. "Are you still mad about losing your legs?" Harry asked.

"Fuckin' A. I still wake up and think that I can walk to the bathroom. I fall out of the bed onto my face. What pisses me off is people think if I got no legs I must be weird."

"You're turning this place into the real thing."

"My mother is."

"You are. And don't worry about getting mad. You should be mad. Just don't get mad at the voters."

Val McCormick, Oak's dad, came in just then. "Hello, Harry," Val had had a few drinks. As always Val was dressed splendidly. A strikingly handsome man, he did a lot of amateur acting in Boston.

"Been rehearsing?" Harry asked.

"I'm doing Lear," Val said.

"Do a line for Ernie. Val, this is my campaign manager, Ernie Marion. Ernie, this is Val McCormick, Oak's dad. Would you do a line?" Harry asked again.

"I'm not sure you want a bit of tragedy in the night," Val laughed.

Ernie said, "I lay in a trench with my dead buddy for a whole day. Can you do a line about that?"

Harry was annoyed with Ernie. When would he get rid of the chip on his shoulder?

"Ernie..." Harry started.

"No," Val said, "I appreciate that, Ernie. *Lear* is about loss. Lear lost everything. It was his own fault, but he lost everything: his land, his power, his mind, and his daughter Cordelia, whom he loved more than anything in the world. These are the lines to the dead Cordelia."

Val stood straighter. His words were charged:

Howl, howl, howl! O, you are men of stones!
Had I your tongues and eyes, I'd use the so
That heaven's vault should crack. She's gone forever.
I know when one is dead and when one lives;
She's dead as earth.

A policeman came in. "Hey, Tommy," Ernie said. "This is Mr. McCormick. He's doing some Shakespeare." The spell was broken. Val left with Oak.

"Jesus," Ernie said. "He's a God damn furnace."

"He's an extraordinary man," Harry said. "Let's close up, Ernie. We have a chance. See you tomorrow. Night."

CHAPTER 14

Two nights later Harry stepped into the headquarters just before midnight. He smelled the whiskey and saw the figures on the floor.

"Who's that?" Ernie said. A woman was underneath Ernie.

"I'll be back in fifteen minutes." Harry said and slammed the door behind him. Harry was so angry he walked up to Pill Hill barely aware of where he was. He walked to The Green and on past the Adams' house, turned and walked back to Pill Hill and down to the village. The lights were on in the headquarters. Ernie was sitting in his wheelchair and there was no sign of the woman.

"What do you think you were doing?" Harry said.

"Fucking," Ernie grinned. "Sorry. It was after hours. I had a few belts and called an old friend of mine and next thing I know we're on the floor."

"I'm so mad I'm not going to say anything more. Don't do that again."

"How about a drink?"

"No thank you. Are you too drunk to get home?"

"Fuck you."

"That's it, Ernie. Get out."

"Sure. No matter how fucking drunk I get, I can wheel this fucker home."

"If you want to work for me then work. If you want to get drunk do that. You can't do both."

Ernie's eyes were large and glazed. He took the pint bottle out of a side pocket attached to the arm of his wheel chair and took several swigs.

"I'm going, Professor. What the fuck are you running for anyway?"

"This is not the time to talk about it."

"You don't know, do you?"

"I'm running to talk about the bomb."

"What about the bomb? It's the only thing that keeps the Commies from taking over the fuckin' world."

"I'm running because if that's the way we think then all we'll do is build more bombs, more planes, more tanks, more ships and forget to think about living life."

"If the Commies walk all over us, what kind of fuckin life will that be?"

"Why are you working for me?"

Harry was still standing. Ernie took another swig of his pint. It was nearly gone. "If I don't do something, I'll be drunk all summer. It's a fucking job."

"Is that all? It's a job."

"That's all. Fifty bucks a week is good fuckin' pay."

"We'll talk about it tomorrow."

Ernie finished the bottle. Harry opened the door and Ernie wheeled himself out on the sidewalk.

"Can I wheel you home?"

"No."

Harry walked back up Pill Hill. Why am I running? Why does anyone run? To be a big shot. To articulate hopes for the country. He walked up Hillage and said aloud, "I'm running to see if I can get my family back together but it looks as if there's no chance of that. I don't know why the hell I'm running. I am. That's enough."

CHAPTER 15

B y nine the next night Ernie was alone in the headquarters. Everyone had left early because Ernie was in a bad mood. Hi Ho had come in and swept up hoping for a quarter but Ernie threw him out.

"Jesus," Ernie said aloud. "It's only ten past nine." He expected Harry to drop in by ten.

The mood of hopelessness always descended so fast. The train rumbled by shaking the chairs and table. The train. Four years ago, Ernie had come back to Boston on the train missing both legs.

The train from Chicago had been loaded with soldiers. Ernie was so mad at being a cripple he got in a fight with a man on the train. An army captain said to Ernie, "Shape up, soldier or I'll have you taken off at the next stop." Ernie shut up.

The next stop was a small town. Ernie sat on the outside seat so no one would sit beside him. He had a blanket over his legs. A woman asked Ernie if the seat beside him was taken.

"Does it look that way?" Ernie said, not looking at her.

"I'm blind," she said squeezing by him.

She was sharp chinned, wore a yellow dress and dark glasses and had once been very beautiful. She smelled of soap and dust.

"I'm Amy Van Hostler."

"Ernie Marion," he said in a tone that meant he didn't want to talk.

She was silent for a long while. Got the message, Ernie thought.

A vendor called out, "Sandwiches, candy, donuts."

"What kind of sandwiches?" the woman asked.

"Egg salad, bologna, ham and cheese," the vendor said. He was a tall teen-age boy. She got an egg salad sandwich. It was wrapped in wax paper. She unwrapped it and offered Ernie half. He declined. She got egg salad on her lower lip.

"I'm headed to New York," she said.

"You have egg salad on your face."

"Oh, thanks," she said. "Most people wouldn't tell me. Where are you headed?"

"Boston. Goin' home."

"You've been away overseas in the war?"

"Yeah. Then an army hospital."

"Oh, I'm sorry. Are you all right?"

"Yeah." Ernie had a pint of whiskey. When it got dark he took a few swigs. "Want some whiskey?"

"No," she laughed. She had nice teeth.

"What's so funny?"

"Well, I'll tell you," she said. She was not intimidated by him. "My parents were Quakers. They are Quakers, I should say. They're both alive. They were very strict when I was growing up. We always wore black like Mennonites. Do you know what a Mennonite is?"

"No." Ernie did not volunteer that he was brought up Catholic.

"No matter. Dad wouldn't buy a car. We had a horse and buggy. I ran away when I was seventeen. I was in love with acting. My sister and I used to make up plays in the barn and I acted at school. Anyway, I ran away to New York of all places. It was the most frightening time of my life. I managed to get a job in a kind of drug store restaurant. I had a room that was so small I slept curled up. It took five years but I got into a show. I was twenty-two. I sang and danced. I loved dancing. Do you dance?"

"No."

"Well I laughed because even though I went to New York and got on the stage, I never took a drink. That's a little too daring. I'm an old fuddy."

"I wouldn't say that."

"Thank you."

"What happened? How'd you go blind?"

"A stupid accident," she said. "At a rehearsal they had creaky risers. I was dancing on the top riser, maybe ten feet up. The riser collapsed and I hit my head on something as I fell. I was unconscious for two days and when I woke I was blind."

"How old were you?"

"Twenty-six."

"What happened then?"

"I sent a telegram to my aunt. She loved my being on the stage. She came and got me. I've lived with her all these years. My parents live on a farm a mile way. They come for Christmas, other than that they don't speak to me."

"Jesus," he said. "All this time?"

"My aunt died last week. I'm going to see two friends I made in New York."

"They dancers?"

"One is. She's an actress now. The other I knew from the drug store. She's married. We've written all these years. Tell me about you, Ernie."

He liked her saying his name. She spoke nicely. Every word was clear. Ernie took several swigs and fell asleep.

When he woke she was asleep. It was the middle of the night. He kept hoping she'd wake. They passed so many towns. The sleeping towns cried out to him. They were filled with returning veterans. He was drawn to the mystery of towns full of people he'd never know, towns filled with voices, with men and women and kids who had lives. For the moment he wasn't angry that they could walk; he wasn't angry that most people had two legs, and that most guys would fall in love and *walk* down the aisle -the aisle. Who cares about the fucking aisle? They can walk down the street. They can walk.

What moved Ernie was that they lived in the towns he was passing and he felt for them. The war was over, and when the sun was up these people would get dressed, go downstairs and live lives he'd never know about.

"Are you awake?" she asked.

"Yes. It's four o'clock. Can't sleep."

"You look forward to Boston?"

"I don't know. I played football in high school. Thought I might get a football scholarship. That's out."

"There's the GI bill."

He didn't reply.

"May I ask why you were in the hospital?"

"Complications."

"Oh."

"They cut my legs off and something went wrong. Complications. They messed it up. Eight months in the hospital because they screwed up."

"I'm sorry."

He nodded. They were silent. She was crying.

"You all right?" he asked.

"Yes. I imagine after being a football player it would be even harder to lose your legs."

"Yeah."

"When I went blind I carried the biggest sack in the world."

"What?"

"A big sack of resentment. I didn't even know it. Everyone I met I'd find fault with. I was convinced they were all against me. I did it for years. Then one day I noticed what I was doing. It was amazing. I spent ten years carrying this big sack of resentment. I'm sorry. I'm talking too much."

The train pulled into Grand Central station. She gave him her address and said to write if he wanted.

———

Harry Hutchinson came into the headquarters smiling at eleven. The fan clinked.

"How'd the speech go, Professor H.?"

"Good. I tried your suggestion. I started with a joke."

"They laugh?"

"No but I did. How about you Ernie?"

"It was dead tonight. Oh, you got a call from a woman who says you're great. Mrs. Samuelson. Says she's sending fifty bucks."

"She's an influential woman," Harry said. "Nuts though."

"Like me?" Ernie laughed.

"Like me," Harry said. "Let's close up. I know better than to ask if you want a ride home."

Ernie wheeled himself through the village and into the Farm. He posted his letter on the corner.

CHAPTER 16

Harry walked the length of the third floor of the Women's Free Hospital, one very long room with a tall ceiling; the beds could have curtains pulled around them but this morning only one of them did. Old women lay in the beds, their worlds reduced to a bed, slippers and a photo or two. It brought the war back to Harry. In France Harry had been in the town of Courbeau where six old women were accused of helping the partisans. The Nazis had hanged the old women on the limbs of trees in front of the Town Hall.

"Hello," a withered old woman called from her bed, her voice a high whisper. She was all bone and wrinkled skin. Her arm was painful to look at, it was so thin. Harry went over.

"Nurse said you're running for Congress," she said. Her eyes were alive.

"I am."

"You look nice," the woman said. "I hope you win."

When Harry left, he stood in the sunlight. It stunned him to think a human being could end up lying in a ward with sixty others waiting to die. He lit a cigarette and it occurred to him that if he ever did win, he might be able to help people like those old women. And winning was not impossible.

He walked down to the village and took the bus to Allston. A girl of about sixteen, with a smile that was innocent and beautiful, sat with her mother. Harry thought the girl was all that was womanhood, and the thought cheered him.

The Allston headquarters was a storefront space beside a paint store on Colley Street before the bridge to Cambridge. Ernie had set up the headquarters and put a friend in charge. She was paid twenty dollars a week.

"Professor Hutchinson, I'm Marge Caposella." Her face was wide and pock marked. Her smile was warm; she was cheerful.

"First of all, thanks for doing this, Marge."

"I owe Ernie. If he says you're ok, you are. My father-in-law knows everybody. We're going to lunch with him, and he's gonna introduce you around; then tonight you'll say a few words after supper at the Italian Hall."

At ten o' clock when Harry got the bus and headed back, only three people were on the bus. Harry imagined himself in Washington hurrying down Constitution Avenue to the Capitol where he'd take his seat in Congress. Imagine speaking before the House of Representatives. Who knows? Maybe Senator Hutchinson some day. President Harry Hutchinson.

It was almost ten-thirty when Harry got back. Ernie was the only one left.

"Marge is terrific, Ernie. She's got about ten speaking engagements lined up. You all right?"

Ernie sat in the wheel chair with his hands on the wheels.

"Bad news, Professor."

"What? My daughter? Something happened?"

"A buddy called from the *Globe*. Your father's going on some big banking conference in London. There was a press conference and your father said you shouldn't be running for Congress. He said you're dangerous. All but called you a communist."

"It's going to be in the paper?"

"Tomorrow's *Globe*."

"I can't believe he'd say that to a reporter. Your friend's exaggerating. We'll see in the morning. I'm beat. Let's go."

They parted at the fire station. Harry walked up Pill Hill too stunned to take it in. He found it hard to walk. His strength deserted him. He sat and rested on a stonewall at the crest of Pill Hill. Later, as he passed the Lawrences he saw the kitchen lights on; he walked up the board path, swatted mosquitoes, climbed the outside stairs and called through the moth-covered screen door, "Edie? Edie?" Bones, the sausage dog, scrambled down the hall barking.

Edie came to the door. "Harry. Come in. One waits for Craig."

She poured him bourbon. They sat in the living room and he told her about what his father had done. "Can you imagine his saying I'm dangerous?"

"Perhaps it will come to naught."

"Perhaps. But I've got a bad feeling, Edie."

Fifteen minutes later Harry left and went home. There was no note from Jillian saying his father had called. Surely father would have warned me.

At six in the morning Harry was at the White Tower reading *The Globe*. The only good thing was the front-page article was below the fold. It had a picture of Harry's father. HUTCHINSON SAYS HIS SON COMMUNIST SYMPATHIZER.

John Putnam Hutchinson, President of the Boston Bank, said yesterday, his son, Professor Harry Hutchinson, should not be elected to Congress. Hutchinson said his son is a socialist who has no understanding of the danger communism poses to this country and the world. Hutchinson went on to say as far as he knew his son had never been a member of the Communist Party.

The article continued. *Harry Hutchinson, assistant professor of American History at Northeastern University, advocates disarmament and the abolishment of nuclear weapons. Hutchinson denied being a member of the Communist Party.*

Harry read it and read it again and again. The article was a disaster. No reporter had ever asked him if he was a member of the Communist Party. My God, to the best of Father's knowledge, I'm not a Communist.

At seven Harry drove over to Cambridge and rang his parents' bell. There was no answer. Of course they were off to London for the banking conference. On the drive back Harry trembled with anger. "How the hell could he have done that?" Harry shouted over and over.

The next few days were the hardest Harry ever experienced; he realized that deep down he had always hoped that some day his father would not only admire him but that they'd have some kind of friendly relationship. That was over. The break was terrible.

By the end of the week the campaign had changed, and Harry knew there was no chance of winning. In the public mind he was the socialist candidate, the communist sympathizer, the disarmament professor. For the *Boston Record American* he was Harry the Red. Several of the women Meg Marion brought to the headquarters stopped coming. Their husbands didn't want them working with a Communist. A Northeastern student who went door to door for Harry in Allston was beaten up. Harry's campaign headquarters window was smashed one night. Several veterans stopped working for Harry. He wondered if he should quit so no one would get hurt. He talked it over one night at the headquarters.

"Don quo na," Old John said.

"If you quit," Edie said, "what would we do in the evenings? You are Odysseus. You must go on."

"You're always saying Washington had guts," Ernie said. "Cause he didn't quit, right?"

Harry nodded. He smoked cigarette after cigarette. So did Ernie and Meg and Edie Lawrence. The screen door let in the night air, but the room was heavy with smoke.

"What would Washington do?" Harry asked.

"He would go on," Edie said. "If you do not, the debate will cease."

"What do you think, Oak?" Harry asked.

"I think you should go on."

"Then let's," Harry said.

The good thing was Harry got publicity for weeks. He was Harry the Red to many and a thoughtful man to others, but he was known.

The Big Four were there every night. John, Oak, Ernie and Edie Lawrence. Ernie's mother, Meg Marion, was taking a night course and was there when she could be.

If there wasn't a lot of work to do, around nine-thirty Edie Lawrence would take out Dickens and read aloud. They would stay until Harry returned from speaking engagements; it was usually between ten and eleven, but even if it was midnight, they'd wait. It was important to be there night after night to swat the mosquitoes, take calls, make calls, do the mailings and, above all, to be there when Harry got back.

Harry lost weight; he was smoking three packs of cigarettes a day and was irritable.

CHAPTER 17

At seven o'clock at night, it was still light and hot in Harry's headquarters which smelled of tar because they had resurfaced the opposite side of the street. Oak had run home from school, done his homework, eaten supper and was back at headquarters where Ernie's nose was out of joint. He had a pain in his non-existent legs. Almost all of his buddies had begged off helping; they didn't say outright that Harry was a pinko, but they didn't come.

Old Mr. Paine of the stationery store came. He was eighty and lean as a fountain pen. Even his wrinkles were elegant; he stuffed envelopes at a table with Meg, Oak and Edie Lawrence. John was in the back office. Harry had had three other small headquarters but now only the Allston one stayed open.

"Yeah?" Ernie said to the woman who came in. His tone was rude. Meg got up and shook hands with the newcomer. Ernie wheeled himself out on the sidewalk and shouted he'd be back in ten minutes.

"I'm Joan Crawford," the woman said. "No, I'm not the movie star," she laughed. "I'd like to help."

"Good," Meg said. "Coffee?"

"No, thanks."

"This is Mr. Paine. He runs the best stationery store in the world."

"How do you do," Mr. Paine said, standing.

Joan was one of those people who couldn't be in the sun; her face was freckled and splotched with white patches from the sun. She wore a pale blue blouse under a dark vest with a gold pin. She was quick and efficient.

"Where are you from, Joan?" Meg asked.

"I live in Chestnut Hill. I'm a nurse. I got so mad when I read the Harry the Red article I had to do something. I'm only sorry it took me so long. Years ago I read Professor Hutchinson's book on James Otis. I've admired him ever since. What about you?"

"I live close by. My son's the campaign manager. Excuse his rudeness. When things are going badly he feels pains in his legs."

"Did he lose them in the war?"

"Yes. He brooded for two years, and then I got him to try Northeastern where he liked Professor Hutchinson's class. This campaign has been the best thing that ever happened to Ernie. We had a chance until the Harry the Red thing. It scared off most of our workers. You're a godsend." Meg's eyes filled with tears.

"I'm sorry."

Louis the Barber came in wearing a white sports shirt open at the neck and dark black pants; his black hair was sleeked back. He looked like a tour guide.

"What, no singing?" Louis said. "You can't win without a song. You people stuff. I'll sing." Louis smelled of shaving lotion. He stood just inside the doorway and began to sing in Italian. The train went by. The floor shook. Louis kept singing.

At the end of his song, Mr. Paine stood and shook Louis' hand. "From *Aida*," Mr. Paine said. "Magnificent. Thank you."

Joan left at ten and only the regulars remained. Edie Lawrence had been quiet all night. "One is sad," Edie said. Ernie had not returned.

"He's getting drunk," Meg said. "I'm furious with Professor Hutchinson's father and even madder at the newspapers. I'm mad at everybody. People really are sheep, aren't they?"

"But there are the noble," Edie said. "Ernie. John. Oak. You."

Meg laughed. "There is nothing noble about me. I just hope Ernie hasn't given up. He could be drunk for days. God, how I hate it when he's drunk."

Harry came in at ten-thirty just as John came out to the front room. "Good evening all," Harry said, "this was not our best day."

"More bad news?" Meg asked.

"More bad news," Harry said, sitting down. He lit a cigarette, took a deep breath and said, "When I was in college I went to a couple of Communist Party meetings. They were open to the public, and I went to see what they had to say. The *Brighton Weekly* had a story today saying I was at communist meetings. How the hell did they find that out?"

"Alas," Edie said, "there is but one story. Make the hero, then destroy him."

"We ha a noo halpa too nagh." John said, coming out.

"A new helper?" Harry said. "That's good. Where's Ernie?"

"He left early," Meg said. "I think he's getting drunk."

"I don't blame him. Let's get some sleep and hope for better news tomorrow. Don't anyone wear red."

Harry drove Edie and Oak home. He walked Edie up the wooden path to her back door. "Will one have a drink?" she asked.

"Not tonight, Edie."

"What your father has done will take time to absorb, Harry. It's like a death."

Harry's sleep was disturbed. A death. Edie was right. It was as if an earthquake had happened inside him. His own father. He needed Jillian. He needed to talk to her; no, he needed to make love. He got up and opened Jillian's door. "Jillian? Jillian?"

"What is it Harry?" She sat up and turned on the light.

"I need to talk, Jillian. I can't calm down. I can't rest. How in God's name could he have done it? My own father." Harry paced, took a deep breath and tried to compose himself. "I'd really like to make love."

"I'm sorry about the campaign, Harry. I asked you not to run. This is hard for me too." Her hair was all mussed, her thin nightgown showed the curve of her breasts. He was throbbing with desire.

Harry drew a chair over to the bed. "My campaign was doing far better than I'd ever have expected until Father put his oar in."

"I'll give you this, Harry, he put his oar in because you were doing well. If by some wild chance you did win, he felt you'd be a danger to the country."

"Cut it out, Jillian. He did it to punish me." Harry's voice was rising. He knew he was losing control. He couldn't get too angry or there was no hope of making love. "My father hasn't forgiven me for not going to Harvard. He hasn't forgiven me for not going to church. He doesn't give a God damn whether I believe in God or not; he just wants me to go to church." Harry slammed his fist on the bed shouting. "My father ruined my campaign because I didn't follow the plan he had for me. He is a small-minded, vengeful son of a bitch. Get that straight, Jillian," he said with such ferocity that lovemaking was out of the question. "What my father did has nothing, absolutely nothing to do with what's good for this country."

"Harry, I'm not going to have you shouting at me."

"You have a marital obligation to fulfill."

"That was over a long time ago, Harry. Please leave."

"Why?" he shouted. "Why the hell should I leave? God damnit, we're married!" Harry got up, flung the chair across the room and stormed out. A moment later he stepped back in, "Did my father tell you he was going to wreck my campaign?" She didn't answer, and Harry shouted with all the force of his being. "Did he tell you he was going to say I was all but a communist dupe? Answer me!"

"No," she screamed. "He did not tell me. Now go away!" He'd never heard such fear in her voice. He slammed the door feeling sure his father had told Jillian before speaking to the reporter.

He couldn't sleep, and at five he was walking the silent streets of Pill Hill. At dawn he stood in front of the Cobbs' castle-like house. Lydia Cobb at Creighton Mental Hospital. Would she ever again be the Lydia Cobb he'd known? Would she ever dance?

He had breakfast at the White Tower, then went to the headquarters and fell asleep on the floor in the back office.

CHAPTER 18

A week later Harry was still brooding but brightened at the sight of Meg Marion. She came into Harry's headquarters just before noon on Monday. She had called earlier to see if Harry could join her for a sandwich at Goldman's Drugstore down the block. When Meg came into the headquarters Ernie spun around in his wheelchair saying, "Hey. What's up?"

Meg wore a white dress, red shoes and carried a white pocketbook. She had on a gold bracelet, pearls and looked stunning. "Harry and I are having a sandwich," Meg said to Ernie. "Then I'm meeting a friend in Boston."

"Who's the friend?" Ernie asked.

"Just an old friend. Ready, Harry?"

When they left, Ernie lit up a cigarette. Something was up. Usually when his mother had a day off, she cleaned the apartment then helped at the headquarters. Something was up.

Meg and Harry sat at the counter at the drugstore and ordered tuna sandwiches and cokes from the wide-eyed red-headed girl behind the counter.

"Is this your first day?" Meg asked.

"Yes," the girl blushed.

"Good for you," Meg said.

Harry lit a cigarette saying, "You look beautiful, Meg."

"I'm a nervous wreck, Harry," she said. "I have an afternoon date with a boy I really liked in high school. We met again at our high school reunion and he called me. He's teaching an intensive French course in Boston. I'd like to take it."

"Do," Harry said.

"But I'd be letting you down."

"Nonsense, Meg. I'm Harry the Red. There's no chance I'll win. I'll stick it out to the primary. Take it."

Meg lit a cigarette saying, "It's not so much French. It's to see if I can still study. And this man is brilliant. I'm not sure I'm smart enough and when will I study? It's three nights a week."

"Take it," Harry said as the red-headed soda fountain girl set down two plates of tuna sandwiches with dill pickles.

"They look delicious," Meg said to the girl, and she beamed.

Harry lifted his sandwich saying, "You are very smart, Meg. I heard you got straight A's in high school."

"That was a long time ago, Harry. But it is a college course. Want my pickle?"

"I live for dill pickles," Harry said. "You could stay, Meg, and help me get the French vote. We probably have about twenty-three French Canadians in my district."

Meg didn't touch her sandwich. "No, it's foolish," she said.

"Learning is not foolish, Meg."

"But going on a date at my age is. We're going on the swan boats then we're having tea at the Ritz. I've never been to the Ritz. I'm afraid someone will say, 'Isn't that the lady who works at the donut shop?'"

"Ah," Harry said waving his pickle. "They'll say, 'Isn't that the Red donut lady?' Revolution at the Ritz."

"Seriously, Harry. It's foolish. I'll call him and tell him that I'll take the course but I'm not going out on the swan boats."

Harry laughed, "You'll go. You'll have fun. French. The Ritz. Romance. The hell with politics. I'll go with you. We'll all go with you."

"You think I should go?"

"I do," said Harry. Harry was being very expansive. He threw his arms out and said, "You look beautiful! The swan boats will love you, ma cherie."

Meg insisted on paying. She left a quarter for the red-headed girl and told her she'd done a wonderful job.

Out on the sidewalk Meg said, "Good luck tonight at the high school, Harry. You'll be great." Harry kissed her on the cheek and Meg headed off to catch the bus to Boston.

Harry's asthma kicked up on the way to the Saunders High School in Allston where all ten candidates were going to speak for ten minutes each. Idiocy, he thought. He was in a bad mood. Idiotic auditorium.

The candidates sat on metal chairs on the stage. Now that he was no longer an unknown assistant professor of history but Harry the Red, the other candidates felt either awkward with him or hostile toward him. Tonight he felt like leaning close to Don Nestor and saying, "Joe Stalin called me last night from the Kremlin. He's endorsed me." He made jokes to himself but hated being treated like a leper.

The crowd was pretty good, almost four hundred people. They had a drawing to pick the order and Harry was to speak second to last.

Josh Cater spoke first. Harry made notes in a small notebook. *Josh is Copernicus. He's discovered that the entire solar system revolves around him. Dark caramel voice.* Harry found Josh interminable. They were allowed ten minutes. After fifteen minutes the moderator asked Josh to finish up. Five minutes later Josh sat down. At this rate, Harry thought, I'll give a breakfast talk.

Next, State Representative Joey H. Kiernan came to the podium. *Ordinary guy approach. I'm goin'. We're goin.' I'm tryin'. Green tie. Blue shirt. The rest of us look like undertakers in white shirts and dark ties. Joey said all he had to say with his first two words. Thank you. Should have quit then.*

Michael Webster began to speak. Michael, thirty-three, was rich, handsome, a Rhodes scholar, a Harvard man, a good trial lawyer and a polished speaker and, if anything, he was too confident. He hadn't been in the war because he had had polio as a boy and suffered a bad limp. It occurred to Harry that Michael was the son his father wanted.

He makes sense, Harry wrote, *but he's dull.* Harry lost interest and began to make notes for a letter to his father.

Our Father. Grandfather said that was the great prayer of life. When I was twelve, you and I drove to the Cape together and you said, "We're all heading to the Father." I asked what you meant and you said the whole point of Christianity was that we're headed back to the Father from whence we came. I had no idea what you meant but was struck by your saying something adult to me. I think it was the only time we ever had a conversation.

You crippled my campaign. Why? I cannot defend myself now that I'm Harry the Red.

Don Nestor got the biggest applause. Harry made notes of Nestor's talk: *"A new era. Not since the dawn of civilization has there been such danger to mankind." You are the danger Donny. He's decided on the grand approach. "We need new Democratic leadership. We lost China. Russia has the bomb. Alger Hiss is a spy. The Russian army stands at two million six hundred thousand while we have six hundred forty thousand. We produce twelve hundred planes a year. The Russians produce seven thousand a year. Now the Red Chinese are challenging us in Korea. There is a Red Tide rising in the world. My job as congressman will be to support those American fighting men in Korea with everything we've got. If Mao sends in Chinese troops, we should use every weapon we've got. Every weapon." Scare the pants off everybody. Standing ovation. They love it.*

It was nine thirty when Harry was introduced. If it hadn't been for his being Harry the Red, people would have left, but they wanted to hear the wild man who'd been denounced by his father.

"Thank you," Harry started. "You may have read in the newspapers that my father disagrees with my political opinions." Harry named the unnamable. They were listening. "FDR is one of my heroes. Every time I get off the Arborway subway car and walk under the stone bridge to Muddy River, I think of Roosevelt's WPA project. I want to bring that kind of imaginative thinking to Washington."

"Let me tell you something about the atomic bomb. The U.S. military wanted control over the bomb. Lots of top presidential advisors agreed with the military. President Truman felt the atomic was so dangerous a weapon it should be taken out of military hands. The President alone decides whether to use the bomb. That was a wise decision. I want to be in Congress to support that decision."

"Harry the Red!" someone shouted. It was like a flash of electricity. Suddenly there was danger in the air.

"Harry the Red," Harry repeated. "The red, white and blue." People laughed and applauded, and the tension was broken. When Harry sat down, he got some boos and some applause. Two people in the back stood up and cheered. It was over at twenty past eleven. Harry shook hands with the candidates who didn't flee from him and went down the stage stairs toward the exit. So many admirers surrounded Don Nestor he looked like a movie star.

Harry escaped to the parking lot where a woman was trying to start her car.

"Flooded," Harry said.

"Oh, Professor Hutchinson! I had hoped to talk to you, but you were surrounded by admirers."

"I was being given advice."

"Could we talk? Maybe a cup of coffee?"

"Sure," Harry said. Reaching out of her car window, she shook his hand and said, "I'm Diane St. George," She had so much life it was no wonder the car wouldn't start; it was flooded with eagerness. So was Harry. Even in the dark her eyes were merry and intelligent. "Want to follow me to my headquarters?" he asked. "We could get a bite to eat and talk. It's just ten minutes away."

"I can't. I broke the heel off my shoe," she laughed. "And now I can't start my car."

"I'll lend you a pair of my wife's shoes. She's about your size. We live two minutes from my headquarters. Wait a couple of minutes, it'll start." It started and Harry felt like a mechanic. She followed him home. Hoping against hope Jillian wouldn't be back, Harry knocked on her bedroom door.

"What is it?" Jillian said not turning on the light.

"Sorry," Harry whispered. "A woman at candidate's night broke the heel off her shoe. Could she borrow a pair of yours?"

"God, Harry! Take my old sneakers, and let me get some sleep." She snapped on the light. "They're in the closet to the right." He took Jillian's good sneakers.

The headquarters was dark. "I hoped my campaign manager would be here. He's the wave of the future."

"You are," Diane said.

"No, I'm already old hat. Want a bite of Chinese food?"

The Chinese restaurant was next door to Atlas Paint two blocks from his headquarters. He felt light beside her. His tiredness had vanished and he relished the steamy, sweet smelling, mysterious night lit by a few car lights, street lanterns and a moon that looked like a golden drum.

Her eyes shone in the semidarkness of the restaurant; merry, mischievous brown eyes that combined with the warmth of her voice and the tumbling playfulness of her laughter changed everything around them: the hot and sour soup was not just delicious, it was hilarious. A passing motorcycle made Diane burst into laughter and tell a story of the crowded Brooklyn street where she grew up. The gentle Chinese waitress became the guardian of their enchantment.

When the meal came Diane said, "What do you're mean you're old hat?"

"My political career is beginning and ending at the same time."

"Because they call you Harry the Red?"

"Because Stalin's got everybody scared. McCarthy and company are whipping up a storm. People stop thinking when they get frightened. McCarthy and I are the same age; he's beginning and I'm ending."

"He's a buffoon," Diane said. "Dangerous but a buffoon." Her eyes were the most expressive he'd ever seen as she leaned forward, her eyes now held fury that made her even more beautiful. "The senator from Maine, Margaret Chase Smith, said she didn't want the Republican Party run on the four horsemen of fear, ignorance, bigotry and smear." Diane sat back and he poured her more wine.

"You were wonderful tonight," she said laughing at her own seriousness. "It never occurred to me the military could have control of the atomic bomb."

"Thank God for Truman," Harry said. "Enough politics. Tell me about yourself."

"I'm an actress. Mondays are dark so I was able to hear you tonight. I was on stage yesterday doing *Midsummer Night's Dream* and found I was thinking of Maine." Her voice was alive; her words popped, swam, lingered, and each was a note he savored. "We close in early October, and I'll go up to a funny old hotel by Higgins Beach in Cape Elizabeth for a whole week. I can't wait."

They talked of Maine; then Diane said, "I saw you writing tonight. Were you preparing your talk?"

"No," Harry said. "I was jotting notes about my competitors."

"Wonderful," Diane laughed. "So did I." She took her notes out of her pocket book and began to read. "The first speaker was Sun God." Diane sat straight, opened her arms and said,

"I'm running on the meeeeeeeeeeeeeeeeeeeeeeeeeeeee ticket." Her voice filled the little restaurant. Diane went down the list and had Harry laughing so hard the waiters were staring. "Nestor the Bomber," Diane said. "And you. You know what I wrote about you?" She didn't wait for Harry's answer, "Hutchinson has integrity."

"You know," Harry said, "I go to bed every night thinking I'm going to get out of the race tomorrow. Tonight I'll go to bed laughing."

They walked back through the silent village. "Mr. Paine's Stationery store," Harry said as they passed. "Val McCormick, a neighbor of mine, said Mr. Paine has a fine watermark stamped on his soul. This is Mackey and Mead's Hardware. Meg Marion, who helps out at the headquarters, told me the saddest story about Mead."

Oh," she said, "tell me."

"I don't remember it well enough," he said, but it wasn't that; he didn't feel like telling a sad story while walking with Diane.

When they reached her car, she kissed him on the cheek and drove off as the train rumbled by filling the street with its power and mystery. Then it, too, was gone like Diane. Her kiss quickened his spirits and he whispered-sang "Shine on Harvest Moon."

The night was still hot but a soft breeze turned the village into a strangely haunting place. Harry turned and looked at the sign, HUTCHINSON FOR CONGRESS.

<u>*CHAPTER 19*</u>

John sat in his Charlestown apartment re-reading a letter he'd written to Helene L'Alma, the nurse who was so kind in the hospital so long ago. He wrote her hundreds of letters and never mailed them. He liked to pick a few at random.

This letter was written when he was in the Massachusetts Mental Institution in 1926. The paper was cracked at the edges and the ink faded; only a few phrases were legible.

December 12, 1926
Dear Helene,
Christmas is coming. I remember the French carols you sang.
We put on a play here. The audience was quiet but Bostonians are reserved.
Mayor Curley is coming to visit on Christmas.

The following night John was back in the headquarters. Ernie had the Red Sox game on. Oak was putting stamps on envelopes. Ned Martin, the announcer, was saying, *Pesky is sliding into third base. Safe!*

"A triple is the best fucking hit in baseball," Ernie said. "Home run is all right but a triple keeps everything alive."

"Hi, Mrs. Lawrence," Oak said.

Edie Lawrence came in wearing a red sari. Her brother was a Canadian diplomat stationed in New Delhi, and she'd fallen in love with the saris he sent. She shook her head as if to announce something important, "One waited for one's husband to celebrate one's wedding anniversary when one got a call saying he would be delayed at the hospital until ten which means eleven. One is forlorn," she laughed dramatically. She had had something to drink and was a little unsteady. "I have come to help."

Dom DiMaggio is leading off. Oak liked Dom DiMaggio because he wore glasses. Edie's cigarette smoke drifted into John's right eye. "I'm sorry, John. One does not want to make you a Cyclops."

"Ooooooooo ayeeee ooops?" John asked. They were surprised because John rarely spoke.

"A race of one-eyed giants," Edie said. "Odysseus and his men were trapped in a cave, and a one-eyed giant was crushing and eating his men, so Odysseus got the giant drunk, sharpened a log and put the giant's eye out."

Out! Ned Martin, the announcer, shouted, *Joltin' Joe is out at the plate!*

"So you studied Greek in college, Mrs. Lawrence?" Ernie asked.

"I love the language and was ravaged by Odysseus."

"What can you do with Greek in the real world?"

"Understand it," Edie said. "We are in danger of being defeated by hubris. In *Antigone*, the blind prophet, Tiresias, says only a fool is governed by self will. Hubris. Our government chose not to tell us of the Holocaust during the war. Why? Hubris. We still don't know the damage caused by the atomic bomb. The government will not release films, photographs, interviews with the Japanese. Why? Only the gods of government can know. Hubris comes with power. Harry is our Greek chorus. He warns us of hubris."

Pesky caught a hard linedrive, Ned Martin said. The little tin fan clunked and made metal ticking sounds. Ernie and Edie smoked their cigarettes. *Goodman will lead off the seventh hitting .303.* They were quiet a while then Ernie leaned forward and said, "How can anyone love language? I don't trust people who use big words."

"I feel sad for those who use the same few words," Edie said. Her voice was low.

"Like what?"

"Like the one-syllable verb for fornication that men use over and over. When you rely on a single word to describe an emotion like anger, you become numb to more subtle feelings. You grow coarse. I say this, Ernie, because you have a good mind; I don't want you to trap yourself. The vulgar word I speak of is an explosive, flexible word which if used indiscriminately deadens the spirit. When I was a child I sang "Frere Jacques" so often my mother made me go outside. Wouldn't it be sad if that were the only song I ever learned? You're very bright, Ernie. Sing lots of songs."

Ernie's brow contracted into a scowl. Edie put our her cigarette saying, "Forgive me, I have said too much."

"No," Ernie said still scowling, "I lost my fu…my legs. I can take a little criticism."

Edie looked at him across the table. Oak and John were silent. "I hope you run for office one day, Ernie. Be like Churchill and enjoy the language."

"I'm no Churchill."

"You may be. Play with the language. Freshman year of college, the first day of our English Literature class, our professor, a formidable woman, strode in and said, 'Avoid clichés.' On that note, Ernie," she said in her deepest voice, "I suggest we get the fuck out of here."

Harry came in just then, paused, smiled and took it all in. A woman in a sari, a young man in a wheelchair, Oak in a t-shirt and a man almost impossibly deformed. "What a team," Harry said, "How can I lose?" Harry's seersucker suit was rumpled and his white shirt looked limp but his straw hat gave him dash.

Harry drove Oak and Edie home. Oak said good night and Harry walked Edie to her door.

"Would one like a nightcap?"

"Yes," Harry said. They sat in the kitchen and Edie poured the S.S. Pierce bourbon into small glasses. She put water in hers and told Harry what she had said to Ernie.

"Good," Harry said drinking his bourbon down. He was about to go when he sensed sadness in Edie, "What is it, Edie?"

"One is glad to be in your campaign, for in general I am of little use. I do not fit." She shook her head and laughed but was trying not to cry. "Craig goes off each morning like a great knight," she said. "He is running a hospital, going to meetings, writing papers for medical journals, curing the sick. He is a wonder. I wait for the knight to return. I tried teaching Greek mythology, but I spent the first month on the first letter of the Greek alphabet, and they sacked me."

"You are the most brilliant woman I know."

"One is a misfit. Ah, it's Craig." Craig Lawrence came in the back door and set his black medical bag down. He was a handsome man in his three-piece suit, who walked with a slight rocking motion, his smile and gray-brown eyes were welcoming.

"Would you like a drink and supper, Sir Knight?"

"I had a bite, but I'd love a drink. How's the campaign, Harry?"

CHAPTER 20

A t seven the next morning, Harry was at the Statler Hotel
in downtown Boston for the Democratic breakfast. There
were five hundred people at tables in the Grand Ballroom and
Tip O'Neill, Speaker of the Massachusetts Legislature, was the
master of ceremonies. He was a big, genial, imposing man with
thick, black hair Harry envied.

"When I first got into the Massachusetts legislature, the Democrats were the minority party," Tip said. "We Democrats didn't
even have an office. When we wanted to speak to the Republican
leadership, we had to speak at the door to their office because we
were not allowed over the threshold. Things are changing mighty
fast." There was a terrific applause. "Look at this lineup," Tip
said. "To my left is the Governor of Massachusetts, Paul Dever.
To my right is a man who has dominated Boston politics for half
a century, Governor James Michael Curley. And beside him John
Hynes, Mayor of Boston. And to the mayor's left, Congressman
Jack Kennedy."

Harry felt very much the odd duck here; he knew there was
no one in the room who hadn't read about Harry the Red. No
one had gone out of his way to say hello. Harry was uncomfortable but fascinated by it all; Kennedy looked so young, maybe
thirty, or thirty-two. Harry hoped Curley would speak but De-

ver spoke. Governor Dever was round and smooth-faced, his dark hair was thinning, his voice was as smooth as his skin. Dever made a plea for unity. "When the primary is over, we need to pull together. This has been a Republican state all our lives and, as Tip said, it's changing. We can fight among ourselves up until the primary, but then we need to put our differences aside and work for the party." Harry thought the Kennedys and Curley would never put their differences aside.

Harry heard that four years ago when Kennedy first ran for Congress he'd come into a room and head for the exit. No more. Kennedy had grown; his star was rising, but Harry could see that Kennedy was uncomfortable sitting beside James Michael Curley. In fact, Kennedy looked stiff as a frozen sail.

Harry was fascinated watching Curley and Kennedy. Kennedy was Choate, Harvard, a war hero and son of a millionaire who had been Ambassador to England. Kennedy's father, Joe Kennedy, did all he could to help his son elected. Young Jack Kennedy sat there in a well tailored navy blue suit. He had a great pile of dark brown hair that gave him an air of dash and romance.

Curley was of a different world. He had left school after the ninth grade to work at a piano company. He had been working since he was ten. Curley's father, a laborer, died at thirty four after lifting a four hundred pound curbstone. Curley went on to be an alderman, a ward boss, four times mayor of Boston, governor and congressman. He was hated and loved as no other Boston politician had been. Curley was old school, a brawler, a city boss, and it was rumored that he took money under the table. Curley looked old. He looked like he belonged in the 1930s and so did his suit. But still, Harry thought, the man has magic.

Two years ago, Harry had been stuck in Boston traffic for three hours because thousands of people drove to South Station to welcome Curley back from his second stay in prison. He had been convicted of mail fraud. President Truman pardoned Curley after eight Massachusetts congressmen petitioned for the pardon. Kennedy was the only Massachusetts congressman who didn't sign the petition. There was no love lost between the Kennedys and James Michael Curley because Curley had driven Kennedy's grandfather, "Honey Fitz", from politics at the height of his career. Harry had been told Curley threatened to expose Honey Fitz's affair with the dancer "Toodles." Curley, a superb showman, promised to give a series of lectures on "Great Lovers in History: From Cleopatra to Toodles." Harry thought, better Toodles than Harry the Red. Jack Kennedy was lucky having the grandfather he did.

Harry knew Tip was friendly and helpful to all Democrats, so when the breakfast was over he hung around. Kennedy had disappeared. It was half an hour before Harry got through the crowd around six-foot-four Tip O'Neill. Tip had a strong handshake.

"Yeah, great, Harry," Tip said. "Push what you did in the war. That's what Jack Kennedy did."

"Is there any way to overcome the Harry the Red tag?" Harry asked.

Two men were trying to get Tip away. "We're late Tip."

"I'll be right there." Tip turned back to Harry. Tip clearly liked people. "Joe Meegan collared me. He's head of the veterans committee. He wants you to quit, but I got a call from another veteran, Poo Donovan, and he said you got a veteran running your campaign."

"Ernie Marion. Lost both legs in the war."

"And you're a veteran. A hero. That's gold. And you know what else is gold? Sticking to your guns. Don't push the bomb, but if it's brought up, be honest. Stick to your guns. Good luck, Harry."

When Harry got outside the rain was pouring down and there wasn't a cab in sight, so he made a dash for the subway. A car horn blared, and a back car door opened. "Get in, young man. I'll give you a ride."

He got in. It was James Michael Curley.

"Thank you, Governor," He said feeling he was speaking to a myth.

"I'm headed home," Curley said. "Can I drop you?"

"I'm going to my headquarters in Muddy River Village. The subway would be great."

"No. We'll drop you. Muddy River Village, Jake." The driver nodded. Curley's face was long, lined, strong, and above all, tired. He must be eighty, Harry thought. Curley exuded something; not power so much as warmth which surprised Harry since he thought of Curley as tough and ruthless. Harry could see Curley's suit was so worn it looked sad.

"Your father detests me, and I detest your father," Curley said. "That's why I picked you up. I can't fathom a father attacking his son in the press."

"Neither can I, Governor."

"In my third term as mayor I spent so much money building hospitals, parks and subways the city was broke, so I asked the Boston Bank for a loan until taxes were paid. They refused, so I called the bank president. He was on vacation; I got your father instead. I told him the city water pipes ran right under the bank and said I'd open the main and flood the bank vaults unless I got the loan. I got the loan."

"My mother said she'd never seen my father so angry in her life."

"The pleasures of politics," Curley said. "I saw you talking to Tip O'Neill. I'll give you the same advice I gave Tip. Learn some poetry."

"Why?"

"I saw you speak last night. I liked the red, white and blue comeback. That was quick, but in general you lacked cadence. You need rhythm. Speaking is music. A poem would have caught them off guard. You need to study oratory; vary your voice. Pause; let them wait once in a while. I got Tip over to the house once and picked out some poems and made him learn them. People love poetry, and they love a good speaker."

"Tom Eliot told my father you were the best speaker he's ever heard."

"What did your father say to that?"

He said, "Don't be an ass."

Curley's laugh made him look far younger.

"I'll bet Tip told you to stop talking about the bomb."

"Everybody has. It has to be talked about."

"Not if it loses you votes. You look at my record in Congress, and you'll find it's as liberal as anyone's, but do I sound liberal when I campaign? Of course not. I want to get elected. Jobs. Wages. Defense. That's it."

"I heard Kennedy spent three hundred thousand on his first congressional campaign."

"Old man Kennedy did," Curley said.

"My entire budget is eight thousand."

"I've run on less. You talked last night about the WPA bridge you walk under. I built that. Next time mention that." Curley had changed since they started talking. Harry had heard that when he was mayor, Curley worked eighteen hours a day and saw a thousand people in a week. Harry could feel the man's energy.

"Remember to thank people," Curley said. "People like to be thanked, and they love to be asked for their vote. Do you go door to door?"

"Yes," Harry said. "But it isn't working very well now that I'm the bogeyman."

When they got to the headquarters, Harry asked Curley if he'd please come in to meet his manager. The driver got an umbrella and held it as Curley got out and hurried to the door.

Ernie had his back to them and was shouting on the phone, "I don't give a *fuck* what you heard. It's horseshit! Print it and we'll sue!" Ernie half turned saying, "Asshole reporter from the *Globe* got a tip you didn't save anybody in the war."

"Tell him to check with the Army," Harry said. "Ernie, I want you to meet Governor Curley."

Ernie's face went scarlet. He wheeled himself forward, "Governor, it's a pleasure. I'm sorry for the language."

"A pleasure to see you impassioned. How did you lose your legs?"

"The war."

"I'm sorry," Curley said. "But I'm impressed. Your boss has more sense than the papers give him credit for."

"I'm going to lose," Harry said, "but Ernie's going places."

"Call me if I can be of help." Curley wrote his phone number on a piece of paper and handed it to Harry.

"Good luck, Harry," Curley said shaking Harry's hand. "Try some poetry."

When Curley was gone, Ernie just shook his head. "Holy Shit. James Michael Curley. Wait'll I tell Mom. Who else did you meet?"

"I'll tell you later. What was that about the *Globe*?"

"Reporter said he heard you weren't in Italy so the hero story is a fake."

Harry got on the phone, "Ed? Harry Hutchinson. Fine, and you?" They talked several minutes before Harry explained about *The Globe* reporter. "Call him and tell him what happened. In the meantime I'll call the VA office and see if we can get the records."

"Who was that?" Ernie asked.

"Ed Keefe. Once Private Ed Keefe. He was the one I pulled off the street in Italy. He runs a general store in Maine."

Harry had no luck finding out where he could get his Army records, so he called James Michael Curley. In half an hour Curley found the man who could locate Harry's Army records. *The Globe* killed the story.

CHAPTER 21

It was late and Harry sat alone in the headquarters because he didn't want to get home before Jillian was asleep. A mosquito buzzed his ear; he hit at it with his cigarette hand, the burning ash fell onto his pant leg and he jumped up.

The shock reminded him of jumping up in his kitchen four years ago and running upstairs to knock on his daughter's door. When she didn't answer, he opened the door and she lay on the floor a bottle of sleeping pills beside her.

It was days later in the hospital that Harry had the first real talk with his daughter. "Can I tell you something, sweetie?" he asked sitting by her hospital bed. Ophelia was curly haired, intense and without much of a sense of humor; she was by no means fat, but ordinarily her cheeks bulged as if she were being funny. Today she was pale, and her light brown eyes dull.

"I love you, Ophelia. I've been a lousy father, but there's time. You have a year of high school left, and we can do things. We can hike. We can take Pill Hill walks together."

"Why don't you and Mom even like each other?"

Harry couldn't answer. Ophelia lay there looking more thirteen than seventeen. Her heroes were Dostoevsky and Kafka, and she scorned anyone who said anything ordinary like hello or good morning but lying in the hospital bed her shield was down.

"I'm not good enough," Ophelia cried. "I'll never get into Vassar."

"Oh, Ophelia," Harry said taking her hand. "That's not important."

"It is!"

"No. We love you—not Vassar."

"Mom wants me to go to Vassar." Ophelia's voice was shrill. Her bee hive voice.

"Sweetie," Harry said. "We try, but get confused." He was making no sense. "I want you to get well, Ophelia. I want us to try to be a family."

"It's too late, Dad." The nurse asked Harry to leave.

Harry sat up that night in the kitchen waiting for Jillian to come home. Jillian came in looking almost sexy in a purple dress that looked as if it were made of expensive wrapping paper.

"How did it go?" Harry asked. She'd been at some big charity event.

"Fine. I'm tired."

"Could we talk a minute?" She sat at the kitchen table declining even a glass of water so it would be brief.

"Jillian, I want us to try to be a family. I want Ophelia to be happy. She nearly killed herself because she doesn't think she'll get into Vassar."

"That's nonsense, Harry. She'll get into Vassar. She's dramatic. All this was an adolescent ploy to get attention. She's got to be queen bee."

"For God's sakes, Jillian! She nearly killed herself."

Jillian turned away and crumbled. They'd been married seventeen years and Harry had never seen her cry. He put his hand on hers. "Let's try, Jillian. Let's try."

Jillian nodded. Except for Ophelia's brief smile that afternoon, Jillian's nod was the most beautiful thing Harry had ever seen.

The train went by, shaking the headquarters. Eleven fifteen. Even though the door was open, it was still hot. Hi Ho stood in the doorway, drunk. "Fuckin' Red," he said to Harry and moved on. Harry turned out the light in the headquarters, shut the door and sat thinking. They had tried to be a family…they had tried, then somehow they just got so busy. Harry with his book on James Otis, Jillian with a score of committees; they got busy.

Another train rumbled by. Harry left the headquarters and saw Hi Ho standing by the waist high fence looking down at the train. Harry had the awful feeling Hi Ho might jump so he went over to ask if he was all right. Hi Ho was standing but insensible.

"Can I give you a lift?"

Hi Ho stumbled; Harry helped him to his car just outside the headquarters; they drove in silence down to the Farm.

"Where can I leave you?" Harry asked.

Hi Ho opened the door, got out, shut the car door and stood there swaying.

Harry drove back to the headquarters. He sat at a table, turned a single light on, took out a piece of his Hutchison For Congress stationery and began to write.

July 22, 1951
Dear Ophelia,

It's exciting to think of you acting and walking by the Thames. I miss you but am glad London has a chance to meet you.

I'm involved in a drama here myself. I'm writing you from my headquarters down in the village. It's right beside Louis's barbershop; I think Shakespeare would have enjoyed it. We don't have Falstaff, but we have Hi Ho who, like Bardolf, lights the way with his nose at night.

My campaign stalwarts are the Big Four: Ernie Marion, Old John, Edie Lawrence and young Oak McCormick. Ernie lives down the Farm; he lost both legs in the war and has a chip on his shoulder, but he's a fine campaign manager. I think anybody else would have quit.

Former Governor Curley gave me a lift one morning and came in to the headquarters. He's enormously intelligent and, again, a character Shakespeare would have liked. You were too young to remember that Curley came out for Roosevelt in 1936 when Al Smith, a Catholic, was running. Curley became anathema in Boston and wasn't chosen as a delegate to the Democratic Convention. He showed up as a delegate from Puerto Rico; Roosevelt was nominated, and Curley returned to Boston to the ovation of thousands.

The village is silent now. I often think of quitting; if I did your mother and I could get over to London to visit, but it's best to stick it out. We'll visit you at Christmas time. What fun it would be to see you on the stage and to take a double-decker bus with you. I think of you every day. You are a marvel. I love you.

Dad

After that night Harry wrote Ophelia once a week. He'd scratch out a letter while waiting for a windbag to finish speaking, or he'd write it at home before he went to sleep.

CHAPTER 22

A ugust 15th, Saturday night, was Oak's birthday and instead
of having a party, he wanted to work at the headquarters. It
was 91 degrees at six-thirty. Harry sat in the stifling room talking
with Edie Lawrence; he was nervous and her laughter—which
began low and chugged like a train starting, picked up force then
ran free—buoyed him. Harry wore a seersucker suit and the
Panama hat Edie had bought for him. She had removed the red
band and put on a blue one.

"Skip the VFW tonight," Ernie said. Ernie's face was red;
beads of sweat sat on his upper lip; his short-sleeved blue shirt
had dark patches under the arms. Ernie hated heat. "The picnic started at four. Those guys will be crocked and they're all in
Nestor's pocket."

"I've gotta show the flag," Harry said. "If I'm afraid to go to a
picnic, I shouldn't be running."

"You got to pick and choose," Ernie said. "Skip it."

"No, Ernie. I accepted two months ago. I'm going."

"Then tell them about what you did in the war. Don't mention the bomb. If some drunk yells Harry the Red, don't take the
bait."

"You know Rosalind Russell's motto," Edie said, "Lord, give
me wings to get to the point."

"Let's go, Oak," Harry said.

"Me?" Oak usually went only on day events with Harry.

"Yes. It's your birthday. You'll bring me good luck."

Oak had slicked his hair to look like Joey Hagan, the best street fighter in Oak's grade. Joey lived down the Farm. Without his mother's green gunk on his hair, Oak had no mysterious curl.

Harry's black Chevrolet rattled. The back seat was filled with posters, bumper stickers, and campaign signs and smelled of rotting apples.

"Oak, when we get back, remind me to find that bag of apples and toss them out." He used the cigarette lighter to light his Chesterfield cigarette. "Now, Oak," he said, "if these fellas have been drinking, they might get rambunctious. Pay no attention. I'll keep my talk short and we'll get out of there."

The VFW was on the parkway; the picnic was being held in back where a row of barbecue grills and three silver kegs of beer stood. Further back was a tent that would hold a couple of hundred people. A small band played under the trees. It was quarter to eight and growing dark; summer was coming to an end.

A tall, red-haired man wearing khakis and a dark blue shirt approached. Oak was sweating, but the man looked cool. "Professor Hutchinson? Great. I'm Jack Cleary, Secretary-Treasurer. Thanks for coming. People are excited. We start at eight. How about a hot dog? Is this your boy?" Cleary shook Oak's hand. Harry asked Cleary if he was the Boston University football star.

"Long ago," Cleary said, "long ago."

"You were terrific," Harry said. "Now I'd like to test the microphone. That's one thing I've learned."

"Sure, you go ahead. We had a raffle earlier. Seemed fine."

The tent was hot, paper cups littered the matted and muddy grass. Oak slipped and landed on his bottom. Harry stood on the wooden platform and tested the microphone which squealed; so he moved further away; there was still static.

Since no one was in the tent at eight, Harry went in search of Jack Cleary who was nowhere to be found. By eight-thirty, forty or fifty men and a few women sat in the tent. Jack Cleary appeared and asked Harry to be patient. Only one other candidate, Don Nestor, had come. Nestor, in a dark suit, nodded to Harry but didn't shake hands; he looked as if he'd been on a beach all summer. Outside the tent people were singing and children were running around.

Cleary got people quiet. "Ladies and gentlemen. It's hot and we're gettin' tired so I've asked our two speakers to be brief. I want to thank them for coming. Our first speaker, Don Nestor, is a decorated war veteran, a lawyer and way out in front of the polls. It is my pleasure to introduce Don Nestor." They gave him a hearty applause.

"Thank you so much," Nestor said. "It's hot, so I'll get right to it. There's only one issue. The issue is survival. Stalin and the Communists want to bury us. We learned with Hitler you don't back away. When someone hits you, you hit back. They need to know if they so much as send a plane in our direction, we'll blow them off the face of the earth."

The audience cheered. They made so much noise people came running into the tent. Nestor was different tonight; Harry wondered if he'd been drinking.

"Come on in," Nestor said to people at the entrance of the tent. "It's a victory party. We're giving it to the Reds." This was definitely a different Nestor. Someone had been coaching him. And not only had he been drinking, he was well oiled.

"We're sick of being stomped on," Nestor shouted. He waved his fist, "We're the greatest nation on earth. We defeated the Nazis, and we'll defeat the Reds." The cheering got louder. The tent was filling. Nestor whispered into the microphone, "The Reds say they're going to bury us. Are we going to let them?" Nestor looked around, waited, then said in a clear voice, "No. We'll bury them instead. Are you with me?"

"Yes!" people shouted.

"If they take one more wrong step, shall we blow them back to the caves they came from?"

"Yes!" they roared and Nestor roared back. "I can't hear you."

"Yes! Yes! Yes!"

"Let me hear you! Shall we blow them off the face of the earth?"

"Yes! Yes! Yes!"

They were all on their feet. Men were shaking their fists, shouting, cheering, and slapping one another. Oak had never seen anything like it. Some men were crying.

The audience was in a frenzy. It was as if World War II had just been won. The band just behind the tent struck up the football song. People were jumping and dancing and singing as Nestor stood, arms in the air, urging them on.

"What the hell could I say after that," Harry was wondering, "I was born in a log cabin?" He'd planned to take Curley's advice and recite "Casey at the Bat", but it wouldn't work. He decided on the direct approach. He whispered to Oak, "I should have brought Ernie to this one."

Jack Cleary finally said, "Thank you, Don Nestor. I've never heard a better speech." More applause. "Our other speaker is also a decorated veteran. He is professor of American history, Harry Hutchinson." There were several boos. Harry went to the microphone and waited until it was quiet.

"Thank you Mr. Secretary-Treasurer. It's an honor to be here. Many of you men were in the war and know it intimately."

"Get the Commie off the stage," a man called. The man stood and shouted. "Is this what we fought for? Get him off the stage."

"Let him talk," several men shouted.

"I won't shut up," the loud man shouted. "We're getting butchered in Korea. This guy's a fucking Red."

"Let me finish," Harry said. "We are fighting for freedom…"
He was too close to the mike and it screeched. Harry groaned.

A stone hit him on the side of the cheek and almost at the same moment a softball hit him in the chest. The softball was rock hard and sent Harry staggering back. A fight broke out in the audience. Harry got back to the mike and began to sing the "Star Spangled Banner"; after a few bars the band picked it up and people began to sing. At the end, men applauded, but the angry man shouted, "Get him off that fuckin' stage or I will."

Harry nodded to Oak. The two of them made towards the opening at the side nearest them. The loud drunk who started it came pushing forward and shoved Harry; Harry slipped in the mud, and the drunk kicked him hard in the back before several men wrestled the drunk to the ground. Two men in their twenties lifted Harry up and helped him to his car.

"Want us to drive you home? Joe can follow in his car."

"I'm all right," Harry whispered.

"We'll drive you. Maybe we better take you to the hospital."

"No really," Harry said. "I don't think anything's broken. I look worse than I am."

"I'm sorry," the man said. "I'm Jerry Cleary. You met my dad. I'm sorry."

"It's the heat," Harry said. "I'll be fine now."

Oak was so frightened he was unable to talk. Harry's suit was all mud, his hat was gone, his cheek was bleeding, and he talked as if every word hurt.

"It's the heat, Oak," Harry said but the effort was so great he stopped talking. They drove to Pill Hill in a silence interrupted by small groans from Harry. Harry parked on Forceps and Oak insisted on going with Harry to see if Dr. Lawrence was home. Craig Lawrence came to the screen door. "Are you all right, Harry? Come in. Come in." Edie Lawrence hurried to get towels.

In the kitchen Harry groaned as he tried to take his jacket off. "Easy," Dr. Lawrence said, "I'll do it." Harry unbuttoned his shirt and his breath came short. Dr. Lawrence touched Harry gently on the chest, and Harry let out a cry.

"I think it's a bruised sternum, Harry. We'll have to take an x-ray. What happened?" Harry told him about the softball.

"When will it heal?" Harry asked.

"Four or five months," Craig said.

"Four or five months!" Harry said too forcefully and gasped in pain.

"There is nothing to do about the sternum except wait," Craig said. "You can't lift anything. Not even a briefcase. You should give up the race and rest."

"I can't," Harry said.

"I'll carry things for you," Oak said.

"How about a drink?" Craig asked. Harry nodded.

"They are such fools," Edie said. Oak had never seen her so angry. She shook. "All in the name of the flag."

"Nestor got them crazy," Oak said.

Harry moaned, "It feels like broken glass inside."

"Oak," Craig Lawrence said, "go into the living room and get a pillow from the couch."

Oak brought a pillow, and Craig said, "Hold it to your chest when you laugh or sneeze. You'll have to sleep on your back. I wish you'd quit the race."

Harry was pale. The shock was wearing off. He'd finished his drink. "Nestor is smart," Harry whispered. "I underestimated him. It was like a revival meeting. Drop the bomb and let's all go home." He stood, coughed and nearly collapsed from pain.

"I'll give you some painkillers," Craig said. "You have got to rest."

"I can't."

"You must. At least take the next three days off. Cancel everything. I'll drive you home."

"It's just around the block," Harry said. "Oak will walk me home. Thanks, Craig. Night all." Slowly they went down the board path to the old gate. Harry groaned when he pulled the gate. Oak swung it wide. They walked around Hillage more slowly than Oak's grandmother walked. Harry rested by Oak's climbing tree, moaned and, after a minute, they crossed the street to the outside stairs of Harry's house; Harry leaned on Oak as they went up the stairs.

"Well, Oak," Harry said. "A birthday to remember."

"Want me to call Ernie and tell him you'll rest tomorrow?"

"Tell him to cancel the luncheon talk and I'll see. Night, Oak."

Oak found his parents sitting up talking. They were on the dining room porch. There were no lights on and their cigarettes glowed. They'd been drinking. He told them what happened. "God," his mother said, "those morons. You can be sure they're all good Irish Catholics."

"They are veterans," Val said. "They are Protestants, Catholics and Jews."

"They are morons!" his mother shouted. "And Harry is an idiot. He's out of his league."

"He is not," Oak said.

"He's out of his league," his mother repeated. "He's a fool to mention the bomb. You don't run for anything unless you can win. And you can't win talking about the atomic bomb."

"Nonsense," Val said. "If Harry's father had kept out of it, Harry might have won."

"Those VFW people are idiots," his mother said, leaving the field of battle for a bit. "Did you see who threw the softball?"

"No," Oak said. "But it wasn't the drunk who started it all. It was a big hairy guy."

"You have to be tough for politics," Nora said. "And Harry isn't tough. I can't imagine why he's running."

"He's running," Val said, "because we are at a point in history where we have to make decisions about how much defense we need and decisions about how much to spend on health and education."

Nora blew out cigarette smoke and said, "Baloney. You sound like you're giving a speech. The Russians are dangerous, and the bomb keeps them at bay. It's as simple as that. And education! Don't make it easier for morons go to college. We should teach them to read, then let them drive trucks and go to baseball games. They're happy. Leave them alone. God! All these liberals like Harry want to improve the *people*. And do it from a distance. People like Harry don't want the *people* anywhere near them."

"You should come to the headquarters," Oak said. "Lots of the Farm people are there or they used to be. And Mrs. Lawrence. Dad came down one night and the Tauntons came down."

"The Tauntons," his mother laughed. "They're being *democratic*. Rubbing elbows with the masses."

A new tone came when his parents were drinking; there was always the danger of explosion so he kissed his parents good night.

In bed Oak shut his eyes and recalled the drunken man at the VFW tent. And in his mind's eye he saw Professor Hutchinson staggering backwards. Oak hated the haters.

In the morning Jillian came into Harry's bedroom looking energetic in a dark blue skirt, white blouse and jacket.

"Craig Lawrence called and told me what happened," she said. "I hope now you'll have the grace to pull out."

Harry sat up hugging the pillow to his chest. He'd just taken a painkiller which wasn't working yet. "I'm not pulling out."

"Look at you. You're a wreck."

"I'm not quitting."

"Don't expect me to pay your campaign debts. This whole thing has been a fiasco."

"That's the kind of talk Washington heard."

"Harry, Washington was a general. You're an assistant professor at—"

"At what, Jillian? A college for bus drivers' children. That's Florence Beam's line." He groaned from the effort of talking.

"A third rate college."

"It's first rate for what it does."

"The campaign is a disaster, Harry. The sooner you face it the better."

"It's the best damned thing I've ever done."

"I have to go. Don't make a mess in the kitchen."

"A mess?" he shouted as she slammed the door. He groaned with a flash of pain that took his breath away and lay still until it eased. Why not quit? he thought. I can barely sit up. I've done all I can. It's over.

The phone rang. It was Ernie. "Sorry to wake you, Professor. Oak told me what happened. Dr. Lawrence just called me. He wants you to quit."

"I'm fine," Harry whispered. "I'm not quitting. I'll call you in a couple of hours." The painkiller was making him groggy. He feel asleep dreaming that Aunt Harriet was sitting on George Washington's horse.

CHAPTER 23

The following Monday night Ernie looked up at a very pretty black-haired woman coming into the headquarters. "I'm Diane St. George. I'd like to help."

"I'm Ernie Marion." He introduced Edie Lawrence, Oak and John. Diane joined in on the mailing; she was good at getting people to talk. She told them about her acting, and Oak told her about the Big Tree in the woods on Pill Hill.

"Next Monday night," Diane said, "I'll get here around six, and maybe you can show me the tree."

At ten thirty that night they were all laughing when a broad-shouldered, handsome man wearing a tweed jacket, burst into the headquarters. He'd been drinking. "Come, lass!" the man said. It was an order. "You said you'd be waiting on the sidewalk at ten."

"Oh, Peter," Diane said. "I want you to meet…"

"I said come." He strode to the table and pulled her to her feet and Diane jerked away shaking. Tears filled her eyes. Ernie wheeled to the table, grabbing the man's hand. Peter turned and was about to hit Ernie when John's ferocious animal-like snarl sounded. They all froze. Then Peter said, "Come." Diane followed him. Over his shoulder Peter said, "She'll not be back."

But the following Monday Diane came at six, and Oak took her to the big beech tree hidden in the sloping woods between Hillage and Forceps Avenue. She wore dungarees, sneakers and a pullover shirt. Oak liked her red lipstick and quick smile. Oak began climbing and said to her, "It has seven realms. I've never conquered the seventh."

"What's your favorite realm?" She climbed swiftly up after him.

"The fourth," Oak said. And that's where they sat and talked.

Her black eyes shone with curiosity. "Do you like the campaign, Oak?"

"Yes, but I wish Harry's father had stayed out of it. Still, it's fun. It must be fun to act."

"It is." Her laughter made her laugh more. "Look," she said pointing. A squirrel was at the end of the branch with the purple-silver leaves. It jumped through the air to the branch of another tree and, falling somehow caught a branch down low, collected itself and went on about its business. "That's better than acting," Diane laughed.

On the way back, she asked how Harry was doing. Oak had told her about Harry's being hit in the chest by the softball. "He gets tired fast," Oak said, "so he probably won't come in tonight."

At ten that night, Harry pushed open the screen door of the headquarters looking exhausted. He glowed when he saw Diane. Harry took Diane off to have supper at the late night Chinese restaurant. Even though it still hurt to laugh, Harry was glad she gave him something to laugh about. Before they parted, she told him she wouldn't be able to come anymore. Monday mornings she'd be taking the train to New York to work on a new play she'd be doing in the fall. She'd return on Tuesday afternoons for her Boston performance. "I can't wait for Maine," she said.

CHAPTER 24

Harry stayed home the next three days working on his Emerson Club speech, then resumed a slowed-down schedule with Oak carrying his briefcase, opening doors, getting coffee and being Harry's right-hand man.

Harry looked forward to his last campaign speech at the Emerson Club annual dinner, a black tie affair. He wore his tux and drove slowly because he still had pain. A car cut in front so he had to pull the wheel to the right and gasped with the pain in his chest.

At the Emerson Club on Beacon Hill they went straight in to the large dining room where waiters in black coats rushed around serving trays of hors d'oeuvres amidst a merry bubble of people having cocktails; not too many, Harry hoped—drinkers were trouble. As he went to the bar to get a glass of soda water, he was stunned to see his father across the room; he'd been sure his father wouldn't come.

Harry didn't touch his supper and his ashtray was filling with cigarettes.

"What's your position on the bomb?" Old Mrs. Forrester asked as if he were her servant.

"I'm agin' it," Harry said.

Finally a white-haired man took the stage and gave a long talk about the history of the club. Harry looked at Oak and rolled his eyes. "Now," the older man said, " I'm delighted to introduce our guest speaker. Professor Hutchison was at Exeter with one of my sons. He is one of the few daring souls to say no to Harvard, which is Harvard's loss. I'm sure you all know he wrote for *Stars and Stripes* while in the army and heroically rescued a soldier during the Italian campaign. He is running for Congress. Please welcome Professor Harry Hutchinson."

The applause was robust, but when it died down there was the clatter of coffee cups and waiters continued to pour coffee.

"Thank you, Arthur, for that kind introduction. I want to correct any misconceptions about my heroism. The man I rescued, Private Ed Keefe, had Turkish cigarettes in his pocket. I couldn't let them go to waste." People laughed. The lights in the room were dimmed, and Harry was lit up on the stage. He spoke for half an hour about Washington's judgment, courage and good sense. Lots of nice sounding murmurs, cigarette and cigar smoke filled the room.

"We need the same kind of restrained leadership that marked Washington's presidency. I want to be in Congress to support President Truman and his effort to find a peace. Thank you."

Most of the audience applauded. Some sat with arms folded. Harry nodded and smiled. He was pleased he hadn't said the words atomic bomb, and yet of course, everyone knew that's what he was talking about. The older man returned to the stage and said, "Now, we will take questions." Harry sensed it was a mistake.

The first two questions were about President Truman's thoughts on disarmament. The waiters re-appeared and clanked around. "Only one more," Harry said.

A distinguished looking man, who Harry found out later was Jack Lowell, a famous lung surgeon, stood and said in a carrying, righteous voice, "Do you think it was a mistake to drop the bomb on Nagasaki and Hiroshima?"

"I think," Harry said, "it was mistake to drop the bomb on civilians. I will always regret that. We sent a terrible message to the future."

"Then sir," said the surgeon, "you are a traitor."

"George Washington was called a traitor," Harry said. "In fact, so was everyone who signed the Declaration of Independence."

"Washington was a patriot!" the surgeon shouted into the din. "You are not!"

People were booing and applauding. Harry caught sight of a black-haired beauty in the back cheering—Diane St. George. Arthur of the white hair said into the microphone, "Thank you all for coming."

"No," Harry said, "we are not done. Please, everyone, sit." He said it with authority and people sat. "Thank you," Harry went on. "What I said in the campaign is that we have not caught up with our science. We have not caught up with ourselves. The atomic bomb was dropped five short years ago and now we find ourselves living in a standoff world, a world of so much fear we have lost a sense of who we are, a vibrant people of generosity, courage and some wisdom. We sit here tonight just a few miles from where George Washington ordered a daring night march to take Dorchester Heights. The British woke stunned; overnight the British hold on Boston had been broken. There was audacity and boldness in Washington's plan and execution. We need that boldness now. We have a great adversary in Soviet Russia but you must remember that Russia lost millions and millions in World War II; they are in the grip of Stalin's madness, but if we are steadfast it will play itself out. We can win the peace." Harry hit his stride and went on.

"This is a new world. You gentlemen are mostly Harvard men, and you ladies have been educated for the most part at Wellesley,

Radcliffe, Smith, and Vassar. Good. Now the world is opening, opening, opening. If your child wants to go to the Massachusetts College of Art and paint, bravo; if he or she wants to dance, bravo; if he or she wants to wash windows, flip pancakes, be a welder, poet, writer, janitor, teacher, linguist, bravo—let us loosen our grip. Let us be in awe of the new world; let us be delighted at the energy that has been released by the splitting of the atom; let us be astonished again at life itself. Let us listen to the Ghandis of the world. Let us know that the world is new and we are capable of seeing it as new and bold enough to take off our blinders and embrace it. That is what my campaign has been about. Thank you. Good night, ladies and gentlemen."

The next moment was perhaps a kind of social splitting of the atom. There was a second of silence and then pockets of people leapt to their feet applauding. One woman raised her hand and fist and shouted, "Bravo" as if it were an opera. It all happened in a moment and in the next moment a quarter of the people were applauding while most sat still. And yet the room was changed. John Hutchinson's banished son, Harry, had touched a truth; the world had changed and realizing that excited and terrified them.

Outside Harry heard his name called. It was Diane with a dashing looking man who wore a cape over his tux.

"Harry," Diane said and kissed him on the cheek. "You were magnificent. This is Peter," she said.

"Superb," Peter said shaking Harry's hand.

Oak recognized Peter as the drunken man who had come into the headquarters and almost hit Ernie. Oak despised the man.

"We've got to run," Diane said hugging him again. "Thank you, Harry," and they were off.

Oak and Harry walked through the Boston Garden and stood by the copper statue of George Washington sitting on a horse. "You were great tonight," Oak said.

"Thank you," he replied and smiled.

That night in bed Harry remembered that as pockets of people were cheering his speech, his father had sat shaking his head in disgust. He fell asleep thinking of Diane.

CHAPTER 25

After ten o'clock Sunday night as Oak watched Old John shuffle toward the door, he realized next week he'd be back in school and the headquarters would be just an empty store; primary day was two days away.

"Goo na," Old John said.

"Hey, John," Ernie said. "Sit down a minute. Professor H is gonna be here any second. He wanted to say something."

A car went by leaving Vaughn Monroe's voice floating in the air singing "Ghost Riders in the Sky." The village shops were closed; the train whistle grew louder, louder then, like the ghost riders in the sky, faded.

Ernie turned off the overhead lights so only two lamps were lit; Edie Lawrence sat finishing a letter. For the past month she had been writing elegant, slightly odd letters to former Wellesley classmates asking for contributions to Harry's campaign and those letters had raised four hundred dollars.

"One wilts," Edie said. "March comes like a lion but September is a cow in heat." Just then Harry pushed open the screen door and came into the headquarters. Ernie and Edie turned off the two lamps and a moment later Oak, his face lit up by the candlelight, carried the birthday cake in from the back. He set it down before Old John and they sang the birthday song. Harry sang:

Mon Cher ami
C'est a ton tour
De te la se
Parlez d'amour

Harry translated. "Now is the time for you to speak of love." Ernie popped the champagne cork and filled the little paper cups saying, "If Hi Ho heard the pop, he'll come runnin'. So drink up."

The flickering light played on Old John's misshapen face.

"Ha da yo no ho ol I am?" John asked.

"How'd I know you were twenty-six?" Ernie asked. "I don't know, but it was lucky because that's how many candles came in the box."

"John," Edie said shaking her head. "You are noble."

Oak was staring at the little candles; he loved the moment when the lights were out and the cake was alive with candlelight and all was still. In that stillness Oak was aware of John's terrible face, of Mrs. Lawrence's breathing, of Professor Hutchinson's kind eyes and aware of the knowledge that, as usual, Ernie was running the show.

For Oak, the twenty-six little candle flames burned brighter than a million stars; each little white flame wavered, fluttered, then was still while drops of pink wax ran down the tiny candles towards the chocolate frosting. Suddenly Oak was afraid Old John wouldn't be able to blow out the candles because his mouth was in the wrong place so he'd have to turn his head and might not succeed.

"Can we all blow them out, John?" Oak blurted.

"Ya," John said. Harry bent down, Ernie wheeled closer, Edie and Oak leaned across the table and they blew out the candles. They cheered.

"Don tun on the li," John said. John, laboring to be understood, told them of his twelfth birthday. He said when the kitchen lantern had been blown out his mother had carried in a cherry pie with twelve candles on it. His grandmother, who was senile, had clapped her hands and sung a song in Welsh she hadn't sung in thirty years. John's dad had picked up the song, and they sang until the candles burned out.

"So," John said, "la have some kay then sin a son." They sang "I've Been Working on the Railroad" and "She'll Be Coming Round the Mountain." Old John couldn't be understood but he was the only one who sang on key.

By ten-thirty they were standing in the dark on the sidewalk. Edie wrapped a piece of the cake for John to take home and they waited for his cab. As the cab drove off Ernie shouted, "Don't be late tomorrow or I'll dock your pay."

CHAPTER 26

Harry's team manned the polls on primary day, a balmy Tuesday, September 9. Oak was allowed to miss school and spent the day holding a HUTCHINSON'S OUR MAN sign outside the Codman School voting place. Eliot Adams walked by Oak and ignored him. Amelia Adams voted later and stopped to talk to Oak. Ernie Marion arranged for a friend to drive him to the different polling places. Edie Lawrence handed out cards.

The workers gathered at Harry's headquarters at eight that night. In addition to Harry and the Big Four, Meg Marion was there along with Mr. Paine, the Tauntons, Levensons, Oak's parents and his grandmother, the Lawrences, Louis the barber, a few Northeastern students, and stalwarts from Brighton and Allston. It was so crowded it was almost impossible to get to the crackers and cheese on the back table. The returns started coming in on the radio at ten and by eleven it was clear Harry had no chance.

Craig Lawrence led everyone singing, "For He's a Jolly Good Fellow." The night train rumbled by, shaking the headquarters. "Speech! Speech!" people called.

Harry stood on a chair and waited for quiet.

"We won a real victory," Harry said. "We talked about beginning anew. We talked about the bomb. No one else did. We talk-

143

ed about a Marshall Plan for the country. We talked about race.
I had a wonderful time working with all of you. I want to thank
Ernie Marion, my campaign manager. I want to thank John."
Harry realized he didn't know Old John's last name. He was Old
John of the Tennis Court. "I want to thank Edie Lawrence and
all the Lawrences. I want to thank Oak McCormick who was my
Sancho Panza." That was Jillian's line but Harry couldn't bear to
mention Jillian. She should have come tonight.

A small group went to the Lawrences' for a nightcap. Craig,
Edie, Harry, Nora and Val McCormick. They sat in the living
room. The night had grown cold, so Craig made a fire.

"One was brave," Edie Lawrence said. Harry sat on the chair
by the fireplace. He didn't want to talk. He got up and went into
the piano room and began to play "Only Make Believe," Val Mc-
Cormick's favorite song. Val and Craig joined Harry.

Edie and Nora were not singers; they talked.

"One is sad," Edie said.

"Yes," Nora said. "But Harry never had a chance. He's not
tough enough." Nora realized that was the wrong thing to say.
"But he did it," Nora said. "Harry got the signatures to get on
the ballot. He gave all those speeches. And Oak had the time of
his life."

"So did I," Edie laughed.

At one in the morning Harry shook everyone's hands, bowed
and left. Edie watched Harry walk down the wooden path to
the gate. Edie Lawrence stood at the door crying; she wanted to
call "Bravo", but knew it was best to say nothing. The gate, on a
slight incline, banged twice ending the campaign.

Harry walked down Forceps Avenue, past the Beams' house,
past the tennis court, and on down by the Women's Free Hospital where the wards were crowded with frail old women who
looked like ghosts. He crossed the street and sat on a broken
bench. The moon was a slice in the sky.

A car came down Forceps and its lights shone on Harry. The lights went out, and Edie Lawrence got out saying, "I saw you headed down the hill. One worried. Are you all right?"

"I hate Shakespeare, Edie."

"One surprises."

"He's filled with these great characters. I am a minor character. How can one be a has-been at forty-one?"

"You are tired. You are bold. You ran. Your headquarters was the most exciting place I've been in my life. We were all cut off, but you changed that. After some rest you will go on with your book on Washington. You promised me a chapter."

"And you'll get it; now you to go home and get some sleep. I need to walk."

"You are Henry the Fifth."

"I would rather be Falstaff."

Edie kissed him on the cheek and left. Harry walked through the Farm and stopped when he saw a figure in a doorway.

"Professor H, it's me, Ernie."

"Still up?"

"Can't sleep. Want a slug?" Ernie handed the pint bottle. Harry took a swig and handed it back.

"You did a great job running the campaign, Ernie."

"Looks like we'll come in fifth. Not bad after all the lousy publicity."

"Not bad at all. And your mother was terrific. She should run for office in the town."

"Someone should. I heard a rumor there's a deal to get rid of the Farm and build fancy apartments."

"It's valuable land here, Ernie. Who's behind it?"

"It's just a rumor. Hi Ho told me. Maybe he dreamt it."

"Well, you get some sleep. I'll keep my ears open." Harry said.

"First thing tomorrow I gotta register at Northeastern, then I'll close things up at the headquarters."

"I'll be in around ten," Harry said.

Harry sat on the bench thinking it had all been a terrible waste. I ran to bring the family together and now we're farther apart than ever. Ernie's tarred with my brush. He'll run for state representative in a couple of years, and they'll say he worked for that nut, Harry the Red. I was so high and mighty; the bomb changed everything and nobody knew it but me. I was going to save Lydia and everybody else. What a waste! For a while it was working, and then Father had to open his mouth.

Harry flung his cigarette down, got up and stamping on the cigarette, saw the glint of an empty pint bottle; he picked it up, flung it down smashing it, then paced and lit another cigarette. He thought of Lydia dancing down the lawn and slitting her wrists. I did nothing to help her. What a waste the whole damn thing was! Truman didn't need me, but it was working until Father put his oar in. "What a son of a bitch," Harry said.

The thought of fall flooded his mind. The same routine, students who can't spell, half asleep; the damn radiator banging and Dean Jackass Whitton sitting in on my classes. I've had it with teaching but there's no damned choice. How much do I owe? Two, three thousand dollars. Thanksgiving at Jillian's parents we'll sit there while her father carves the turkey wishing it were me he was carving then Christmas and Jillian's four inch glass Christmas tree on the dining room table God the trouble with running was not just Father's coming out against me how the hell could he where was I tired need to go to bed stop feeling sorry for myself why not feel sorry I'm married to a stone I chose the stone but it was different in the beginning it was exciting hard to believe twenty years ago all those rallies the songs she Washington Hiroshima how the hell could we go from Valley Forge to Hiroshima in so short a time she was stiff in bed but not when she had a few drinks it's over campaign is over moon is round tonight maybe go off to India just France campaign my debts why doesn't she get herself a stud when can I finish my book Pulitzer show her show them all Dad I won the Pulitzer hang up on him it's cold Hi Ho sleeps out every night in the winter it's unnatural not to screw I'm horny Harry the Red is horny horny horny so I lost I got into the race didn't I and everything went to pot but I'll give myself a C no an A for effort my damned chest still hurts like hell couldn't screw if I wanted to can't lift a briefcase without screaming pain is going to go for months why did I get so nervous speaking in the campaign the bomb shhh don't talk it'll go away how many bombs have we got now ten twenty thirty fifty I did speak up didn't I son of a bitch threw the softball nothing compared to my father if only I had won Father would have knocked on my door in Congress tell him to wait I'm busy be proud of me why did I run Lydia poor kid tired it'll look better tomorrow Thanksgiving sitting at that table is like having supper at the morgue how's your book coming Harry it's coming well I'm on the part where George is in bed with Martha and the bed's squeaking thundering oh did I offend you I'm sorry your daughter and I don't squeak anymore so it's on my mind especially at Thanksgiving so I lost I'll teach pay my fucking debts that's funny fucking debts get through the year and then who knows maybe... "Who's there?"

A drunken man lurched towards Harry.

"Hi Ho. Can I help you?" Hi Ho stumbled, twisted and fell on the bench. "Go way," Hi Ho said flailing. Harry thought, yes, I'll go away. It'll all look better in the morning. It's nothing compared to what Washington faced; he was a little wooden too. What a waste it all was.

CHAPTER 27

He woke the next morning at six, dressed, had coffee and called a cab. At seven he was in Harvard Square. His parents' house was opposite Longfellow's long, yellow clapboard house. Longfellow, Harry said to himself, no one reads you any more. You're like me. Disappearing. He walked up the gravel path admiring the perfectly manicured lawn. The house was a light yellow, like Longfellow's and nearly as big. Sixteen rooms for his mother and father and a small carriage house for the cook and gardener.

Harry's parents were in the breakfast room. Harry's father wore a dark blue suit; his gray hair was as perfect as the lawn; he still played three sets of tennis twice a week and was trim. Harry's mother was given to plumpness. Although she had only orange juice and a poached egg for breakfast, Harry knew the moment his father left for the office, his mother had a large second breakfast.

"Harry," his mother said. "What a surprise. I'm sorry you lost."

"Good morning, Harry," his father said, nodding but not rising. "Have some coffee." Harry sat down and poured coffee.

"I'm glad the campaign is over," his mother said. "I've never seen you look so tired."

"I just wanted you to know," Harry said to his father, "what you did to me was despicable."

"What I did," his father said, "was tell the truth. I did not expect the *Globe* to put it on the front page."

"What you did was despicable," Harry repeated. His voice was getting high. "To go out of your way to destroy my campaign was the lowest thing I can imagine."

"Then you have no imagination," his father said. "We are in a life and death struggle with the Communists, and, because you don't understand that, you do not belong in Congress."

"Now, let's not quarrel," his mother said. "Your father was just doing what he thought best." She spilled her coffee and was about to ring the bell for the maid.

"Leave it," his father said. "Harry, you are naive. I felt it necessary to say something about your politics."

"What utter hypocrisy," Harry said. "You're angry I never became the puppet you wanted for a son."

"Get out!" his father shouted. "You are an ass. You've always been an ass."

"Please," his mother wailed.

"*You* are the ass," Harry shouted. "Calling a press conference to denounce your son. What a total ass."

"I said get out. You are too stupid to argue with."

His father stood and faced Harry. "Get out!" he shouted and pushed Harry.

"Do not push me," Harry said enraged. He felt murderous. "Do not push me!" He was shouting as loudly as he could. "You pushed me all my life. You touch me again, and I'll smash you so badly you'll never get up, you God damned bully. You are no father. You are a disgrace to fatherhood. You're nothing but a God damn puppeteer and the God damned strings are broken."

CHAPTER 28

Two weeks after the primary, Harry was surprised when Jillian suggested they have supper together; she was rarely home at suppertime. They ate broiled sole, new potatoes and corn in the dining room by candlelight.

"Last of the corn," Harry said.

"It tastes it," Jillian said. She wore a red dress, gold earrings and pearls, her small nose looked attractive tonight, but her chilly voice kept his ardor in check.

"How much do you owe?" she asked.

"It'll be fine," Harry said.

"How much?"

"Three thousand."

"You are irresponsible. You had no right to go into debt like that. God, what a fool!"

"I'll take care of it," Harry said. He was too tired to hold his temper. "I'll take care of it!" he shouted flinging down his napkin. He stalked out of the house, walked down to the village and got a cab. He checked his wallet. Fourteen dollars.

"Charlestown Square."

Twice he almost told the driver to turn back but he was too angry. The cab cost five-fifty. Harry got out in Charlestown Square and he stood in the darkness under the elevated as the subway train rumbled and squealed overhead. The YMCA was behind him and he could get a room for three or four dollars. Harry walked down Main Street as another train roared overhead sounding like rusty thunder. He stopped at number forty-two, a two story brick building, rang the bell, and a suspicious looking woman opened the door.

"Yes?"

"I'm here to see John."

"He know you're coming?"

"He's a friend. Helped in my congressional campaign," Harry said.

"John? What did he do? Scare the opposition?" Her nose wiggled. "Upstairs. First door on the right."

Harry felt her watching him as he climbed the stairs. The banister was oak and rock solid. He liked banisters. The best part about going door to door in Allston and Brighton had been the triple-deckers with the banisters. As a child he slid down the banister in his home on Brattle Street in Cambridge. His father caught him once; it was the only time his father had hit him.

Harry knocked; there was no answer.

"He plays the radio so he don't hear. His ears are no good," the landlady called up. Harry guessed his coming was an event; he doubted John had any visitors. The door opened and John stood there in his overalls and gray shirt.

"Unnn. Pra faa saa Haaa saaa."

"Can I come in, John?"

"Hunnnnnn," John said welcoming Harry in. The main room was filled with large baskets overflowing with wool so the room smelled of lanolin. John had both a spinning wheel and a loom. The Red Sox game was on the radio.

"How's the game going?" Harry asked.

"Ba Door ga a dou bllll. Taaad the gam."

"It won't stay tied for long, John. I'm afraid the Yankees are going to sweep us, but maybe there'll be a miracle."

John's mouth looked like a frozen hole. It changed slightly and Harry knew it was a smile.

"I had an argument with my wife. Forgive me for coming."

"Na . . . goo. Wann a drinnn?"

"Maybe a small one with a lot of water."

John turned the radio down. The elevated train passed by not ten feet from John's windows making the whole room rattle.

"How can you stand that noise, John?"

"An na baaaa. Ga usta ah."

John took an unopened pint of Old Grand Dad whiskey from a cupboard by the sink. "Oh," Harry said. "Don't open it, John."

"Unnn. Ah don drinn. For com pana." Harry was touched.

"I want to have a party, John. A small party for you, Ernie, Oak and Edie Lawrence. And Meg Marion, but I think she's taking night classes. I want to thank you all for helping in the campaign," Harry took his drink. The glass was a kitchen glass. "Go on spinning, John." Harry sat in an old, blue, stuffed chair; the spring was uncomfortable. The couch was covered with shawls.

"Did you make those John?"

"Unnn."

"I like the patterns and the colors. Where do you sell them?"

"Fan Ha Maaa."

"Faneuil Hall Market. The shop next to the Greek breakfast place?"

"Ya."

"You're amazing, John. Go on spinning or I'll feel I'm ruining your evening." John's misshapen hands moved swiftly, easily.

"You know, John, I feel terrible about losing, but it's nothing compared to what you've gone through."

"Ah ha hap."

"Who helped you?" Harry asked.

John went over to the corner where there were three small black trunks stacked one atop the other. He opened the top one and Harry could see it was crammed with envelopes holding letters inside; John handed one to Harry.

The envelope was written in pencil. The writing was large and almost illegible. Harry studied it and finally made it out. Helene L'Alma, 17n rue Corbet, Paris, France.

John handed Harry a small faded newspaper clipping from a French newspaper. It was the photo of a nurse, a beautiful young woman, standing beside a building Harry took to be a hospital.

"Helene?" Harry asked and John nodded.

Joe DiMaggio made a great catch of a Ted Williams line drive, and the Sox lost. John turned off the radio.

"Wha part?"

"Oh, the party," Harry said. "Just a little supper for the five of us. It won't be complete unless you come."

John was back at the spinning wheel. Harry looked around the room: a spinning wheel, five barrel sized baskets filled with wool, a loom, shawls, a blanket, a cat sleeping on the couch; it was the opposite of Harry's home which was so orderly. Harry felt Jillian would prefer him to sleep on the rug so the bed wouldn't be rumpled.

"Sav your mon a."

"I want to do it, John, and it would mean the world if you'd come. I'll pick you up."

John kept spinning. "Ah don go to rest oh rans."

"You'll go right upstairs to the private dining room; no one will see you or Edie. It's a men's only restaurant. Let me tell you my plan."

Harry's drink relaxed him and he accepted John's offer of a cheese sandwich. There was a large old-fashioned icebox by the sink. The elevated train went by; Harry got a glimpse of a sad looking woman on the train; she wore a blue coat, looked very tired and was gone in an instant.

John continued spinning and he must have talked for an hour. He told Harry that he'd been so burned and battered that when he was in the hospital all he wanted to do was to die. He could neither write nor speak so he couldn't tell the doctor that he wanted him to give him an injection to take his life. It was Helene who made the difference; she was young and newly married, and he realized later that she had had the kindness to take her wedding ring off her finger. For two years Helene was the flame that kept him going. The other nurses laughed at him behind his back. He heard one of them describing him as a worm, and another nicknamed him Humpty Dumpty, but Helene was always encouraging. She'd teach him French phrases; she'd read him novels in English saying it was just so she could practice her English. She read him Dickens and Dostoyevsky and Balzac. She came in on her off days to check on him always with a smile, always with "Bon Jour, Jean." He liked being called Jean. He fell in love with her and knew, of course, it was going nowhere, but it was she who saved his life.

When the Army felt John could be moved, he was flown to Texas to a veterans' hospital that specialized in orthopedic surgery; John spent another two years there. When he came home, he was alone because his parents had died. No one recognized him. He couldn't bear to stay in his own town, so he found an apartment in Charlestown. When the thugs had threatened him outside the Charlestown bar and had begun to push him around and beat him, he had hit one of them so hard, the fellow died. The judge had been kind enough to send John to the Massachusetts Mental Hospital. There he made friends with three older women, and they'd play cards together; they didn't have real cards so they had imaginary cards and they'd all burst out laughing when each of them came up with four aces. They had even put on a Christmas play, just the four of them. They made it up; it made little sense and no one cared. While he was at the mental hospital, a Catholic chaplain became interested in him. John was not a Catholic; he had never even been to a church. The chaplain arranged for John to go to a little town in Chile called

Nirivilo, a town that time forgot. He lived in a tiny, cold room out back of the priest's house. One Sunday the priest took John far out into the country; they walked miles to a house where a family had been living for several generations. They sipped matte, a sweet tea they drank out of a metal straw. The grandmother of the house was spinning; she saw John's interest and offered to teach him to spin. He spent seventeen years in Chile.

Harry spent the night on John's couch and went by trolley to Northeastern the next morning.

———

The following Tuesday night at Locke Ober's Cafe in Boston, Harry escorted two hooded monks up the side stairs to a private room on the second floor. Ernie wheeled himself through the diners to the elevator.

Harry had ordered a buffet so they wouldn't be bothered. The round oak table was laid with silver, handsome gilt-edged plates, silver candelabra, flowers, wine glasses, water glasses and brandy glasses. A Caesar salad sat at each place. On a sideboard against the wall were silver chafing dishes full of lobster Newburg, beans, codfish, squash, mashed potato, gravy, peas and carrots. Harry left orders that no waiter was to come in without knocking and tipped Freddy, the elegant and famed maitre'd, fifteen dollars to make sure all went smoothly.

Edie Lawrence looked no less absurd than John in her long brown hood. "One feels like Friar Tuck," Edie laughed.

When they finished their salads, looking wan but happy, Harry raised his wine glass. "I was going to save the toast for last but you all know politicians can't shut up. James Otis was a lightning bolt of the revolution. You were the lightning bolts of my campaign. I'm prouder of what we all did than anything else in my life. Thank you."

There was raucous applause. Edie Lawrence was crying.

Ernie said, "I liked the donuts best."

"One is bereft," Edie Lawrence said. "I sit at home at night wondering what to do. One is empty without the campaign."

"You can work for Ernie when he runs," Harry said.

"Ma ta," Old John said.

Oak was intrigued with it all. The beautiful room, the food, Edie and Old John in monk's robes. He, too, felt empty when night offered only homework.

The wine flowed. Old John said he liked Edie's Greek myths. Edie said, "Harry led us into the labyrinth where we confronted the beast."

"So, Professor H," Ernie said. "Are you going to finish the Washington book now?"

Harry avoided the question and said, "I suggest something like charades. Each person acts out a moment in the campaign and we all guess, but you can use words."

Old John stood up and swept with an imaginary broom.

"Hi Ho," everyone shouted.

Ernie sounded very English saying, "I'm down at Harry Hutchinson's campaign headquarters. It's all so democratic."

"Betty Taunton!"

Oak stood and clipped with imaginary scissors.

"Louis," Ernie said.

Harry stood and jounced. No one got it and he made the hooting sound. "The train! The train."

Edie said, "It's my turn." She stood and said nothing. No one guessed. "Then I will be blatant," Edie said, and spoke into an imaginary microphone. "Ladies and gentlemen, I am running because it will be fun to be in Congress. There will be other congressmen there and we will all be congressmen."

"Don Nestor!"

They reminisced. Over coffee it was clear Ernie had drunk too much. He was saying to Oak, "I'm still trying to find out who threw that softball. I'm gonna make that bastard pay."

"No," Harry said. "It's done. As Edie said, we went into the labyrinth. Things happen in the labyrinth. We're here to celebrate. Now my friends, it is late. To bed! To bed! Tomorrow we begin another day."

At eleven thirty, two French monks led the little gathering out into the chilly Boston night.

CHAPTER 29

Harry had been driving too long. The rain was so heavy he pulled over; then he saw the big faded sign across the street, Higgins Inn and underneath, Cape Elizabeth, Maine. He made it. It was orientation at Northeastern, and he had three days off.

In the morning he walked down to the beach where the breakers were six and seven feet high and the sea looked like an eternal herd of white horses thundering onto the sand. Down to the right he saw a woman standing on the rocks above the sea; a wave crashed onto the rocks and soaked her. It was Diane St. John. He felt wildly excited and suddenly guilty and embarrassed; doubtless she was here with her man. He felt like an ass.

"Harry!" She called and came running. Her black hair was soaking; her face alive. "Harry!" She said hugging him. He gasped in pain.

"Oh," she said pulling back. "Are you all right?"

"Bruised sternum. I'm fine, fine, fine." He took her hands. "I'm so glad to see you."

"Are you staying here?"

"They had a room free."

"Twenty-eight of them," she laughed. "Have you had breakfast? I'll change and we'll go to The Egg."

She changed into dry dungarees, an old shirt, a wool sweater, sneakers, and an orange beret.

"My Aunt Harriet would have loved your beret."

"Here," she said, giving it to him. "It looks better on you."

They walked along the side of the road past rose hip bushes, old houses and big fields. The Egg was crowded with locals: plumbers, electricians, carpenters and women who had dropped their children off at school.

"I love this place," Diane said.

The pancakes were crisp. Harry wanted to turn somersaults.

"You look like an old salt," Diane laughed. He was wearing khakis, a blue corduroy shirt he'd had for years and worn sneakers. He laughed but didn't like being called an *old* salt. As he reached for the syrup he saw her engagement ring.

"Oh, yes," she blushed, "I'm getting married to a wonderful director, Peter Brathwate. He's an Englishman; you met him at the Emerson Club."

"Yes," he smiled remembering the man. The son of a bitch had been handsome. Harry felt both betrayed and foolish for feeling that way. Diane could be his daughter. He cut a pancake and said, "I'm just staying the day. I'm headed up the coast." When they'd finished he walked stiffly beside her along the sandy edge of the road.

"Is Peter coming up?" he asked.

"No! He hates places like this. Is your wife coming up?"

"No," Harry said. "She hates places like this," and laughed despite himself.

They walked in silence, and he stole glances at her. Her hair was dark black and shoulder length; her face well shaped, her forehead open and unlined, and she walked with the easy grace of a dancer. The smallest things made her smile: a gliding gull, the bell of an old woman's bicycle, the smell of the clam flats. They walked by Len Libby's candy store.

"Come on," Diane said pulling him into Len Libby's. It was as clean as a hospital. The air conditioning was up so high it was freezing. Every surface was immaculate. The counter shelves were laden with boxes of chocolates and bon bons; pale green bon bons, light orange bon bons, yellow, pink and rose bon bons. A young woman behind the counter smiled showing her braces; she was thin and wore glasses.

"Chocolates or bon bons, Harry?" Diane asked.

"Too early for me."

"Too early? It's never too early for chocolate. In college I had to write a paper on how and why time came to be. I wrote that the whole purpose of time was to discover chocolate." Diane bought the pound box.

When they left Len Libby's, Harry asked, "How did you do on the paper?"

"I got an A for originality and an F for feasibility. My grade was rounded off to a B plus."

"He wasn't very good at math."

"He was a she. I gave her a box of chocolates at the end of the term."

They sat on the sand dune opposite Len Libby's. The bright air smelled of sea. "Opening a candy box," Diane said, "is like lifting the curtain on stage. It is a moment of high drama. Are you ready, Harry?"

He nodded. She lifted the lid. "Behold," she said, addressing an invisible audience. "Behold these glorious chocolates. Gaze on each shape, each ripple. See each royal chocolate sitting in its own paper home. Is this not wonderful?"

The thought of Jillian sitting on a sand dune playfully admiring a box of chocolates was so absurd he almost laughed. But he didn't. He couldn't speak. They sat in silence. Diane stared into the box of chocolates and slowly put the lid back on. They walked on without a word and turned down the road leading to the beach and Higgins Inn. A gull soared above them. Diane was crying.

"What is it?"

"You," she said. "I wish I'd met you long ago," she hesitated then looked away and shook her head. "Oh, this is stupid."

"How long are you staying?" he asked.

"Three days."

"Me too."

"I thought you were going up the coast."

"Nonsense. Why would I go up the coast?"

That afternoon they walked to the boarded up lighthouse down the road from the inn. Sitting on the grass, Diane got Harry talking about the campaign and what his father had done. It was getting just a little chilly when she asked if he knew about the Kanda acting method. "It gets to the core of things," she said. "You can't do Shakespeare without getting to the core. Want to try it?"

"Me?"

"Yes. Shut your eyes and think of reading what your father said about you in the newspaper. Now let it go and just let any image come to mind. It can have nothing at all to do with you."

Under her guidance Harry found himself telling a story. "It's 1870 in Ireland. I'm eighteen, strong and drunk, sitting in a dark cottage where my father is telling me to keep my gob shut about the landlord. This is the way it will always be, my father says. But for once, I rebel. I'm drunk and enraged and set out for the landlord's manor. I get to the manor house, fling the great door open and bellow for the lord. Charles appears. Charles is the lord's son, and we're fast friends. He's back from Oxford, and changed but we've been friends since boyhood.

'I came to tell your father we're not dogs,' I say to Charles, 'I will not be treated like a dog. Where is the old bastard?'

'Ian,' Charles says reddening. Charles is dressed in a fop suit the color of ashes. 'My father is Lord,' Charles says. 'And thank

God for it. You and your people need a firm hand to keep you from behaving like animals. If the truth be told, you are a stupid people and we English are your blessing. Now get out and don't ever come to the front door again.'"

"What do you do?" Diane asked.

"Slink off," Harry said.

"You are Ian. How do you feel?"

"Enraged."

"Let's hear your rage. Acting is real. Let's hear your rage."

"I shout," Harry said. "I begin to shout." Harry was shouting. "I'm shouting so loud I think my face will burst. I smash the son of a bitch with my fist."

"What are you doing now, Harry?"

"Smashing the son of a bitch. I smash you, you unjust bastard," Hitting the ground Harry groaned. His chest was all splinters of glass, but he was in a fury. "You were my friend!" he roared. "You betrayed me. You are caught in the trap we both despised." Harry was shouting, panting, smashing his fists on the earth. "Charles is bleeding. He's lying on the floor bleeding and panting. His fop clothes are torn. We've broken though the trap, the wretched old fucking pattern of lord and servant, slave and master."

Harry lay breathless on the grass. The sea pounded in. He was in terrible pain.

Diane lay beside Harry. "It's good you ran for Congress."

CHAPTER 30

When they got back to the inn, Harry took three aspirin, napped for three hours and met Diane in the lobby at one. "I have a picnic ready," Diane said. "Is that all right?"

"Great. Where will we go?" Despite his awful pain he had never been so happy.

"A deserted house with an orchard. It's a long walk along the rocks."

"I'm ready," Harry said. "I love rock walks." Every step would hurt, but that was no matter.

"I love apples," she said.

Harry wanted to say I love *you* but just smiled. They walked along the beach, climbed the rocks and made their way along the rocks for an hour before they came on a field with an orchard of trees filled with small, gnarled apples at the edge of the sea. The picnic was simple: two chicken salad sandwiches and a bottle of wine. Diane had insisted on carrying the small cloth bag.

"Do you know who owns the orchard?" Harry asked.

"No. I suppose it goes with the farmhouse up the hill. Hungry?"

"Famished."

They sat by an apple tree twisted by years of wind from the sea. The apples had dents and bumps. They were red and yellow like the leaves.

"Little sour," Harry said, "but good."

"A few days ago," Diane said, handing Harry a sandwich, "I lay here and let my mind wander. I imagined being this tree, and I know on some snowy day next January I'll be hurrying along in New York and I'll think of this tree and it'll cheer me up."

"Me too." He was aware of Diane's fullness. Everything about her was full. Her face, her breasts, her dark black hair. Her eyes had such life and spirit Harry couldn't stop looking at them.

"I'd love to see you on stage," Harry said. "I'll come down to New York to see you."

They ate their sandwiches and lay down side by side looking up at the sky.

"What does that cloud remind you of, Harry? See the cloud that's opening? I had a dream last night about a girl who found out how to go into an entirely new world. The trouble was that anyone who went into the new world forgot about the old one so they never came back."

"Did she?" Harry asked. He loved lying beside Diane. He felt freer than he ever had.

"She wanted a reminder of her other world so she took a little strip of leather with her. It was only about four inches long and very narrow. Maybe it was a book mark."

"When are you getting married?" Harry asked.

"We think February, but if Peter gets to direct in London it will be spring."

"A new world," he said and propped himself up on his elbow. "God, you are beautiful."

"I want to show you the house," Diane said sitting up. "Come on." She took his hand and they walked through the orchard up the hill to the house, a forlorn, peeling white farmhouse; half the chimney had fallen, a few bricks lay on the shingled roof, a second floor window was open. The front porch looked strong. The breeze pushed an old gray rocking chair which Diane tried, and it held. Harry sat on the stairs.

"I wonder who lived here last," Harry said.

"I'd guess a woman who came here to paint," Diane said. "Maybe she got old and died, and her family doesn't care about the place."

Harry was imagining marrying Diane and the two of them fixing the place up and living here. Diane would come back when she wasn't acting, and Harry would be finishing his book on Washington and then writing books he hadn't even thought of.

"Or doing something completely different," he said aloud.

"What did you say?"

"I was imagining living here and doing something completely different."

"Like what?"

"I don't have the foggiest. It's just time for something different."

"Does it make you sad?"

"Oh, no. It's not a sense of giving up at all. Quite the opposite. It's time to wander into that new world you dreamed of. I'll probably go on writing, but who knows. Imagine restoring this orchard, growing vegetables, writing something new and interesting. Who knows? Until now it never occurred to me there were possibilities. Could I be sly as Odysseus?"

"What do you mean?"

"I don't know." He had a wild idea.

"I want you to be careful, Harry. You're really tired. I can see it in your eyes. I wonder if you shouldn't just recuperate for a year."

"I might." He put his arm around her. "And you?"

"I love acting, but I want children. I'm thirty-three, time's running out, but I'm so scared of being married. Oh, Harry, I'm so scared."

He held her and said, "Marriage is a great journey." Or it could be, he thought. She kissed him on the lips.

"I love him, Harry. I wish you and I had met a year ago. I do love him."

CHAPTER 31

Wednesday morning they held hands walking through South Portland. The air was crisp. Harry felt relaxed in khaki pants, a green wool shirt, and the orange beret. His chest hurt less. Diane wore dungarees, a red turtleneck and Harry's army leather jacket.

"I love Whitman," Diane said. "And Dickinson. But Shakespeare's my favorite."

I love you, Harry wanted to say. Instead he said, "What's Shakespeare compared to you?"

"It's true," Harry went on. "Those old warehouses stood straighter the moment you went by."

"No more of that, Harry Hutchinson," Diane laughed, squeezing his hand.

He was astonished by her. Millions and millions of years had to pass for her smile to exist and as any fool could tell, it was the high point of existence. Her smile was full and quick and bright. Harry felt he understood art for the first time in his life. Art was a response to beauty or to something so alive the artist *had* to create. He told that to Diane and she stood in front of him. "That's exactly what you did with the campaign, Harry. You responded."

"Not to beauty, to the bomb."

"To beauty," Diane said. Her black eyes flashed and then were full of tears. "To beauty. You respond all the time. To the beauty of this street, to the beauty of people and morning and life."

"I'm starved," Harry said. "I'm taking you to a really fancy restaurant. It's down on the corner."

Walking near the docks, they passed a shoe store where the shoe store man was fitting shoes for a large man who smoked a cigarette. Diane lingered. "I want to do a play set in a shoe store. A little girl comes into the shoe store with her mother. The girl is happy because her mother is usually too busy to take her places. Every pair of shoes in the store hopes the little girl will pick them." They walked on.

"Voila," Harry said. "D'Amatos. The best submarine sandwiches in the world. If you marry me, we'll move to Maine and live on D'Amato's sub sandwiches."

D'Amato's was small and crowded. They took their sandwiches to the single empty booth. "There is something in these subs that makes them irreproducible," Harry said wondering if there was such a word. "I think it's the oil." Harry went on at length about each ingredient. He loved being in D'Amato's with her.

"How did you find it?" she asked.

"I come up every year and wander around Portland."

He longed to be alone in bed with her, to make love to her, to have his hands run over her skin, her breasts…but it was a miracle just to be with her.

"It's the bread," Diane said.

"I think it's the oil," Harry repeated.

"Maybe the tomatoes," she laughed.

"The oil."

"The pickles."

"Oil."

"Shakespeare doesn't have enough food in his plays," Diane said. "He was a passionate man, but I don't think he loved food."

"Falstaff loved food."

"You sack of guts," Diane cried. "You bull's pizzle. This cup of sack tastes like Pepsi Cola. Let's rob a stagecoach."

"Then let's buy ten Shakespeare plays and find out what foods he liked and make a picnic of them."

"In *Macbeth* there's meat and drink and roots."

"Roots?"

"Yes, roots. And in *Twelfth Night* there's pickled herring, capons, mutton and ginger. They put ginger in ale in those days." Harry took her hand, "Shakespeare was intrigued with politics."

"Power and love," Diane said. Her eyes. What was it about her eyes? They were hawk's eyes but full of fun.

"Macbeth couldn't resist power," Diane said. "Who can?"

A little girl held her father's hand while he ordered. The girl looked at Diane and smiled. She had straight brown hair and looked curious and intelligent.

"She has vision," Harry said.

"Yes," Diane agreed.

They left D'Amato's and walked hand in hand down to the docks where a fishing boat was unloading. They sat on a bench with only two surviving slats and watched two fishermen, maybe a father and son, carry big white plastic buckets of fish to their truck. Harry wanted to say so many things but felt it better not to. He had been in love with Jillian but never like this. With Diane the whole of creation opened; he wanted to imagine and laugh and be silly, to make love, to marry her.

Diane started to cry. "I'm frightened of being married. What if it doesn't work?"

"Are you in love with him?"

"Yes, I think so. I am. My mother is excited. The whole idea of marriage. Oh, Harry I'm so frightened." He put his arm around her.

"I want to have children," she said.

"I've never understood Shakespeare before," Harry said. "If he hadn't met someone like you he could not have created Juliet, Cleopatra…"

"Ha, Harry Hutchinson," she laughed. "You are my Anthony. You tower o'er the world."

CHAPTER 32

They spent much of the last afternoon walking on the beach holding hands. The ocean was stirred up, the day blue and clear.

"I wish I were a porpoise," Diane said.

"And I," Harry said.

"Or an owl."

"And I."

"Or a codfish."

"And I," said Harry.

Diane was booked on a six o'clock plane from Portland. She'd rented a car, so Harry followed in his. At five o'clock they sat at the airport.

"When does your play open?" Harry asked.

"First week in December."

"You'll be wonderful."

They were intent but barely aware of what they were saying. They sat side-by-side holding hands. He was aware of her eyes, of her whole self. He felt as if the world had turned to smoke and he was watching the last wisps. There was no way of catching it; he just had to savor each wisp.

"I loved D'Amatos," Diane said.

"It's the oil," Harry whispered.

"That little girl with the straight brown hair."

"Had vision," Harry said.

"Like you."

"I'm afraid of getting married, Harry."

"But you love him?"

"Yes."

"Then being afraid is perfectly natural. It'll be fine."

They made each gesture in slow motion as if they hoped time would fall asleep.

When the plane was boarding, Diane kissed Harry. She looked at him with brilliant black eyes full of tears and walked down the stairs out onto the tarmac; she turned, waved, climbed the stairs to the plane and was gone.

Harry drove back to Higgins Beach, put on a sweater and his leather army jacket and walked on the beach. There was a whisper of a moon and far out at sea he saw the lights of a ship. The waves tumbled in. Suddenly losing Diane engulfed him, and he was unprepared for the shock of it. For the first time in his life some door inside him had opened and Diane had tumbled in like a great ocean wave, and now that she was gone the furies took her place. Jillian, Dean Whitton, his debt, his father, the possible destruction of the Farm and above all the loss, the loss of the most wonderful woman he'd ever met.

Late that night he drove back home. He arrived at one in the morning, switched on the lights and saw the hallway and living room were as perfect as always. There was a note on the kitchen table saying, *Wash, dry and put away your dishes. Jillian.*

Longing for the ocean he woke at four, dressed in old clothes and sneakers, crept down the stairs and went outside; the wind was up and leaves were whirling all about. He walked down Forceps to the tennis court, Old John's other home, and stood resting his head on the wire mesh fence and dozed. He started to awake. He'd had a vision of the tennis court burning. All the lightness he had with Diane deserted him. He felt awkward, frightened for himself and the world, and tired. So very tired.

He walked down to the village to the White Tower where he sat over coffee at the counter. At four-thirty the skinny boy with black hair and a grin came in. The same boy Harry had seen the night he decided to run for Congress. Chickie, one of Oak's friends.

"Fuckin' cold, Harry," Chickie said. For a moment Harry thought Chickie was talking to him.

"Whatta ya got, Chickie?" Harry, the short order cook, asked. "Two paper routes this morning?"

"Yeah. Bud's gonna make me Head Boy next year; then I don't leave the fuckin' shop."

"You walk or do it on the bike?"

"I walk. Better than gettin' on and off the fuckin' bike all the time."

Breakfast renewed him, and when Harry walked back up Pill Hill, he was feeling ready for battle.

CHAPTER 33

The printer called Harry every other day demanding the seven hundred dollars his campaign owed. When the phone company threatened to cut the home phone off, Jillian called Harry at Northeastern.

"I haven't got the money," Harry said.

"I will not lend you a penny. You got yourself into this, now get yourself out."

Harry began staying up all hours writing articles and proposing others to raise the money. He was getting by on four hours sleep and looked it. Although he was flattered that his Introduction to American History course was popular, he was angry. Dean Whitton not only added a new course for him to teach, but saddled him with writing a brief history of Northeastern due in the spring.

"Jillian," Harry said one morning, "there are no socks in the drawer."

"I told Gladys to send them all out. The washing machine is broken." Gladys cleaned house and did the laundry.

"I need socks."

"Get some downtown. No one will notice you're not wearing socks."

That surprised him. Jillian, the proper one, saying no one would notice he wasn't wearing socks. Harry came home the next afternoon and the Hermans, who lived next door, were having a birthday party for their grandchildren. Jillian had been nice enough to go down to the village, get some balloons and fill them with water so the children could have a water fight. Jillian said the children would love it if Harry went over and threw a balloon or two. He did and the children had fun splattering him. What had gotten into Jillian?

A week later Dean Whitton called Harry into his office at ten in the morning and said that he needed a précis of Harry's history of Northeastern the following morning.

"The morning," Harry said. "I've barely started; it's impossible."

"A précis, Harry, maybe five pages. It slipped my mind, but the committee has got to have it for a nine o'clock meeting. Now, if you'll excuse me."

"That son of a bitch," Harry fumed. As he walked up Pill Hill he was aware the maple leaves had burst into color, but he couldn't enjoy them because of that son of a bitch Whitton. Harry worked on the précis until five in the morning and then got a couple of hours sleep. At seven he staggered through breakfast, called goodbye to Jillian and was off to Northeastern.

Jillian came down to the kitchen and stood staring. There were crumbs on the table, not just on his plate, there were crumbs all over the table. She felt an explosion of anger, the crumbs were like little sparks flying through her brain and her limbs, and burning through her stomach.

"That bastard," she shouted. "That stupid bastard." She trembled and made growling sounds. Her fists clenched and unclenched, "How dare he!" When she calmed down she looked at the crumbs and then his egg-stained plate sitting on the table beside his orange juice glass and his knife and fork, and then she looked back at the crumbs. Over twenty years she had trained him to never so much as leave a peanut butter jar out. This was an affront. She washed his plate, his silverware and his glass and wiped the table over and over saying, "That bastard. That stupid bastard."

Later that morning, Jillian rode her horse, Big Boy, in the woods in Dover. She felt an affection for Big Boy she had never felt for Harry, and as she trotted through the woods she realized she had expected that once the campaign ended Harry would be back to normal. Instead he'd come back from Maine wearing an orange beret in which he looked ridiculous; she had told him so, but he kept wearing it. She'd come home at night and find him singing or dancing with a pillow. Inspecting his bathroom one morning, she found a toothpaste that had stripes on it, some kind of children's toothpaste. A waste of money. When she challenged him, he smiled and said life was short. Every morning he bellowed in the shower even after she told him to shut up. Things were getting out of hand. Last Friday she'd come home to find a van parked outside with two men sitting in it. She'd gone into the kitchen and found Ernie Marion, in his wheelchair, and Harry drinking beer out of bottles. The following Saturday afternoon, instead of doing yard work, Harry had taken Oak to see the Boston Celtics. He had the Lawrences over for cocktails. Would the campaign never end?

Trotting through the woods, she realized if she didn't act now Ernie Marion would be sitting around her kitchen night after night drinking beer. Had Harry gone crazy? The next thing she knew, he'd have Old John in the house. My God!

By four that same afternoon, Harry had taught three classes, attended an endless faculty meeting and seen a doctoral student. He was bleary when Angela came into his office.

"Oh, Angela, I'm just on my way out."

"It won't take long, Professor." Angela was one of his favorites. She'd been working as a secretary for seven years and had decided to go to college. She told him her parents, who lived in the North End, were not pleased. Her mother said, "You'll be thirty when you finish and then what? You'll be an old maid." Angela's face was long and lovely. She wore her hair unfashionably short. She was a beautiful young woman.

"Sit down, Angela, what is it?" Harry's office looked like an old bookstore that had been squeezed into a closet. His desk was piled with papers, books, magazines and his own notebooks. The radiator clinked and hissed and refused to shut off. Angela sat on the only other chair. She wore a dark sweater and smelled of lavender.

"It's my paper on Sam Adams," she said. The office was so cramped their knees were practically touching and Harry was suddenly full of desire. He looked at her and thought of Diane. "What about it?" Harry asked.

"I got a B. I want to know what would make it an A." She held her paper out and as Harry reached for it his chair tilted, he lost his balance and his hand shot out and landed on her breast. He pulled his hand back so fast he fell backwards onto the floor.

"Are you all right?" Angela asked.

Harry blushed and laughed. "My dignity is shot," he said getting to his feet. "I was up most of the night. We'd better meet Wednesday at three o'clock."

When Harry got home he was surprised to find Jillian making supper in the kitchen. She had fixed him a martini. A miracle! Harry drank half the martini and he was so tired it went to his head. He told her of his day. "And the whole day ended with my hand on Angela's breast," he laughed and explained what happened.

The following day, Friday, Jillian called Craig Lawrence. "Craig, I'm worried about Harry. I'm afraid he's having a nervous breakdown."

"Why? What's wrong?"

"A lot of little things and some more serious. Northeastern has a very strict dress code for its faculty and Harry's going off with his orange beret and sneakers, and one morning he didn't even have socks."

"That seems pretty harmless."

"It is, but as I said there are other things. The other day the Hermans were having a birthday party for their grandchildren, and Harry stalked over there and began throwing water balloons at the children; he terrified them. There are a hundred things but I'm calling you because he has molested one of his women students."

"Are you sure?" Craig asked.

"He told me himself. I've called Dean Whitton and we've talked it over. Whitton doesn't think the woman is going to bring charges, but he may have to let Harry go. It's awful, Craig! I came home a week ago and Harry was in the bathtub fully dressed. When I asked what he was doing he said, 'Valley Forge, my dear, Valley Forge.' Craig, I'm terribly worried. He should be sent to Creighton Mental Hospital for a rest."

That Friday night Harry was walking by the Lawrences' enjoying the leaves swirling around their yard. Bones, their sausage dog, was in a dither.

"Harry," Edie called. "Come in for a sherry." Over a drink she told him his first chapter of the Washington book was elegant.

"The challenge," Harry said, "is to make it all new, to avoid cliché. Washington's a cliché. When you think of Valley Forge you think of men dressed in rags, cold and wet, their feet freezing in the snow. Last week, all in search of a telling phrase, I put two inches of cold water in the bathtub, dumped in all the ice I could find, put on old clothes and my cracked boots, and I stood in the tub for an hour. All in search of a phrase."

"What did you come up with?" Edie asked.

"Cold and wet."

CHAPTER 34

Oak glanced at the clock. Nine thirty. Half hour to recess. He was thinking of Professor Hutchinson because he'd seen him going over the hill this morning wearing an orange beret. Primary day was seven weeks back. It was almost Halloween.

"What is the Immaculate Conception?" Sister asked. Lee Conroy put her hand up.

"Yes, Lee," Sister said.

"Mary was born pure," Lee said. Lee had red hair and was so beautiful Oak was surprised every time he looked at her. Her red-gold hair was like fire. Her face was freckled. He'd like to see her naked.

"Yes," Sister Mary Joseph said, her face hard as a shield. A wide, whiskered, lined shield bordered with a stiff, white, starched, collar-like material. Black-eyed shield. The shield opened its lips and spoke, "Mary was conceived without sin. Is that clear?"

Everyone was silent. Oak had no idea what that meant. He didn't know what conceived meant. Sin was lying, stealing, murder and coveting someone's wife. He was sure no one coveted Florence Beam.

"Jesus and Mary were the only two people who lived their whole lives without sin," she said.

Who sins? Oak wondered. Dad and Mom don't sin, but Mom should go to mass. Gram doesn't sin. I'd like to see Lee Conroy naked. It was a sin to lie that day. Dad asked who broke the record? Did you do it? No. No. I lied. Mrs. Lawrence wouldn't sin or Dr. Lawrence or Monica or Carrie. Florence Beam is mean but she wouldn't sin. Who sins? It's seeing girls naked and lying and stealing. Chickie gets drunk. He steals. That's a sin. Is fighting a sin?

"Now," Sister said, "let's move on to English. *The horses galloped to the town.* Who will diagram that for us?"

Gail Mullen raised her pale hand. She had black circles under her eyes and was tired because she carried the weight of knowing all things. Gail went silently to the board, drew a straight line and wrote the sentence while explaining that *horses* was the subject and *galloped* was the predicate and *to the town* was the prepositional phrase. Then she diagramed the sentence, which acted as a sleep potion for Oak.

"Master McCormick," Sister said. "Diagram this sentence. *The horses, tired from riding all day, galloped into the town which was in an uproar because of the opening of the train station.*" Oak went to the board, stiffened and thought of Professor Hutchinson's rigor mortis speaking position. Oak did all right until it came time to make the strange right angles under the main line.

"Can someone please help?" Sister said shaking her head at Oak. "Master McCormick, if you can't diagram a sentence, you can't understand your own language. Sit down and pay attention."

Robert McPhee came to the board. He was a saint disguised as a boy. His skin was smooth, he never had any cuts or scratches, and his clothes were never torn. Maybe he would marry Gail Mullen. Robert diagramed it just right. All those lines. How did he do it?

The big hand of the clock sprang to the twelve and the bell rang. "Get in line," Sister Joseph said. "Get in line or there'll be no recess."

They marched down the wide wooden stairs to the basement to go to the lavatory. It wasn't called a bathroom. It was a *lavatory*. They said the word as if it were a secret. Oak was beside Ziggy. Ziggy was bigger than any of the boys. He had blonde hair and green eyes. Ziggy had moods. He was in one now and shoved Oak. Oak shoved him back. "No shoving, Master McCormick!" Sister shouted. Ziggy grinned.

They stood at the entrance to the boys' lavatory. Sister let six boys go in at a time. Robert McPhee and other good boys went in the front part of the lavatory. They stood with their backs to the door and peed against the black wall with the water streaming down it. The wild boys went around back where Sister couldn't see. Oak went around back. So did Chickie.

Chickie got his cards out—baseball cards he flipped against the wall for nickels. The person whose card was closest to the wall got the nickel. Joey, Chickie, Smelly and Oak threw cards. More boys were streaming into the lavatory. Older boys. Two of them got into the card game.

"You've had enough time back there," Sister Mary Joseph called. "Come out of there!" She stood at the doorway to the lavatory. The boys ignored her.

"I got a leaner!" Chickie said. His card leaned up against the wall. Chickie collected his nickels.

Sister Mary Joseph came around back like an explosion. "Get out of here!" she yelled. They flew like pigeons. It beat diagramming sentences.

That afternoon Oak, sitting in his tree, told Harry of his failure to diagram the sentence.

"We're in the hands of diagrammers, Oak," Harry said. "What we need are poets and tree climbers. Actually they're one and the same."

"I like your beret, Professor."

"Merci, Oak."

Harry went home in time to catch the phone. What he heard came as a shock; there was some relief but mostly shock.

CHAPTER 35

When Jillian came home Harry was smoking a cigarette at the kitchen table.

"They're letting me go at Northeastern," Harry said. "Dean Whitton called. No warning. No real explanation. It's just best for the university he said. Son of a bitch."

"What will you do now?" Jillian said. She stood in her riding outfit reminding him of an impatient horse.

"I fall in the fall," Harry said. "I am but a leaf on the tree of life."

"No wonder they let you go. Orange beret, sneakers. Hi Ho could get a PhD if you had your way. God, you never wake up Harry. Stalin killed millions and you're the happy Red."

"Ah, a political speech," Harry said. "Did you come across a newspaper on the riding trail? Is it the first you've read this year? For your information, I'm a socialist not a Communist."

"What are you going to do now, Harry? You expect me to go begging to my father to give you an allowance."

"Jillian, your whole life has been a game with your father. You married me to rile him. Sadly, it was the only reason."

"No, Harry. I fell for Saint Harry, savior of the masses. It all seemed so daring."

"And that lasted a year."

"Six months, Harry, then I saw what a sentimental business socialism is. I told my father some day you'd wake up. Instead you ran for Congress and made a complete fool of yourself."

"I worked like hell, and you never even came down to help."

"I came down that once and it was full of freaks and children. I'm going to shower."

"The campaign was actually quite successful, Jillian. I stirred things up."

"My father said you were stupid enough to quote Marx in a speech."

"Groucho, not Karl. Your father kept you up to date on my campaign?"

"He called when you said particularly stupid things. Leave the kitchen neat. I'm going out to supper at the Washburns'."

"I'm going to the McCormicks' party."

"Get a job."

"Thank you for your continued support and encouragement."

Harry stacked his corrected papers neatly on the table. "The solace of home," he said to the kitchen. "My wife takes me in her arms and says, 'Harry we're in this together. Let's get drunk and make love.'" He stubbed his cigarette out and went to the bottom of the stairs.

"I need a bit of air, Jillian," he shouted.

"I've told you before," Jillian called back, "don't smoke in the house."

"Make sure you're naked when I come back," Harry called. "Hereafter I want you naked at all times." She slammed the bathroom door and Harry went for his walk.

"Hello, Val," Harry called as Val McCormick pulled into his driveway.

"How's everything, Harry?" Val called getting out of his car.

"Fine, Val."

"Hope you and Jillian can come over tonight."

"Jillian can't come. She has nothing to wear. But I'll be there."
Val waved and went inside.

Harry walked along Pill Hill past the Lawrences, and as he
passed the Cobbs, he thought of Lydia Cobb at Creighton Mental Hospital. He walked by The Green and on to the Adams'
house. Amelia was deadheading flowers.

"How's the book coming?" Amelia asked. She had on gardening gloves, a purple hat, a short green coat and looked like a Girl
Scout.

"Amelia," came the strained voice of Eliot Adams. He appeared at the doorway. "Amelia! Come in here!"

"Is that you, Harry?" Eliot said coming down the outside
stairs. That was a surprise because Eliot detested him. Eliot was
dressed in a tweed jacket, wool trousers and crimson tie; his red-gray beard gave his face color, but even smiling he looked as if
the wrong team had scored.

"How are you, Harry?" Eliot said shaking Harry's hand vigorously; his high voice reminded Harry of bagpipes.

"Fine, Eliot. And you? Have you played any bagpipes?"

"What?" Eliot said.

"Nothing," Harry said. "I was just thinking of bagpipes."
Harry was sweating; the wing tips of his shirt collar had curled
up, and his tie was askew.

"I was just having a glass of beer, Harry. Come in and join
me."

Harry felt dizzy and hoped for crackers and cheese. He felt
weird; his head was filled with noise. "Thanks," Harry said.
"Maybe ten minutes. Jillian expects me back." It was the first
time Harry had been invited in.

They went in the back way. The entrance room had a deep
blue linoleum floor that spoke of laundry done and put away.
Harry saw a single banana sitting in a wooden bowl looking like
a little yellow canoe. The kitchen smelled of roast chicken and
mince pie. Eliot opened the refrigerator.

"How about a Ganset?" Eliot listened to all the Red Sox games.

"Hey, neighbor," Harry said, imitating sportscaster Ned Martin. "Have a Ganset when you're having more than one."

"Are you a Sox fan, Harry?" Eliot asked with interest.

"I like bagpipes," Harry said as Eliot poured a glass of beer. Why the hell am I talking about bagpipes? I couldn't care less about bagpipes. Now Eliot will go on and on about God damn bagpipes. I should go. I'm going to say something awful.

Eliot led Harry into the living room which was pleasant and neat as a museum. Just like our house.

"Harry," Eliot said in his high voice, "sit in the Morris chair."

"No, thanks, Eliot. The sofa's fine." It was obvious it was Eliot's chair.

"I like to sit here when the day is done," Eliot said, his bagpipe voice making every word a drama.

"Cheers," Harry said. "Here's to bagpipes."

"To bagpipes," Eliot laughed. Eliot's teeth looked to Harry like the grandmother's in Red Riding Hood. No, Harry thought, not the grandmother, the wolf.

"My father played the bagpipes," Eliot said. "In fact, he played them at the Harvard Yale game in 1898."

"No!" Harry said, taking a cracker and cheese.

"Yes. High point in his life."

Must have been a moron, Harry thought. The phone rang.

"Damn it," Eliot said. "Amelia must be back outside. It's getting dark. What's she up to?"

"Does she play the bagpipes?" Harry asked.

Eliot went into the hall and Harry heaped his plate with crackers and cheese. Lightheaded because I haven't eaten. Haven't eaten at all. He ate four crackers heaped with cheese.

"Sorry, Harry," Eliot said returning. "It was for Todd. It's getting late. He should be back by now." Eliot's voice tightened and his cheeks reddened. "I don't like some of the boys he plays with."

"Todd's playing football on The Green," Harry said. "I saw him on my walk."

"Oh, good," Eliot said drinking his beer. "That's good. Jimmy Douglas there I suppose?"

"Yes, and Oak McCormick."

Eliot sat stiffly. He drank his beer and looked at his glass in silence. "How's the book coming?" Eliot said.

"Writing a book is like joining the Army."

"You've got a good subject, Harry, but Napoleon would be my choice if I wrote a book."

"Washington was a better man," Harry said. "He knew he wasn't God." Harry began hearing bagpipes again. I need a real meal. "And how are you, Eliot?"

"Keeping occupied. I had lunch today with Ian Burns, my roommate at Harvard. He's in real estate." Eliot shook his head and sighed. "Your Washington book reminds me of what this country once was. It's changing now. Even the Hill. The Irish are moving in."

"You mean the McCormicks?" Harry asked. "You know Val was at Harvard."

"I don't like the Irish," Eliot said.

"What did Washington fight for?" Harry said, unable to keep his annoyance from showing. "A democracy where all men…"

"For God's sakes, Harry, don't preach. The Irish are drunks," Eliot said. "The Catholic Church is a feudal institution that has no place in a democracy."

"I'm not a supporter of any church, Eliot," Harry said trying to be calm, "but it sounds as if you want walls to keep the neighborhood pure. I think I heard that tune in Germany."

"I want peace, God dammit!" Eliot said. His voice rose so high his words ran together like the notes of a bagpipe. "I want Pill Hill the way it was. I don't want drunks running around.

I don't want my son exposed to the idiocies of the Catholic Church. I don't want Jews, Poles, Italians or Negroes ruining a perfectly nice neighborhood. God, we'll have Gypsies next. Let them have their own neighborhoods." He sipped his beer and said, "I just want to keep the neighborhood as it was." Eliot smiled and changed. He leaned forward as if sharing a confidence. "Harry, I want to let you in on a way to improve the town and to make some money. If you can come up with ten thousand dollars, I can help you turn it into thirty thousand. That'll give you time to do your book."

"I'm afraid I don't have any money."

"Let me finish," Eliot said. "Ian Burns told me that he and a few others are going to clean up the mess at the bottom of the hill. Bulldoze the place and build first-rate apartments. Highrise, high rent. The selectmen are behind them. It's all set. It's going to sail through."

"Bulldoze the triple-deckers? You mean the Farm?"

"Yes," Eliot said, his anger was gone now. Eliot was speaking with his whole body. His hands were open. "The place is a disgrace. We clean it up, make some money and you finish your book."

"What happens to the people who live there?"

"Who cares?" Eliot said, his face turning red. "They're town drunks. Let them live in Allston. They look as if they come from Allston."

"Eliot, we're talking about two or three hundred people. Some of my Northeastern students live there. A lot of the men down there were in the war with us."

"The war was a blessing, got them out of the bars."

"It got some of them killed. Ernie Marion's a student of mine. He lost both legs in the war. You're going to just boot him out?"

"Harry," Eliot said, "those people will be happy living anywhere."

"How do you know, Eliot? Has anyone consulted them? It's their home, for God's sakes."

"They are too stupid to care, Harry. Listen, Harry. Amelia likes you. She'd like to see you write your book so I'm letting you in on this for her sake. If you're not interested, let's drop it."

"You were very kind to have me in," Harry said standing. "Can I show you something? Then I must run," Harry said. "Now this chair is the subject of a sentence I'm going to diagram for you. A declarative sentence. The sentence is *They are bums.*" Harry began to move the furniture. Eliot was too startled to protest.

"Now the subject of the sentence is *they*. The verb is *are*. The object of the verb is *bums*. These cushions I'm throwing on the floor are the *bums*. The hidden compound subject of the sentence is *money and power*. I'll put these end tables over here to represent that. The illusion here is the goodness of you and your friends. The reality is greed which this chair will represent." Harry pulled over a big stuffed chair. "Now, Eliot, if you'll just help me move this couch, I'll show you the hidden adverbial phrase."

"You're a God damned ass, Harry. Go see a psychiatrist."

Harry lifted the couch and put it at an angle. He knocked over a lamp. The bulb smashed. Harry went to pick it up and bumped a table and the ashtray fell off. Harry started to laugh.

"Get out, Harry," Eliot said in a stifled scream.

"This is the way English should be taught," Harry said. "Listen, Eliot, I hate to, but I've got to dash. I'll leave the diagram so you can study it." Amelia came in and looked at the furniture all jumbled together as if children had been making a fort.

"Where's Todd, Amelia!" Eliot shouted. "It's time to eat!"

"He'll be right along," Amelia said. Amelia went to the back door with Harry.

"Are you all right, Harry? I could call a cab."

"Amelia!" Eliot called and she hurried back. Harry took the banana from the bowl and left.

<u>*CHAPTER 36*</u>

H arry went to the McCormicks' party; he danced with Oak's grandmother and she faltered and nearly fell. Because Harry had been drinking and felt responsible, he left the party early.

At four in the morning Oak heard his mother whisper, "Wake up! Wake up!" Oak was sleeping on the second floor porch just off of his mother's room.

"Harry Hutchinson's in our garden," Nora whispered as she shook Oak awake. "It sounds as if he's digging and singing."

"Nora," Harry called. "Are you awake? Fall is falling." Nora crept back into her bedroom and Oak called down, "Mom's asleep, Professor Hutchinson."

"Time to get up, Oak. What kind of tulips does your mother like best?"

"I think she likes red."

"Red it is."

Oak went into his mother's bedroom.

"Get me a cup of tea, dear," she said to Oak, "and tell your father."

"I'll get tea," Oak said. "You wake Dad."

When Oak returned, Val stood in Nora's bedroom in a white terry cloth robe smoking a cigarette.

"I think I'd better call Craig Lawrence," Nora said. "Is Harry still down there?"

Oak opened his mother's porch door, and they could all hear Harry singing.

I've got a loverly bunch of coconuts;
There they are all standing in a row.

"He's having a nervous breakdown," Nora said. "You think it's too early to call Craig Lawrence?"

"He's planting tulips," Val said. "There's no harm in that."

"At four-thirty in the morning?"

"It's twenty to five," Oak said.

"Hello! Hello!" Harry called from downstairs. "Oak!"

"God," Nora said. "He's in the *house*. He's coming up. Oak, tell him we're asleep." Val fled to his room. As far as Val was concerned when the party was over, it was over. He did not want to chat. Oak went to the hall banister. Professor Hutchinson was on the first stair calling. "Oak! I've planted red tulips. Ask you mother where she'd like the yellow ones."

"All right."

Oak went back and his mother glared. She whispered, "Tell him I have a terrible cold."

I've got a loverly bunch of coconuts;
There they are all standing in a row.

"He's coming up," Oak said.

"Tell him no!" Nora said. She took off her glasses and slipped under the covers.

"Val," Harry was calling. "We need to plan my next campaign. Oak will be my campaign manager. Val? Are you awake?" Harry was on the second floor landing, halfway up the stairs. "Oak," Harry said. "These windows are John LaFarge windows. Did you know that? That's Edie Lawrence letting her dog out. Come on, Oak. We'll plant her some tulips."

"It's so early," Oak said coming to the banister.

"I need you, Oak. The bag of bulbs is too heavy for me."

The two of them lugged the burlap bag of tulips into the Lawrences' yard. There must have been three or four hundred bulbs. Bones, the sausage dog, shook his long body and barked madly.

Florence Beam opened her bedroom window and shouted. "Keep that dog quiet!"

"Florence," Harry called. "You sack of guts. You must have the best box springs on earth." She slammed the window shut.

Edie Lawrence opened her bedroom window and called, "Will one desist, Bones?"

"Good morning, Edie," Harry called. "I'm planting tulips. What's your favorite color?"

"One likes all colors," Edie said looking down at Harry.

"Good. All I've got is a mix."

Florence Beam charged across her lawn to the fence in a robe and slippers. The sky was filling with gray-purple light.

"What did you say, Harry Hutchinson?" Florence shouted. She stood at the fence. Harry was digging in the Lawrences' garden forty feet away.

I've got a loverly bunch of coconuts;
There they are all standing in a row;
Big ones, small ones, some as big as your head.

"Harry!" Florence shouted. Harry went on digging

I've got a loverly bunch of coconuts.

Bones ran barking at Florence Beam. Florence's dog, Puddy, barked back. Craig Lawrence came out on the back porch in bathrobe and pajamas.

"Apologize!" Florence shouted.

I've got a loverly bunch of coconuts.

Oak helped dig.

"Harry Hutchinson!" Florence called.

"Florence," Harry called back. "I'm planting tulips. I'll be over when I finish here. Have breakfast ready."

"Good Morning, Florence," Craig said. Florence did not take her eyes off Harry.

"If you come into my yard, Harry Hutchinson, I'll call the police."

"French toast and bacon," Harry said. "Two eggs. Poached eyes on ghost."

"Good morning, Harry," Craig said. "Hello, Oak."

"Morning, Craig," Harry said. "Let's roast marshmallows in the yard."

Craig came down the porch stairs. "Harry, please come into the house."

Harry looked up. "I'd love a cup of coffee, Craig. We need to plan the campaign."

"Let's go into the kitchen, Harry. It's freezing out here."

"Just as soon as these are planted, Craig. I've changed my mind. I want Oak to go to Harvard. It's the best club in the world."

"Please, Harry."

I've got a loverly bunch of coconuts;
There they are all standing in a row.

CHAPTER 37

It took half an hour to get Harry into the Lawrences' kitchen by which time all the Lawrences were dressed and helping with breakfast. Edie Lawrence was at the stove. Monica was pouring orange juice, and Carrie was being kind.

"I think it's nice you planted tulips, Professor Hutchinson," Carrie said.

Harry and Oak were sitting at the kitchen table. "Florence Beam's box springs must be made of good grade steel," Harry said.

"One is grateful to you, Harry," Edie Lawrence said from the stove. "I never manage to buy tulip bulbs, so they never get planted."

"Jillian will be furious," Harry said. "She bought them for her riding club. She's leaving me for a stallion."

Craig Lawrence was on the phone in the hall.

"Do you know this song, Carrie?" Harry asked. *I've got a loverly bunch of coconuts.*

Oak caught Monica's eye. He lifted his eyebrows and she smiled.

Bones barked and Carrie joined in singing with Harry.

"There's Old John walking down the sidewalk," Carrie said. "I've never seen him going to the tennis court. He's always just there."

"Let's plant tulips on the banks of the tennis court," Harry said, and sang, *On the Bonnie Banks of Loch Lomond.*

"One must eat first," Edie said flipping a pancake.

"It won't take ten minutes," Harry said. "Then the pancakes will be ready and we'll eat as a team. Come on Oak, Monica, and Carrie. We'll be right back, Edie."

The sky was a mixture of black, purple and gold. The wind picked up and Harry's parade was accompanied by the music of shaking leaves. Oak pushed the Lawrences' wheelbarrow, which held the sack of tulips. Craig Lawrence put the phone down too late to stop Harry.

"He's planting some tulips at the tennis court," Edie said. "They'll be right back."

"How do you know?" Craig said. "He's having a nervous breakdown. I've been talking to Jillian. Harry's been acting strangely for weeks. I've seen it myself. Jillian thinks Harry should be sent to Creighton."

"Send Jillian to Creighton." Edie said. Edie stood with a spatula in hand. Her neck seemed to grow. Her head shook. "Send Florence Beam to Creighton. Send us all to Creighton. He's planting tulips so send him to Creighton. Is that the best you can do?" Edie shook her head and started crying. She turned back to the pancakes. "Truman dropped the bomb. Send *him* to Creighton."

Craig put his arm around her. "Edie, he's having a breakdown. He needs rest."

Edie sobbed and shook him off. She half-noticed she'd made a large golden pancake. "Creighton will destroy him. He'll give the book up."

"He's sick, Edie. He needs care."

"I need care," she said. "You're so busy being the almighty healer, you notice nothing."

"Edie, I'm getting dressed and going down to get Harry. I don't want the children with him."

"You are not going down to the tennis court. You are not getting dressed. You will sit down and talk to me until they get back."

Craig's face widened. His brown eyes betrayed his uncertainty. Edie had never issued a command.

"I'll pour you some coffee," she said.

Craig stood in pajamas and robe unable to decide. He stood as if there were mud inside him.

"The children are perfectly safe," Edie said. "It would be better to be thinking about raising money so Harry can finish his book. He needs encouragement."

Craig sat down at the table and sipped black coffee. "You don't understand these things, Edie."

"I understand you are at the hospital twelve hours a day. I understand that you are told a hundred times a day how wonderful you are. And you are." Edie was unaware the pancake was smoking in the pan. Craig pointed to the smoke and she turned to flip it over. She added some margarine and turned back. "There are some of us who live very different lives. We're Antigone's brother, rotting in the sun. One goes too far," Edie laughed. "You don't understand anything but your world. For you, Craig, life is a project. Everything is a project. You love projects. Maybe we should commit *you* to Creighton. You think you are the most tolerant man in the world, but you are oblivious. Everyone can't be magnificent. Everyone can't be like you, Craig. We all begin to think we're crazy because we're not like you and Nora McCormick."

"I am running a hospital, Edie."

"And I am undone. You are gone seven days a week. Vacation comes and we go off and do projects. You write papers, hike with the children, do your paintings."

"Edie, this is not the time to be talking about vacation. Harry is having a nervous breakdown. He needs help."

"I need help. The children need help. Carrie is eight years old and she spends every afternoon bent over the piano like Lydia Cobb. It's become a horrible project. Carrie hates the piano but she thinks she has no choice. She won't listen to me. She wants to please you. By the time she's in high school *she'll* have a breakdown just like Lydia Cobb. I do not want you sending Harry to a mental hospital."

———

Old John was raking the leaves on the tennis court.

"Hello, John," Harry said. Old John looked at Harry in his wrinkled brown suit followed by Monica and Carrie Lawrence and Oak pushing a wheelbarrow.

"Hi, John," Oak said.

"John," Harry said. "This is Tulip Planting Day on Pill Hill. We wondered if you'd let us plant a few tulips on the tennis court border. Maybe by the far corner of the fence."

"Annnaannnnn be niiiii."

"It *would* be nice," Oak said. "Thank you, John," Carrie and Monica chimed.

"I just have two spades," Harry said. "Oak and I will dig. Monica and Carrie will plant. Just a dozen or two. Is that all right, John?"

Old John nodded.

Old John came over to watch Oak digging. "Baaaaaaaaaa soool. Gaaa some od leeeee." Old John pointed to the little field between the Beams' house and the tennis court.

"Yes," Oak said. "I'll get some old leaves."

"Gaaa bukaaa in baaannn." Oak got the bucket from the barn

and began to gather decaying leaves in the little field behind the barn next to the Beams' backyard.

"Good," Harry said. "We will enrich the soil." Harry was down on his hands and knees digging the holes.

"John," Harry said. "You know this one?" Harry sang *I've got a loverly bunch of coconuts.*

"Look at the sky," Monica said. "The sun's coming up."

"It's a lemon meringue sky," Carrie laughed. Her laughter was quick as tiny silver bells. Oak was hoping they'd get Professor H home and after a good sleep he'd be all right and they'd laugh about it later.

Puddy, the Beams' dog, barked at Oak, and Florence Beam came out the back door. "Puddy!" she called. She was wearing a bathrobe over her nightdress. "What are you up to, Oak?"

"Just getting some leaves, Mrs. Beam."

"What are you doing getting leaves at this hour of the morning? Is Harry Hutchinson there?" Her face turned red.

"John," she called storming through the little field to the tennis court. "John! What is that man doing?"

"Hello, Florence," Harry said. "Is my breakfast ready? I want the bacon *crisp*."

"John," Florence said to Old John who was standing over Harry. "I do not want tulips planted on the tennis court grounds. It's six o'clock. This is outrageous."

I've got a loverly bunch of coconuts.

Florence was shaking with fury, "Harry Hutchinson, you are not a member of the tennis court association. If you don't stop this minute, I'm calling the police."

"And I mean crisp," Harry said and went on digging.

Oak brought the leaves over; he and Harry stuffed the rotted leaves into the holes and Monica and Carrie put the bulbs in and covered them up.

"Mrs. Beam's mad," Carrie whispered. Carrie smiled but her eyes were wide with fright.

"Now," Harry said. "Next spring, tulips will sing their song." *I've got a lovely bunch of coconuts.* On his hands and knees, his pale face smeared with dirt, Harry opened his arms to the rising sun.

As they left the tennis court, Craig Lawrence came down the sidewalk in his dark blue, three-piece suit.

"Here ye, hear ye," Craig said clanging an imaginary bell. "Pancakes ready."

"I'll be right along," Harry said. "Florence is fixing me bacon."

"Come on, Harry," Craig said. "Edie's waiting. Please."

"Please," Carrie said breaking into tears.

"All right," Harry said stooping down and giving Carrie a hug. "No need for tears. I'll have the bacon later."

Edie greeted the entourage at the door saying, "All who enter will be stuffed with pancakes." They sat on the small white stools around the narrow table; Edie serving pancakes, said, "One has beautified the tennis court."

"It will be the talk of Pill Hill," Harry said. "We had an encounter with Florence." Harry described the incident. They laughed and ate.

Ten minutes later the doorbell rang. Bones barked. Carrie opened the back door. A young policeman stood there. "Can I see your father?" he asked. Craig went to the door.

"We got a complaint about a Professor Hutchinson trespassing on the tennis court. The complainant said the trespasser is here."

"Come in officer," Craig said. The policeman looked uncomfortable; he was clean-shaven, slender, and looked as if he'd graduated from high school yesterday.

"Quiet, Bones," Craig said. "Quiet!"

"I am Professor Hutchinson," Harry said rising. Harry's suit was smeared with mud. He had washed his hands but not his face.

"I need to talk to you, sir," the policeman said.

"Officer," Craig said, "There's been a misunderstanding. We had a tulip planting to spruce up the neighborhood. Professor Hutchinson was our guest."

Edie came forward. "Officer, one is drowned in pancakes. Could we tempt you?"

"No, thank you."

Edie went on, "We are enchanted with the Tulip Brigade, and we are indebted to Professor Hutchinson."

The policeman was lost in the dark strangeness of her voice. This was a crazy house. Professor Hutchinson in his muddy suit was so pale he looked as if he might faint. Three dirty children. This strange deep-voiced woman offering pancakes and Dr. Lawrence who somehow looked like a hospital.

"We got a complaint," the policeman said again. "The planting was very early." He felt stupid standing at the edge of the kitchen talking about who planted tulips.

Carrie said, "We had to start early, before people come to play tennis. We asked Old John. He's the caretaker."

"You asked him?" the policeman asked Carrie. All three children said yes.

"He said it was all right?" The children nodded again.

Ten minutes later the policeman went down to the tennis court. He questioned Old John and John said, "Yeaaaaaaaaaaannnnna. Diaaaaaa."

CHAPTER 38

After the policeman left, Harry went into the Lawrences' living room and began playing the piano and singing,

I've got a lover ly bunch of coconuts
All standing right in a row.

Oak, Carrie and Monica stood giggling and singing. Harry excused himself, got a drink from the pantry and sat down at the piano stool and began to cry. Craig Lawrence came in from the kitchen and sent the children out to the yard to play.

Oak was on the back stairs with Monica and Carrie.

"He looks tired," Monica said.

"Mom said he is having a nervous breakdown," Oak said. It was terrifying to see Harry cry. He was like a baseball coming apart. Dr. Lawrence should walk him home and put him to sleep.

"I worry, Craig," Harry said looking at the piano keys. "I worry. I see Carrie at the piano when I come home in the afternoons. I saw the same thing with Lydia Cobb. Lydia's back bent like Pill Hill. She broke. I worry about them all. Todd Adams, Carrie, Monica, Oak, Ophelia. All of them. I worry about them." Harry got up and swept his hands up over his head just as he had last night at the party and did his dance finishing by collapsing on the rug. Craig sat down on the rug opposite Harry.

"Harry, I think you should go to Creighton. For a while. You're exhausted and you've been under a tremendous strain." Harry's face looked so sad. The tears had run into the muddy places. He'd wiped his tears and spread mud all over. He sat there in a battered brown suit, his thin black tie looked like a dead snake.

"Strain," Harry said. "Strain?"

Edie came in saying there was an urgent call for Craig.

"Be right back." Craig said.

Harry was crying again. He started singing, "*Harvard, Harvard, Harvard.* I've been fired, Edie. You think I'm nuts?"

"I think you are wonderful. I want you to do your book."

"Book?" Harry said wiping his nose. "It's gone. Who the hell is interested in Washington? Washington was nuts. I'm nuts." Harry jumped up. "My God! I could have killed old Mrs. McCormick," he shouted and ran out the front door. Harry hurried across the yard. Stopping to get his breath by the gate, he turned and called Oak. "Come on, Oak! Errand of mercy."

Oak hesitated. Where was Dr. Lawrence? Why didn't he come out and take care of Professor Hutchinson? Harry's sadness was gone.

"Come on Oak. I must apologize to your grandmother."

Patricia was in the kitchen sitting over a bowl of Cheerios when Professor Hutchinson burst in.

"Good mornin', Patricia," Professor Hutchinson said. "Don't eat too much. Florence is frying up crisp bacon." Harry swept into the butler's pantry.

"Wait!" Harry said looking at a painting. "Who did this?"

"I guess Dad," Oak said. "He does paintings late at night."

"Hide it, Oak. Hide it or they'll send your father to Creighton. Your parents are crucial, Oak. Without their parties, the Hill would explode." Harry sighed and stared at the floor. "I am afraid for your father."

"Let's use the back stairs," Oak said.

Oak's grandmother was sitting at her third floor kitchen table having toast and a soft-boiled egg. Oak came in and said Professor Hutchinson wanted to say hello. Harry came in, knelt on the linoleum floor and took Mrs. McCormick's hand and kissed the back of it. Mrs. McCormick's large blue eyes widened, her lips smiled in shock and her hands flew to her head.

"I am so sorry, Mrs. McCormick." Harry said, "I danced poorly last night and you almost fell. I beg forgiveness."

"Oh no," Mrs. McCormick said. "It was fine."

"You are gracious. I'm so sorry."

"It was nothing, really."

Harry stood up. "I would like to sing you a song."

"No, that's all right," she said not knowing what she was saying. "There's coffee. Oak, get a cup for Professor Hutchinson."

"Is there a song you like?" Harry asked sitting down at her large pale, oak kitchen table. He frightened her. He looked worse than a bum.

"After The Ball," Oak said.

"Would you join me?" Harry asked, leaning forward to Mrs. McCormick.

After the ball is over, Harry sang. His voice was high. He was slightly off tune. Harry sang it right to her. His hand moved slowly towards Mrs. McCormick and didn't stop until he hit her glasses. He lost the tune and found it. Her smile was fixed. Her eyes went from Harry to Oak.

After the break of day
After the dancers leaving
After the stars are gone.

Harry laid his head on her table and began to sob. Oak was unable to move. He thought he should get his father or call Doctor Lawrence. He should never have taken Professor Hutchinson up here. He was out of control. Mrs. McCormick's hand touched Harry's. "You need some breakfast," she said. Harry sat at the table wiping his tears looking like a little boy who'd been in a fight in the schoolyard.

"Tears of life!" Harry said. "Tears of suffering. *You* have suffered, Mrs. McCormick. Didn't Val say his father died when Val was a boy?"

"Yes," Mrs. McCormick said. Oak was surprised at how calm his grandmother had become. He expected her to be laughing nervously the way she did when Oak's dad came up after he'd been drinking.

"Cornelius," she said, "my husband, died on Christmas Eve. He came up the stairs and collapsed. He was gone in a day. That was 1919. He was a good provider."

"Provider," Harry said. "I admire him. I am no longer the provider. Who will provide for my family? My daughter is sane, Mrs. McCormick. That is a terrible curse. It seems, Mrs. McCormick, I have contracted leprosy. No one wants to be near me."

"It's probably just a cold," Mrs. McCormick said. "My sinuses act up in the fall and spring."

"Tell me of your husband," Harry said. "One day he's fine, and then he's gone and you are without your love."

She put some toast in for him and stood up to make scrambled eggs.

"Yes," she said. "I often say it's a terrible thing to live so long you don't remember your husband's face."

"You carried on. And Val was just a boy."

"Val was eight. He never really knew his father."

Craig Lawrence came into Mrs. McCormick's kitchen smiling. He'd never been up to her kitchen before. Nor, of course, had Professor Hutchinson. Harry had calmed down.

"Good morning, Mrs. McCormick," Craig said in his most cheerful doctor-of-the-house manner. He looked jolly but his brown-green eyes were concentrated and serious. "I hope you're well."

"Yes, thank you, Dr. Lawrence," she said. She thought the world of Dr. Lawrence.

"Would you like some coffee?"

"No, thank you, Mrs. McCormick. I have to get to the hospital. Harry, I wonder if I could see you downstairs."

"No thanks, Craig," Harry said. "We're having a nice talk. May I be so bold as to ask when you were born, Mrs. McCormick?"

"August 27, 1873," she said. "Oak, get more cups. Please sit down, Dr. Lawrence." She hadn't had this much company in ages.

She scrambled the eggs and put them on a plate for Harry. Harry smiled and pushed the plate to Oak. Harry stood up and gestured for Mrs. McCormick to sit at the table. Craig Lawrence sat at the far end of the table. Harry remained standing.

"We do not live alone," Harry said as if he were addressing a class. "We are held by our ancestors." Harry turned back to Mrs. McCormick. "You were born only a decade after the Civil War, Mrs. McCormick. Your parents lived at the time of Lincoln. Their grandparents were alive when Washington was president. I am almost having coffee with Washington."

Mrs. McCormick laughed. "When I was a girl we had a neighbor who had lost his leg in the Civil War. I think it was one of the big battles. He saw Lincoln once on a boat on the Potomac."

"This is marvelous, Mrs. McCormick."

"My father came over from Ireland," Mrs. McCormick said. Her strong-boned face was wrinkled. Her false teeth straight and dully white. She thought Harry drunk but she liked talking about the past. And Dr. Lawrence was here. She was enjoying the attention. "My father thought the world of Lincoln. But my father didn't like the colored."

"That," Harry said, "is the oppressor's invisible hand at work. That's going on in this very neighborhood. We sneer at the people at the bottom of the hill and they sneer at themselves."

"Oh," she said. "They drink a lot down there."

"And we drink a lot up here. *This*, Mrs. McCormick, is history. We on the Hill think of the working class the way they thought of the Indians of India." Harry's eyes had a shine. He leaned onto the table and looked like a madman.

Val McCormick stood at the entrance to the kitchen. The party was swelling. Val was dressed in dark trousers, a gray tweed jacket, blue shirt and tie. His eyes were a little blood shot.

"Good morning, Mother," Val said. "Good morning, Harry. Craig."

"Would you like some coffee, Val?"

"Yes, thank you, Mother."

Craig said, "After coffee, Harry, I'd appreciate your coming downstairs."

Harry was playing with the glass salt and pepper shakers he'd taken from the table.

"We are the destroyers and the destroyed," Harry said. "Val, you studied history. Is not the Hill a destructive place?"

"I think it's great," Val laughed.

"Something is rotten in the state of Pill Hill," Harry said salting the table. He unscrewed the top and poured salt on the table. "Here, Mrs. McCormick, is Pill Hill. A well educated, mostly old Yankee neighborhood. But not a place for the truly odd. I, Mrs. McCormick, am odd. But here is the secret, Mrs. McCormick. We are all odd. We must huddle." Harry shook pepper onto the salt hill and started to cry. Craig Lawrence took Harry by the arm and helped him up.

"Ah," Harry said. "Look out the window. Old John's fixing up the fence on the tennis court. He's my hero. Old John, the oddest of the odd. The most genial man in the world. There's no meanness in the man. He's the king, Oak." Harry looked at Oak then abruptly pulled loose from Craig Lawrence and hugged the boy.

Oak was embarrassed but knew he'd been given some honor. It was over now. Dr. Lawrence was taking charge.

"We better go, Harry," Craig said.

"I must depart," Harry said. "I need to plant more tulips." He bowed to Mrs. McCormick. "You have been so kind, Mrs. McCormick. Thank you."

"Oak," Val said, "You keep your grandmother company." Val followed Harry and Dr. Lawrence out of the kitchen.

"Oak," Harry said on the stairway. "I want Oak to come with us." Val called Oak.

"Oak," Harry said, going down the stairs, "We *descend the* gallows." And he started singing.

Dr. Lawrence took Harry aside in the downstairs hall. "I talked to Jillian, Harry. And I called a friend, a Doctor Murchison who runs Creighton Hospital. I want to take you there right now."

"No," Harry said. "My schedule won't allow it. Besides there's a waiting list."

"What do you mean?"

"Eliot Adams is in line ahead of me. And Florence Beam. And Val who puts up such a fine front. And you, Craig. Anyone who's as normal as you must be nuts. I'm sorry, Craig, but it's off to Creighton with you."

"The ambulance will be here in half an hour," Craig said.

There was bigness about Craig Lawrence that got bigger when he was serious. The hall wall leaned forward to hear Craig Lawrence's every word. "I talked to Jillian," Craig said. "She agrees it's best."

"The ambulance will be here in half an hour!" Harry shouted. "I must say good bye to Jillian. She'll be so sad her hair will turn gold. That's Oscar Wilde, Oak. I need to pack, Craig. I'll run for mayor of Creighton. This time we'll win, Oak."

"Harry," Craig, said, "Jillian will bring you everything you need."

"No, Craig. I must say good-bye. Send the ambulance to my door."

Craig looked at Val. They could restrain Harry but it would be a nightmare.

"Fine, Harry. Say good-bye to Jillian."

Edie Lawrence came in the McCormicks' front door and bumped into Harry.

"Tea at Creighton. Edie?" Harry said and left.

CHAPTER 39

"You're sending him?" Edie asked. She wore a dark skirt, a white blouse and navy blue sweater.

"He's having a nervous breakdown, Edie."

Val said, "Let's all go into the living room and sit down."

Oak knew the living room was a bad choice. The living room furniture didn't relax until late afternoon. Everyone looked stiff as the chairs and there was no liquor to loosen the mood.

"Do not send him, Snell." Snell was the special nickname she called Craig at times. She never explained it. "Do not send him. You are making a terrible mistake."

"He's sick," Craig repeated. "He is having a nervous breakdown. And it's no surprise after all he's been through."

"He is not sick," Edie said. "He needs help. One needs friends. One needs friends to gather round. Antigone needed friends."

"Don't make a Greek tragedy of it, Edie," Craig said. They both sat on the green couch.

"It *is* a tragedy!" Edie said. Her voice often had a hint of self-mockery. Not now. Her voice was low and deep, almost a moan.

"Antigone was left alone," Edie said. "No one stood by her. No one dared. No one is standing by Harry. He's lost his job.

He's at his wit's end. The book is his salvation. He needs friends, not a medical prison."

Oak sat still. It was as if black ice was cracking.

"It is not a prison. It's a hospital," Craig said. Craig was angry now. "It's a hospital for the disturbed."

"I'm disturbed," Edie said. "Everyone's disturbed. One thinks that is part of being human."

Val had been quiet. He lit another cigarette. "Edie," Val said, "Craig has seen this kind of thing a hundred times. I think Harry is beyond our help."

"Val," Edie said. "You are the last person in the world I'd expect to turn your back on Harry. He needs rest. We could raise some money to help him finish his book."

Craig stood up and went over to the fireplace. "He is having a breakdown, and we are not qualified to help him."

"But we are. We just don't have the courage."

Oak had never seen Mrs. Lawrence like this. The living room was alert. The air stood still.

"He's not crazy," Oak said.

"Who will pay for Creighton?" Val asked.

"He's still on the Northeastern payroll," Craig said. "They might pay."

"You do not understand," Edie said. "If you send him, it will break him."

"Isn't there some way he could just rest in a quiet place for a few weeks?" Val asked. "Then send him to Creighton if necessary. All he's done is plant tulips."

Craig shook his head. "He needs institutional care."

The phone rang and Oak got it. It was Jillian Hutchinson asking if Harry was with Dr. Lawrence. Harry had disappeared.

"We've got to find him," Craig said. "Val, can you look on Hillage Avenue? I'll get the car. He may have gone down to the village."

Oak found Harry in the tennis court barn talking to Old John. They were sitting on wooden chairs in the middle of the dark barn. The stone floor sloped to a drain in the center where there was a small circular oil stain from a car that used to sit there. The barn was filled with a silence that had been accumulating since the horses left thirty years ago.

"Come in, Oak," Harry called. "Ambulance here yet?"

"No."

"Cold here, John," Harry said shivering. "Chilly this morning. They think I'm nuts because I was planting tulips. They want to put me in a mental hospital."

"Maythyeeeee are nooooz."

Oak pulled over a third wooden chair and joined them sitting in the semi-darkness. The silent horse stalls were full of mystery. Light leaked through windows that hadn't been washed in long years.

"John," Harry said. "You are my model of a man."

"Unnnnnnnnnnnnnnnnnnnnnnnnnnnn."

"You are. No fuss. No tantrums. You just do your work."

John's shoulders jounced and he made laughter sounds.

"I'm serious, John. You're a good man," Harry said rubbing his arms to get warm.

Old John got up and went to the horse stall behind him. He got a dusty horse blanket for Harry.

Oak felt torn. Both Dr. Lawrence and Oak's father were looking for Professor Hutchinson, so maybe he should leave and tell them where he was. Harry was sad again.

"I wish we could change places, John," Harry said. "I'd like to do your job for a year and you do mine. You'd be great for the students." He pulled the old blanket about his shoulders.

"Puddy!" Florence Beam was out on the sidewalk calling for her dog. They heard Val McCormick saying, "Florence, have you seen Harry?"

"I've seen him all morning. He's drunk. If he comes in my yard, I'm calling the police."

Val peered into the barn. He stood adjusting his eyes.

"Join us, Val," Harry said. "You know John." Old John got a sawhorse and gestured for Val to sit on his chair.

"Thank you, John," Val said.

"I'd like John to see the painting you did last night, Val," Harry said. "Why don't you get it, Oak?"

"I better not go now," Oak said.

"Harry," Val said. "Perhaps we could raise some money so you could finish your book."

Harry didn't seem to hear. "Speak to the Pill Hill Association," Harry said to Val. "There is a move afoot to bulldoze the tenements at the foot of the hill."

"The Farm?" Val asked.

"Yes. Eliot Adams told me. You met Ernie Marion, my campaign manager. Talk to Craig and get a meeting of the Pill Hill Association set up fast. Get Ernie there. Could you do that Val?"

"Of course."

"I havvvvv coffaaaa," John got up to get his thermos. Harry stood and took John's gnarled hand and held it in both of his. "Time to go," Harry said. "Thank you again, John."

"Delicious smell. Florence is burning leaves." Harry said as they started up the sidewalk. Harry and Oak walked up together. Val was behind them. A pile of maple leaves burned in the middle of the Beams' yard. Daniel Beam stood by with the hose. Florence piled on more leaves.

"October incense," Harry said. "Florence," Harry called. "Is my bacon crisp?"

Florence ignored him.

I've got a lov er ly bunch of co co nuts, Harry sang and walked into the Beams' yard.

"Get out of this yard or I'll call the police," Florence said.

"Morning, Harry," Daniel Beam said. Daniel in khakis, jacket and old shirt, was a kind, quiet man, a surgeon. Daniel held the hose in one hand and a pipe in the other. Harry began to sing the Harvard football song. He started to march around the burning leaf pile singing *Harvard Harvard Harvard, victory today.*

Florence shouted for him to go. Harry took the hose from Daniel, turned the nozzle and squirted Florence Beam. She was so startled she didn't move.

"Here, here!" Daniel said. "Give me that, Harry."

Puddy barked. Harry squirted Puddy. Florence ran to the house. Harry gave Daniel the hose and left the yard singing the Harvard fight song.

"Good day, Miss Hatcher," Harry said. She'd seen him squirting Florence Beam and looked straight ahead. Her bulldog snarled. "You are a lovely sight this morning, Miss Hatcher. Next fall I hope you'll join our Tulip Brigade."

The Hood's milk truck squealed to a stop. Behind it came the ambulance.

Monica and Carrie Lawrence opened the Lawrences' gate and went onto the sidewalk and stood by the ambulance. Craig Lawrence spoke to the ambulance men. They ran down the sidewalk and grabbed Harry. Craig Lawrence hurried behind.

"There is no need to hold him," Craig said. "Harry, I'll walk you to the ambulance."

Florence Beam opened her bedroom window. "I've called the police, Harry Hutchinson."

"When I say crisp, Florence," Harry called, "I mean crisp."

Edie Lawrence was at the gate.

"I want him arrested," Florence called.

"For God's sakes," Edie said. "Shut up, Florence!"

Harry called to the dour milkman. "Two heavy cream and two coconut milk." The milkman stared.

They put Harry in the back of the ambulance and strapped him to a stretcher.

"Harry," Craig said. "I'll follow along in my car and get you settled."

"I'm sorry, Professor," Oak said crying.

"Don't be, Oak. We got the tulips planted." Harry sang, *I've got a lover ly bunch of coconuts*. The men shut the door.

Dr. Lawrence shook his head and went to the tin green garage. Edie Lawrence was crying in the yard.

"He is destroyed," Mrs. Lawrence said. Carrie and Monica started to cry.

They watched the ambulance go off, followed by Dr. Lawrence in the old purple Buick. Oak stood on the sidewalk unsure what to say or do.

Oak had agreed to help Mrs. Adams with her garden. Todd and his dad, Professor Adams, were going up to look at Exeter Academy for the day. Oak walked across Pill Hill and down Svensons' driveway, it was a short cut, unaware of what he was doing. He thought only of the ambulance driving away.

When Oak got to the Adams' house, Professor Adams was on the back porch pointing at Hi Ho the bum and screaming at Mrs. Adams.

"Get him out of here!" Professor Adams was yelling.

"Could you give me five dollars, Eliot?" Amelia said. She was standing on the driveway with Hi Ho.

"I will give you nothing. Get rid of him!"

"I'm so sorry, Mr. Regan," Amelia said to Hi Ho. "I'd like to pay you for coming."

"I didn't work," Hi Ho said. "Sorry, I was late." He left. Eliot Adams slammed the back door and retreated to his study.

Todd was in the yard raking. "Dad woke with a cold so we didn't go," Todd said. Oak told Todd what had happened to Professor Hutchinson.

Eliot Adams came back to the porch. Oak and Todd were around the corner of the house but they heard him.

"Amelia," Professor Adams said in a high, excited voice. "I just got a call from Florence Beam. They've taken your friend, Harry Hutchinson, off to Creighton Mental Hospital this morning. There was a drunken party at the McCormicks' and Harry went crazy."

Professor Adams went back into the house. Amelia Adams had on a rumpled old blue hat, big gray garden gloves. She wore pants and a wool shirt that was probably an old one of Eliot's. She looked very small.

"I better go," Oak said.

"I'll come over this afternoon if I can."

"Good."

Oak went home and climbed the Big Tree. He sat on his usual branch in the Fourth Realm. He caught sight of Old John repairing the fence on the tennis court. Perhaps unconsciously, Oak knew Old John's mangled body mirrored the soul of the neighborhood. A soul full of tears, scars, awful deformities and beauty.

Oak sat in the tree for the rest of the morning. Hungry for a peanut butter sandwich, he climbed down and walked up Forceps Avenue. A foursome, all in white, was playing doubles. Old John of the Tennis Court was working on the wire fence. Oak kept walking. Edie Lawrence was in her yard raking leaves.

CHAPTER 40

"My boots are dead," Harry cried in the padded cell. He cried for days. He smashed his hand against the padded cell so they put him in a straight jacket. He refused to eat, and they force fed him.

After three weeks he began to eat, and on Christmas Day he sang carols with some of the patients in the main room they called the Sitting Room.

New Year's Eve Harry heard one of the nurses saying, "Happy New Year," when she left. That night his roommate, Elijah, wailed to the Master of the Universe and fell into noisy sleep. Harry slept for a few hours and woke sweating. Somewhere he heard car horns blaring. Parties. The McCormicks' party came back to mind. Before going to the McCormicks' party that night, Harry had gone to the closet to get different shoes and he'd come upon the boots. The moment he picked up the boot he'd been back in Hiroshima. The boot. He'd picked up a boot in the endless rubble of Hiroshima and there was a leg sticking out of it. It had taken Harry some moments to realize it was a human leg because it was black, hard and full of ashes. He had stood holding it while an army major shouted at him to put it down. Harry had just stood there holding the boot. Somehow Hiroshima and his boyhood were fused in the boot. The major shouted again and for Harry it was his father shouting. "You are four years old and old enough to be responsible. You stole the cookies and lied about it. You will stay in the closet until I say you can come out."

The terror of the closet came back. "I'll be good," Harry said standing with the boot in Hiroshima. "I'll be good." The major stood there saying, "For Christ's sakes, Captain Hutchinson, put the fucking boot down. You can't touch anything. What the hell is wrong with you?"

"Be my friend," the four-year-old said to the boot in the closet. Hours later his father opened the door. "Come out and tell the truth about the cookies." Harry knew he had to keep his friend, the boot, a secret or his father would take it away.

"Christ," the major said. "Get him the hell out of here. And take that fucking boot out of his hand."

CHAPTER 41

Harry shook all New Year's night at Creighton. Towards dawn he began flailing, and they put him in a strait jacket and locked him up. He screamed all New Year's Day. "It's my boot, Daddy!" he yelled over and over. He cried and shook and screamed and fell asleep and had a nightmare that the boot exploded and destroyed everything. There was no closet to hide in. There was nothing anymore.

The second day of January Harry woke before dawn, frightened but clear-headed, aware that whatever wild thing had happened inside him was over; all his apocalyptic imaginings were gone. He looked clearly at his predicament. He was on the floor of a padded cell in a strait jacket. His shoulder ached and his right arm was asleep; he jiggled it to bring it around.

Harry imagined looking down at himself, a thin, balding man in a white night shirt on the floor trussed up in a strait jacket. "I'll run again as Mad Hatter Harry." The terror cut the joke short. "I'm in a mental ward. My God, I might never get out. Oh my dear God. This is a nightmare."

When the doctor returned that morning Harry was ready.

"Professor Hutchinson?"

"Yes, Doctor."

"How are you feeling?"

"Hopeless, but I'll behave. I had a nightmare about a boot I picked out of the rubble in Hiroshima. It brought back a memory of my touching a Japanese woman who'd been poisoned by the radiation of the atomic bomb in Hiroshima. She began to bleed and nothing could stop it. I killed her. When I remembered that, it felt as if the world exploded inside me but when I woke up I knew I was fine. I snapped but somehow I'm myself again."

"If you're violent we'll have to put the jacket back on."

"I understand."

The doctor left and returned with the two orderlies who helped Harry to get to his feet; they took off the strait jacket. Harry's arms hurt so much he groaned.

"Please follow me," Doctor Popham said. The orderlies followed close behind Harry. The quiet corridor of the old mansion had dark oak floors. They went into a medical office with a large desk, a couch, and a tall white gurney for patients to lie on. The orderlies were on either side of Harry.

"Professor, I'm going to give you an injection, then we'll bring you down to the Sitting Room."

"There is no need for the injection, Doctor. I'd rather stay clear headed. I'll behave."

"You are unwell, Professor." They gave him the injection. For the next three weeks he was so heavily medicated life continued to be a haze and a horror, but when the medication wore off he felt trapped, humiliated, angry and often hopeless and yet relieved. He was sane. If he could just get out of here.

Edie was finally allowed to see Harry the last Monday in January. She had pestered Craig until he called Dr. Murchison, the head of the hospital, and arranged for her to visit. The nurse, a gaunt woman, made Edie think of Cerberus, the three-headed dog that guarded Hades.

"Dr. Murchison said I could see Professor Hutchinson," Edie said to the nurse.

"It won't do you any good," the nurse said. "He hasn't said a word in weeks."

"Thank you," Edie said, hoping to shed the three-headed dog nurse.

Harry sat like a wet doll in the corner of the Sitting Room which had been the old mansion's living room. The patients, all on medication, moved about like sleepwalkers.

Harry's tongue hung out. His eyes were glazed. "Eee," Harry said, unable to stand because he was so doped up.

"It is so good to see you," Edie said. She sat on the couch and took his hand. He nodded and kept nodding, then closed his eyes. After ten minutes she squeezed his hand and said good-bye. Harry opened his eyes and smiled, then slumped back into a stupor. Edie was so shaken she tried to see Dr. Murchison. Because he was busy, she called Craig. "Craig, I want to see Dr. Murchison right now. Call him and tell him."

"Edie, he's busy."

"You got Harry in here. They have all drunk of the river of oblivion. If this is the best medicine can do, then medical schools would be better off having witch doctors. I want to talk to Dr. Murchison. No, I've changed my mind. I want you to call him and make an appointment for tomorrow or Wednesday for you and me to sit down with him."

At five o'clock Wednesday afternoon they sat down in Dr. Murchison's office. Once the study of a wealthy man, its oak bookcases lined the walls; leaded windows looked out on a frozen garden. Murchison, who had deep-set eyes, a sleek balding head, horned rimmed glasses, a rigid looking nose and ears that were bent in the middle, had been at Harvard Medical School with Craig. Edie had on a broad-brimmed hat and dressed in a simple black dress with pearls. All three were smoking.

"Craig, wonderful to see you. And Edie, it's nice to meet you. How can I help?" The Lawrences sat in dark blue leather chairs in front of Dr. Murchison's vast glass-topped desk. Edie felt as if she were in school again.

"Gerry," Craig began. "Edie and I are worried about Harry and hope he can get out as soon as possible."

"I'm afraid it will be a long time," Dr. Murchison said. " I see little hope for his leaving before a year."

"A year!" Edie said. "This was supposed to be a rest, a month or so."

"I'm sorry, Edie. He's violent." Dr. Murchison sat back and took a puff of his cigarette.

"He's never been violent," Edie said. "Maybe the medication is all wrong. What has to happen for him to be out by April?"

"I'd say it's unlikely. He can't control his anger."

"Of course he can't. He shouldn't be here," Edie said. "He just needs rest so he can work on his biography of Washington." She saw he dismissed her. "For Harry, this is Hades." And she wanted to add that Murchison was Charon. "There are things one knows," Edie said. "Harry Hutchinson should not be here."

She heard little of the rest of the meeting. On the drive home Edie smoked and brooded. She finally said to Craig, "You put him there. I want him out in three months."

"Edie, these things have no time table. Harry's sick."

"He is not sick. He's discouraged. Everything's fallen apart for him and he's exhausted. You said yourself people sometimes react violently to medication. They doped him up and he went wild."

"Edie, what do you know about mental illness? Medicine is just beginning…"

"You are all so sure of yourselves. I know Harry. You and your cigarette-holder friend have decided humiliating captivity is best for Harry. He needs friends. He needs quiet. He needs peace. I got a glimpse of Lydia Cobb when I first came to see Harry. She looks like a sleepwalker. It's so sad to see her."

"She's on medication because she's a danger to herself."

"She's in danger because her father insists she be something she's not."

Craig pulled into the tin green garage, shut the car off and turned to Edie. "I can't interfere. Gerry knows what he's doing. Harry needs help."

"He needs friends," she shouted. "Why can't you understand that?" she cried. "He drank too much, planted some tulips and hosed-down Florence Beam so now he's branded a lunatic."

"Mental illness is an illness just like any other."

"You've ruined him."

"Edie," Craig said as calmly as he could. When Craig got mad his shoulders and chest expanded. "I had no choice. Harry had a nervous breakdown. His family has a history of them. Jillian called me five or six times before the tulips incident. Harry was behaving oddly. He went to work with his umbrella open when it wasn't raining. Jillian woke up one morning at three and heard Harry having a conversation with a man with a deep voice. She went down stairs and it was Harry talking with himself. He started playing Monopoly in the bathtub. He left the play money in the water. Then…"

"She made it all up," Edie said wiping the tears with her hand. She lit a cigarette and took a deep breath. "Jillian hated the campaign. It was an embarrassment to her. But now she can write it off as a mental disorder." She was crying.

Later they fixed drinks and started arguing again. At ten o'clock Edie said, "Call Dr. Charon tomorrow. Tell him I'm visiting Harry on Friday, and he is not to be on medication. I'll sleep in the sewing room tonight."

Friday Edie went into what she called the Hall of Oblivion and found Harry on the back couch of the Sitting Room. Looking pale, he wore khakis that were too big and a green flannel shirt. His eyes were clear. Dogface was standing twelve feet away.

"How does one fare?" Edie asked.

Harry just shook his head. Several times he tried to speak and shook his head. She did not get a word out of him that visit. Dogface smirked as if to say I told you.

For the next two visits it was the same. Dogface no longer hovered but went about her business while keeping an eye on Harry.

On the fourth visit Harry said, "It is so God damn humiliating. So God damn humiliating. Jillian, my father, Dean Jackass and the newspapers all vindicated. Hutchinson is a nut. We always knew it." He shook his head and would say no more, but she left encouraged. She visited twice a week, and by late February Harry seemed more himself. He was tired and discouraged, but himself.

Edie said, "Harry, Dan Cobb died last night of a heart attack." Lydia's still on medication, but she came over yesterday, and I think she's going to be fine."

Harry let out a breath saying, "Thank God. What a bastard he was."

That evening Craig Lawrence came home at ten. He and Edie had a drink in the kitchen. "How are the children?" he asked.

"The young are fine. I have hope for Harry." Edie poured another bourbon for herself. She spilled some on the table.

"I wish you would drink less," Craig said.

"I wish you'd come home earlier."

"I try."

"I drink."

CHAPTER 42

One Monday in March Edie came in to the Sitting Room with a smile and a shiver. Under her long wool winter coat she wore an orange-brown sweater over a lavender blouse. Harry felt the rustle of her life.

They sat on the back couch which Harry considered his, and, as always, the patients slumped in chairs or walked in a haze. The room smelled stale.

"I bear news that may be good. Jillian called me. She told me to tell you she's decided to get a divorce," Edie said.

Harry's eyes widened.

"Did she say why?" he asked.

"She said she realized your whole campaign was part of a long term mental illness. She thinks if you didn't have the responsibility of marriage, it might lighten your burden and some day you might get well."

Harry laughed so loud Dogface glared. "Perfect," Harry smiled, "she's getting a divorce out of the goodness of her heart."

"Her charity knows no bounds," Edie said.

"This changes everything, Edie."

"Have you thought of the future?"

"I think about it all the time. I don't know where I'll live. I haven't got a job. I have campaign debts."

"They are dwindling."

"What do you mean?"

"Ernie's organized a committee both to erase your debts and save the Farm. I think Craig is feeling guilty. Maybe that's unfair but he's on the committee and so are Val McCormick, Meg Marion and Betty Taunton."

"Betty Taunton? Is she getting crocked and phoning people?"

"She is. We meet at Ernie's once a week. Betty says it's *democratic* and she's right. I had never been on one of the streets in the Farm let alone gone into one of the apartments."

Harry took her hands and shook his head. "You're a wonder."

Edie laughed. "I felt so lost when the campaign ended I was drinking by nine in the morning; then Ernie called and asked my help. I am renewed."

Only after Edie left did Harry feel the force of what she'd said. Jillian was ready to divorce him. He had had a wild hope being at Creighton might achieve just that, but now that it was going to happen he felt uncertain and alone. Humiliation came back with the force of a winter storm.

That afternoon Harry had a consultation with Dr. Popham whom Harry liked because he was a listener. Harry told him about the possible divorce. "It opens a new world," Harry said.

"A good world?"

"Yes. But a sad world. I fell in love with an actress just after the campaign. She's married now. I should have fought for her."

"What will you do?"

"I don't know. I can't think. I feel ashamed."

"Of what?"

"Of everything. My life. I'm not just a failure, I'm a leper. I'll never get another teaching job."

"Is that so bad?"

"Of course it is. I'm damaged goods. I've been awarded a God damned scarlet letter. Anyway, can I get out by June?"

"You've been through a great deal and you could snap again."

"I don't think planting tulips is snapping."

"I've told you I think it's fundamentally an issue between you and your father. Do some writing on your book; that'll show us you're back on track and we'll see. We have a library that's really just a small room with a few magazines. You could write there."

"I'd like the quiet. This place is a madhouse."

"Yes," Popham said. "I'm glad to go home at night."

At supper Harry usually sat beside Kurt the Blinker, a handsome lawyer of about thirty-five who blinked when he looked at someone and then wrinkled his nose. Kurt often growled and laughed hysterically, but there were times when he was both rational and charming.

"Are you a Red Sox fan?" Kurt asked Harry. The lima beans looked limp, the Salisbury steak was hamburg, but the mashed potatoes were quite good.

"No," Harry said. "Just plain black socks."

Kurt laughed so Harry could see his half-chewed lima beans.

"I wanted to play left field," Kurt said. "But Ted Williams was there. Williams lives in left field. He goes home and sleeps in a house at night but he *lives* in left field. We have to find our mythical place, Harry. What's your mythical place?"

"I know Oak's mythical place."

"Oak?"

"A boy in my neighborhood. He loves being up in a tree. That's where he's alive. This past summer I ran for Congress. Looking back, I think my headquarters was my mythical place."

CHAPTER 43

Harry wrote each day but not a word on Washington. Today he sat at the wooden table and began to write.

March 26, 1951
Dear John,
Thanks for visiting. It was great to see you.
My roommate, Elijah, would have fitted into our campaign headquarters very well. He has a gray-black beard, small black eyes that sear, and he's always speaking to God. Sometimes in English. Sometimes in Hebrew but mostly in a tongue no one understands. He whistles for his dog each night before bed. His dog is invisible and requires little maintenance.

You told me about falling in love with a nurse when you were in the hospital in France. She was married and you said you've never forgotten her. I fell in love with a beautiful woman and lost her to an Englishman.

Harry ripped the letter up and began again.

March 26, 1951
Dear John,

This morning I had my bi-weekly interview with Dr. Popham. Evidently he has two heads and switches them. The Tuesday head uses Old Spice and offers me a stick of Spearmint gum so we're chummy. The Thursday head is very formal—no gum. Both heads say I can write my way out of here, meaning I'm to work on my Washington book. I'm sure Craig Lawrence suggested that. I'm writing in what they call the library, a small room with a table, two chairs and some old LIFE magazines.

I'll start by writing letters and then, hopefully, move on to Washington.

The bulb went out. Harry went across the hall, slipped into the staff room, unscrewed a bulb and returned to the library. One day I'm running for Congress and the next I'm sneaking bulbs in the nut house.

March 26, 1951
Dear Jillian,

I applaud you for being without a doubt one of the great bitches of all time.

I see your bitchy hand behind my stay here. I did, in fact, snap, but it was brief and could have been handled by a psychiatrist. What still infuriates me are all those little notes you put on the jars. PUT PEANUT BUTTER AWAY! One week after I'd come home from the war you flew into a fury because I'd left the peanut butter jar on the counter. I had been to Hiroshima on special assignment for Stars and Stripes and you were shouting at me for leaving a peanut butter jar on the counter. We had a family meeting and you spoke for about twenty minutes about putting things away. Where the hell was your perspective? I could never live in the museum again.

Harry ripped it up.

March 26, 1951
Dear Diane,
  The days we had in Maine were the happiest in my life. Losing you is like a death, and I'm not doing well with it. As I think of you, I can smell the seaweed and hear the breakers rolling in. I've never talked with anyone as I did with you. There was such music between us. Just walking back from breakfast was magic. The sun was closer, the air sweeter, the moon and stars were brighter those few days.

Harry stopped because he was crying. He ripped Diane's letter up. The bell rang. "Ah," he said. "Lunch with the zombies."
  Returning to the library at ten the next morning, he tried again.

March 27, 1951
Dear Jillian,
  Edie told me you've agreed to a divorce. Thank you. My campaign didn't help our marriage, and I'm sorry for that. I'm also sorry that when I came back from the war I had little empathy for all you'd been through while I was away. You and Ophelia deserved atten-tion, but I was caught up in my career and my self-importance.
  After Ophelia's suicide attempt we all pulled together but once again got lost in work and projects. But we tried. Give us that. Di-vorce will let us start anew.
  You can do just about anything you want to. If you had run for Congress you would have won. There are exciting things out there for you, and I wish you well.

Harry pushed the letter aside. He wondered how to sign it. Sincerely? Yours, the madman? *Love?*

The letter Harry could not write was to his father. Harry got up and paced in the little room with its sad green walls, eight steps one-way, eight the other. He composed a letter in his head. Dear Dad. God, no. Dear Father. Dear God the Father, I still cannot understand how you could denounce me in public.

Harry wanted to smash one of the chairs against the wall. He could not write that letter. Instead he wrote:

Green walls
Snow falls.
As I write
I watch the light.

———————————

That afternoon Harry met with Dr. Popham whom he thought of as Spearmint.

"Stick of gum, Harry?"

"Thank you, Doctor."

"I've been waiting for the chapters on Washington."

"I've started with letters."

"To whom?"

Harry felt ornery this morning and wanted to say, never mind you nosy bastard, but instead he said, "To a friend and to my wife. I started one to my father."

"And?"

"He's a sad son of a bitch."

"Sad?"

Harry turned red, his breath came short. "My father destroyed my campaign. Am I supposed to take it in good stride?"

"The father figure, Harry…"

"Spare me Freud. My father came out publicly against me. We had never gotten along, but that's God damn mean. Someday I'll come to terms with it. I'll start back on my Washington biography tomorrow." But he didn't.

CHAPTER 44

On a cold April Monday morning Edie arrived at Creighton with Ernie and two of his friends who lifted Ernie in his wheelchair up the outside stairs.

"I'll be out in a half hour," Ernie said to the men and followed Edie in his wheelchair into the Sitting Room. As usual, Harry was on the couch in the corner.

Harry shook Ernie's hand, gave Edie a peck on the cheek and sat down. He was pale and clean-shaven; his eyes were clear and his hands were in constant motion.

Edie, wearing a cape and light green dress, sat down saying, "Lydia's going back to high school in the fall. She's going to dance camp this summer. She wanted you to know."

Harry calmed down and smiled.

"The guy teaching your Early Founders course is making a name for himself," Ernie said.

"He is?" Harry asked.

"Yeah, he puts everyone to sleep in about three minutes. Actually, half the class dropped out because he reads from a book. He doesn't lecture. He just reads from a book for fifty minutes."

"That's an outrage," Harry said. "I'd better take the class back over. Ernie, get my things, we're leaving," he laughed. "How are things in Korea?" Harry asked.

"The Chinese Communists," Edie said, "have half a million men in Korea and they're overwhelming the UN forces. Craig has a friend in the State Department who says MacArthur wants to drop thirty to fifty atomic bombs on Manchuria and Chinese cities."

"There's a measured response," Harry said.

"Yeah," Ernie said, "Nutty Nestor's all for it."

"You see," Edie said, "how important your campaign was."

"MacArthur's putting the pressure on Truman," Ernie said. "He's saying when soldiers are dying you should use whatever you got to protect them and that means the bomb. He's saying he'll widen the war unless the Chinese meet with him; with *him*, not the President."

"What's Truman doing about it?" Harry asked.

"Nothin'," Ernie said, "so far."

The political talk aroused Harry. He stopped fidgeting, got some color in his cheeks and was more animated than Edie had seen him in weeks.

Two weeks later when Edie told Harry the news that Truman had fired MacArthur, Harry leapt up and whooped. Dog Face glared, and Harry went over to her and asked, "Aren't you glad he fired MacArthur?"

"Truman should be impeached," Dog Face said and turned away.

"Alas," Edie said. "That's what Nestor says and most of the country agrees."

Harry was so excited he paced back and forth saying, "Truman's tough. He'll weather the storm."

"And so will you," Edie said.

On April 19ᵗʰ Edie smuggled in a radio for Harry. "MacArthur returned in triumph like Caesar," Edie said. "He's addressing Congress at noon."

At noon Harry sat alone in the library making a wooden boat out of popsicle sticks. He bent a stick for the bow and cursed when it snapped. He bent the next more slowly. The radio, hidden under some magazines, was turned on low but Vice President Alben Barkley's voice was clear as he introduced General MacArthur. The ovation was long enough for Harry to cut two short pieces for the stern.

MacArthur's voice was low and compelling, "I address you with neither rancor nor bitterness in the fading twilight of my life."

Harry murmured, "The emperor has got them in the palm of his hand."

He squirted some glue onto the keel, got his fingers sticky and cleaned them with a rag he dipped in a bowl of water. As Harry considered making a mast, MacArthur was saying that the Joint Chiefs of Staff had been completely behind him.

"Bullshit," Harry said. "Behind dropping thirty to fifty atomic bombs? Bullshit."

The mast was made of a long sliver from the popsicle stick and he cut a little piece from the tail of his shirt for the tiny sail. He worked more slowly because MacArthur's speech was building in a way that Harry could only admire.

Harry's fingers were stuck together as MacArthur paused then said in a voice so vibrant Harry didn't breathe, "I still remember the refrain of one of the most popular barracks ballads of the day . . . 'Old soldiers never die, they just fade away.' And now, like the old soldier of that ballad, I close my military career and just fade away."

The ovation was worthy of the second coming, and Harry was on his feet cheering before he realized what he was doing.

That evening as Harry walked down the hall to supper, Dr. Popham joined him. "I shouldn't tell you this, Harry, but you're a history professor so I will. MacArthur spoke to the Congress today. It was the greatest speech I ever heard."

"What did he say?" Harry asked.

"He said if you fight a war there's no substitute for victory."

"Ah."

"I've never been so moved," Popham said.

"Victory?" Harry asked. "How?"

"Go after the Chinese. Hit them with everything we've got."

"Atomic bombs?" Harry asked.

"Everything we've got. Truman made the mistake of his life. You don't fire God."

"But Truman did?"

"Yes, and he'll pay."

"Maybe I should be the doctor and you the patient."

"See you later, Harry."

Before bed, Harry said, "Elijah, I made a wooden boat out of popsicle sticks today. It's terrific."

When Harry woke the next morning, Elijah was two inches from his face. Harry jerked back saying, "Jesus, Elijah! What is it?"

"The flood cometh." Elijah's face was long, his jowls heavy, his eyes lit up with a sad fire.

<u>*CHAPTER 45*</u>

"Have you written a chapter for me?" Dr. Popham asked. "I've been waiting two months."

"Bracing," Harry said.

"I'm sorry?"

"Old Spice," Harry said.

Popham smiled. "Splashed on a bit too much?"

"No, I haven't written a chapter."

"Harry, I thought we had an agreement. You write a few chapters of your book. You show progress and we work towards getting you out."

"I'm busy mulling," Harry said.

"You're not mulling, Harry. You're making things out of sticks and clay."

"Soldiers," Harry said. "And cannons and tents. I'm re-creating Valley Forge in clay."

"Ah," Dr. Popham said. "Stick of gum?"

"Thanks," Harry said, reaching for the spearmint. "I can use the tinfoil to suggest the ice."

Popham leaned forward and rested on his elbows. "Your wife asked me if you'd gotten her letter."

"I did," Harry said, folding the silver foil and putting it in his pocket. "She wants to get divorced as soon as possible. She wants to sell the house and give me a quarter of the sale."

"Is that fair?" Popham asked.

"Of course not," Harry tried to keep his voice even. "I paid for the house. One minute I'm her nut husband and the next she wants to get divorced so I'm suddenly fine. Who's paying for my stay here anyway?"

"Your wife is a forceful woman. Somehow she got Northeastern to pay, but I shouldn't have told you."

"She loves to save a buck. She's rich and has never contributed a cent to the running of the house."

Dr. Popham smoothed his hair and said, "I think you're not writing your book because you're afraid to leave. Stop stalling and write the chapters."

Harry left the office and went back to making clay soldiers.

CHAPTER 46

"Meg!" Harry said. He stood and spontaneously hugged Meg Marion. Harry was so delighted to see Meg that for a moment the sad mental hospital living room half filled with drugged patients was forgotten.

"I smuggled in a piece of Boston Cream pie," she said.

"Here, sit down," Harry said. "You look wonderful, Meg."

"I had my hair cut," Meg said. She looked younger. She took her coat off and was wearing an orange blouse, black skirt, pearls and a thin, elegant watch.

One of the patients, Elijah, began to chant just as another patient, a young woman of maybe twenty, threw up on the rug.

The ogre nurse led the young woman away, and a janitor began clearing up the mess. Elijah kept chanting.

Meg started, "I hope you leave here soon..."

They got talking and she told him she'd been raised by her French Canadian grandmother who wanted Meg to go to college on scholarship. There was no money. Meg's high school sweetheart was Robert McFee, who'd gotten straight A's from the moment he'd left the womb. But in senior year the lure of the boy they called the pirate, Johnny Steenrod, was too much for Meg. Johnny Steenrod had a black leather jacket, a motorcycle, and he really did have a black patch over one eye. He'd lost an eye in a fight. Johnny was exciting. He took Meg to places on his motorcycle: Nantasket, Newport and even New York. They screamed together on roller coasters, they went to smoky bars and parties the like of which she'd never seen. She left high school and they married and Ernie was born. She said, "The marriage was a nightmare. Johnny got drunk and was killed on a motorcycle."

Meg took a breath and said, "Robert McFee went off to Johns Hopkins, and I lost all touch with him. He came into the donut store during the campaign. He was the one I had a date with. Remember, I told you we were going on the swan boats and then to the Ritz. Well, it was Robert who was teaching the French course in Boston. Robert's divorced. I'm going to Paris with six of our French class members, and I'll spend the last three days with Robert."

"There," Meg said. "There you have it." Her eyes were now filled with tears.

Harry sat smiling and shaking his head in wonder. "I'm just so happy for you, Meg."

"Harry," Meg said, "Ernie thinks you can leave here but you're hanging on. Forgive me. I shouldn't…"

"Oh no," Harry said taking her hand.

"Harry, you changed our lives. All of us, Edie Lawrence, Ernie, me, Oak, John. We want you to be happy. We want you out of here. Ernie—well he's grown up, Harry." Meg looked right at Harry, her light green eyes were determined. "Professor Hutchinson, I want you out of this place. Now, I've got to run."

They stood, she kissed him on the cheek, put on her coat and left.

CHAPTER 47

John had seen the young men twice and wondered if they were the same ones who had jeered at him on the subway car. He remembered the rage on the boy's face when he had grabbed his hand and twisted it until the boy gasped with pain; he'd humiliated the boy. Perhaps he was out for revenge. Boy? He was seventeen or eighteen.

John worked in the tennis court barn mending the spare net. Oak had come in for a chat and time had gotten away, so it was after six when he got on the Huntington Street trolley. He saw the boys at the Park Street subway station and they saw him. The four of them looked as if lightning had hit; they froze, then huddled by the concession stand. John got the car to Charlestown Square where he saw one of the boys but not the others. The boy was tall, wore a black jacket and had shiny black hair. John didn't want them to know where he lived, and although he was very tired and dragging his right leg behind him, he walked slowly up the hill to the Bunker Hill Monument where he sat on a bench waiting for the boy. A woman hurried by carrying a bag of groceries, and her child raced to catch up. The sky was gray-red but would soon be black. Cars rumbled over the hill with their lights on. John waited fifteen or twenty minutes and seeing no sign of the boy, made his way down to Washington Street to his apartment.

Supper revived him; he put on the Red Sox game and got to his weaving. The landlady often complained he had the radio on too loud so when he heard the knock, he assumed it was she. He unlocked the door and the four boys pushed in. Two grabbed his arms while another hit him in the face with the butt end of a baseball bat. John kicked the boy and pulled loose. The fourth boy, behind John, brought a bat down with all of his strength, cracking John's skull. John slumped to the floor.

When the police arrived, the landlady said she didn't get a look at who did it. "He musta' known them. I didn't let them in." They knew she was lying because she was frightened, but there was nothing they could do. Outside one of the cops said, "He's better off dead. Looked like a werewolf."

Ernie heard the news on the radio. "A badly deformed man, known only as John to his landlady, was beaten to death in his Charlestown apartment last night. The police are investigating." Ernie called Edie and together they went to Creighton to tell Harry. Dr. Popham told Harry he could go to the funeral.

Three days later, Edie, Oak, Harry and Ernie were in the minister's office at St. Matthew's Church in the South End. Ernie held the urn with John's ashes. It was nine-thirty; the funeral service was at ten. They were the only ones attending. The Episcopal minister, Fred Sanderson, a heavy man with an unruly black mustache, asked, "Did you bring his baptismal certificate?"

"No," Harry said. "All his records were lost. John was crushed and burned in World War I. When he finally got home, some drunks attacked him. John hit one of the men and the man died, so John wound up at the Massachusetts Mental Institution. A chaplain there took him under his wing and got him sent to Chile where he learned to weave. He came back and lived in Charlestown, and that's all we know."

"Was he baptized?" the minister asked.

Harry said, "I'm sure he was, but we have no records."

"I'm sorry," the minister said. "You'll have to go elsewhere."

Ernie wheeled forward saying, "Listen you son of a bitch…"

"Ernie!" Harry said. "We'll leave."

In the van no one said a word. Edie burst into tears. Ernie sat beside the driver, slamming his fist against the door.

"Fuck." Ernie said.

"Amen," Edie sobbed.

Harry said, "It is just as well. We'll have our own proper service when we decide where to bury John's ashes." They tried to talk but no one really wanted to. Harry was brought back to Creighton where he went to the library.

That afternoon Oak climbed the Big Tree where he sat on the branch of the Fourth Realm and cried. They had bashed John's head in. He'd never see Old John pushing the roller over the clay tennis court again or talk to him in the barn and hear his strange muffled sounds. Oak cried so violently he had to hold onto the trunk of the tree.

Oak remembered what had happened last Easter. After the eight-thirty mass he had gone into the Turk's spa for an ice cream. On Sundays the Turk's place was so crowded with men standing around it was hard to get through them. Oak went to the long white marble counter, got the Turk's eye and asked for a vanilla cone. The ice cream was frozen flat on top, had ridges down the side and tasted like no other vanilla. Oak got the cone and was suddenly aware he was part of all these people standing around. He didn't know them but knew he was part of them. He left the spa and knew he was part of the people walking on the sidewalk, part of the people going to the Protestant church across the street, part of the people in the cars going by—part of everybody everywhere and he felt light and happy.

Oak heard the thunk of someone hitting a tennis ball. John was dead. It was the fighters and killers who did well in the world.

While Oak was in the tree, Edie was home doing the wash. Later she helped Carrie and Monica with homework and called Craig asking him to come home early. Eight was early. They had a drink in the living room, and Edie told him what the minister had said. "My God," Edie said, "is that the best Christianity can do? John went through hell most of his life and this ass can't even do a funeral service."

"I'm sorry, Edie," Craig said. He was on the verge of tears himself. "John was a good man."

"He was more," Edie said. "He was a bright man, a weaver, and the bravest man I ever knew."

The next day Ernie called James Michael Curley at home. "Governor, it's Ernie Marion. I was Harry Hutchinson's campaign manager."

"Of course, Ernie. I remember you well. What can I do for you?"

Ernie explained about John's murder. "I think the cops have dropped it. Is there any way to put the heat on?"

"I'll make some calls, but the best thing might be to get some people to write letters to the newspapers. Give me your number. I'll get back to you."

The following week Ernie got a dozen people to send letters to the Boston newspapers asking why there wasn't an investigation into John's murder. The Lawrences were friendly with Bjorn Thestron at MIT who had received a Nobel Prize for Economics; his letter made an impact.

The police got John's landlady to talk. She told them that four boys around seventeen or eighteen had knocked on her door and forced their way in. They said if she said anything, they'd kill her. They called the lead boy Jimmy. He was big, wore a black leather jacket and had so much black hair piled up on his head it looked like a crow's nest.

Night after night, Ernie couldn't sleep right. He'd wake imagining shooting one of the boys in the kneecap before getting the last name of the Jimmy character. A Charlestown cop had played football with Ernie, and Ernie called him to find out the latest.

"We think we know who the kid is, Ernie," his friend said. "His name is Jimmy Manning. His parents say they don't know where he is. We're pretty sure one of the other three is a kid named Bobby Foster. We had him in, but he didn't crack so we had to let him go. The landlady isn't sure about Foster so we had no choice. Foster works at the car wash in Brighton."

Ernie had his driver park around the corner from Brighton Avenue. "Wait here," Ernie said. Ernie wheeled onto the Brighton Avenue sidewalk, a wide street with trolley tracks running down the center. On the right hand side a steep hill led to St. Elizabeth's Hospital, and on the left, set far back, were triple-decker houses. The Brighton Police Station, a great old stone building, anchored the street. There was no one on the sidewalk, which pleased Ernie; he wheeled himself toward the big kid coming from the car wash. Ernie judged the boy to be six feet and maybe two hundred pounds. The boy walked with a swagger; Ernie guessed it was his big black boots that gave him confidence. Ernie stopped his wheelchair and looked up at the leaves in the maple tree above him. When the boy was about to pass, Ernie blocked his way.

"Hey, watch it," the boy said.

"Fuck you, Foster," Ernie said. As Foster reached down to push Ernie out of the way, Ernie grabbed Foster's shirt and hit him so hard he broke Foster's nose. Ernie held onto Foster with his left hand and hit him again and again, then grabbed Foster with both hands, flung him to the sidewalk and fell on top of him. Ernie hit him until he was afraid he might kill him. Foster was gasping, blood running into his mouth.

"I'm a friend of the old guy you killed, Foster."

"Jimmy killed him" the boy gasped.

"Where is Jimmy?" Ernie hit him again.

"The Y."

"Which Y?"

"Huntington Avenue."

When Ernie got home, he washed the blood off his hands and face, changed his shirt, went into his bedroom and shook. He felt horrible. He had nearly killed the kid. Twenty minutes later his anger came back as he thought of John having his head smashed in. Ernie went to the closet, unlocked a small wooden box and took out his service forty-five. When Meg came home that afternoon, Ernie was cleaning his gun on his bedroom table.

"What are you doing with that?"

"Cleaning it. What's it look like?"

"You're going after John's killers, aren't you?"

"I'm cleaning the gun." He'd spread newspaper on the bureau and was squirting oil on the gun. Meg stood there almost unable to speak. She took a breath and said, "You're going to throw your life away on some hoodlums?"

"I'm going to shoot one of them in the knee cap. Then I'm going to smash his face so bad he'll look like John."

She began to cry, "Your father drank himself to death, and now you're going to shoot someone. Please, please don't."

Ernie picked up the gun and wiped the barrel with a cloth. "I called Sam; he'll be here with the van at eight."

"Could you please come into the kitchen and let's talk?"

Twenty minutes later Ernie came into the kitchen. She had made coffee and put donuts on a plate.

"Is it worth going to prison to get revenge?" She was sitting at the table. "You know what this would do to Professor Hutchinson, don't you?"

"He's done for anyway," Ernie said.

Meg looked at him, her face white with fury. "He changed your life. Now you want to throw it away. He thinks the world of you, and because of him you made a name for yourself. You managed a congressional campaign at twenty-six years old. Professor Hutchinson came in fifth which was a miracle after what his father did. And now you treat him like dirt." Her eyes were blazing with anger. She heard the knock on the kitchen door and went to get it. "Come in, Mrs. Lawrence. Thank you for coming."

Edie Lawrence was dressed in a long crimson skirt, a white blouse and paisley shawl. She looked elegant, gaunt and pale. Edie sat down at the blue wooden table opposite Ernie. "Your mother was kind enough to call," Edie said. "You cannot go and shoot this man, Ernie. You cannot. That is no tribute to John and it will destroy Harry. It will, Ernie. He seems his old self, but he needs time. Everything in his life has crumbled except us. We've stood by him…"

"And John's got his head smashed in."

"God damn, Ernie," Meg shouted. "Listen to her. I called because you won't listen to me."

Ernie, red faced, furious, began to laugh, "Jesus, it's a fucking Greek tragedy."

"It is," Edie said. "It is so sad. Can we not weep over John and kill someone else?"

"Just let the bastards go?" Ernie said.

"No," Meg said. "You told me the police were getting close."

Edie lit a cigarette and said, "They're getting close because of you, Ernie. You got the letters written to the newspapers."

"It was Curley's idea," Ernie said.

"And you called Curley."

The mood had changed; each of them felt that and let out a collective breath. Ernie lit a cigarette. "The kid who bashed John's head is hiding out at the Y downtown." Ernie's face sagged. He felt a terrible sadness because he'd nearly killed Bobby Foster. Ernie went to the phone and called the Charlestown Police Station.

Jimmy Manning was caught that night. The next day the *Boston Globe* reported that all four boys had been arrested and one of them, Brian Foster, had been treated for severe lacerations and a broken nose.

CHAPTER 48

Sunday afternoon the air was cool for the first of May and Edie, wearing a blue dress and wool sweater, shivered as she was hanging out the wash. The sky was clear, a robin sat on the Lawrences' tin green garage, and a gust of wind nearly blew a towel from Edie's hand. Craig, who worked seven days a week, was at the hospital.

Florence Beam, hanging out a white sheet in the next yard, boomed out to Edie, "We're on the high seas."

"Yes," Edie called, "there's Moby Dick."

Florence dropped the sheet and charged the fence like a great bull. "How dare you call me fat," she said. Her face was red and she shook.

"Oh no, Florence, I had no intention…"

"How dare you. Look at you! You heron."

It took twenty minutes to calm Florence down, and Edie retreated to her house. She called Craig at the hospital. "I am undone," Edie moaned. "All is misery." She explained what happened.

"Don't worry," Craig said. "She just needed to spout off."

"I'm undone," Edie said again. "I wanted to work in the garden. I cannot go out now."

"Raise the main sail and head for Nantucket," Craig laughed. "Really, Edie, it was unintended and she'll realize that. Oh, did you call about the theatre tickets?"

Edie made a cup of tea, peered out the window and was cheered to see Harry's red and yellow tulips bending in the wind. There was no sign of the great white whale. She took her tea down the narrow hall where the phone sat on a wooden shelf, lit a cigarette and called, "Diane, is that you? It's Edie Lawrence. Do you remember me from Harry's campaign?"

"Edie! Of course I remember you, Edie. How wonderful. Are you in New York?"

"No, but we will be in three weeks. Craig has a medical conference and we're staying at the Fairchild Hotel. We'd love to go to your show Friday, May twenty-fifth, and take you out to dinner afterwards."

"I'd love it. I'll put two tickets aside. How's everything? Is Harry doing well?"

Edie sighed, "He's had a long winter. I should have written."

"Is something wrong?"

"Harry's in an upper-class mental hospital."

"Oh my God! What happened?"

Edie could hear the shock in Diane's voice. She told Diane the story of the tulips night.

"They put him in an institution for planting tulips?"

"It's a long, complicated story." Edie said. "But he's fine now; in fact he's a little too fine."

"What do you mean?"

"The doctor wants Harry to work on his Washington book, but Harry keeps putting it off. He's put it off for months. He sits in a little room they call the library and writes letters he tears up. And he makes things. Two weeks ago he made a little boat out of popsicle sticks. Ernie brings him model airplane kits."

"Why doesn't he work on the book?" Diane's voice sounded as if she was holding onto a rope that someone was trying to pull from her hands.

"If Harry writes a few chapters, the doctor will probably say he's ready to leave, and then where does he go?"

"He'll go home."

"Jillian's agreed to a divorce. When Harry gets out they'll go to Reno and Harry will return and have no home. Northeastern let him go, and he feels the campaign was an awful failure. He doesn't say so, but I think he's scared to death of leaving."

"I'm coming up to see him. We're dark tomorrow. I'll take the early train."

"We'll meet you," Edie said, "Ernie and I. Harry would love to see you."

"I can't believe he's in a mental hospital." Diane was crying now. "I'll see you tomorrow. Thanks, Edie."

Edie hung up feeling terrible. "How awful. I should have called her months ago." She'd tell Diane about John tomorrow.

CHAPTER 49

After her performance that Sunday night, Diane tried to sleep but kept turning over thinking about Harry in a mental hospital. He's in a mental hospital for planting tulips. Can someone be locked away for planting tulips? Dear God, they can put someone away for that?

She switched on the light, put on her robe and went out to the combination kitchen-living room to make toast and tea. She sat at the formica table dipping her toast into her tea. Dear Harry. Did he have a nervous breakdown? I've got to see him. She began to think of Ernie. He reminded her of cut glass because he was tough and honest. Ernie, Old John, Edie Lawrence and Oak, seeker after the Seventh Realm.

Unconsciously she was drawing a tree with her fingertip on the table. She was a tree climber. The family story was that when Diane was three, her mother was taking her on a walk on the East side. There were three small trees on a corner and Diane said to her mother, "Look at the forest."

They moved to Brooklyn where they had a large tree in the backyard; the tree became her world, her stage, her ship, her flying carpet and her circus. She'd balance on a limb, leap to a higher branch, pull herself up and bow modestly to the applause of the thousands of leaves. In the eighth grade she ran away to the Ringling Brothers Circus and hid out for two days. Discovered, she was sent home and whipped, not literally whipped, whipped with her mother's voice. Her mother, Julia St. George, grew up in the Depression and had seen her family lose everything. She wanted Diane to grow up with money and power. "My God," her mother said when Diane was brought home, "You want to wind up marrying some carnival man? You want to have a miserable life like your father's?"

"It was a circus," Diane said, "not a carnival. I want to be a trapeze artist."

"Artist! My God, Diane, wake up. You have talent. You're going to college. Then you're going into the theatre and you'll love it. By the time you're thirty, you'll be known and have your pick of men."

Her mother's voice fascinated and terrified Diane; her mother's voice could rise and fall then narrow to a point sharp as an ice pick. Her mother's scorn sliced through all Diane's defenses and cut into her soul. Nothing she did was ever good enough. Even at Columbia she wasn't good enough, but then came a grand moment. Diane was Juliet in a production that the *New York Times* covered saying Diane was the best Juliet in years.

Tonight Diane traced the tree on her table and heard her little clock ring two o'clock. Juliet. *The Times* critic had come backstage and congratulated her. The night after the review her mother had a scotch and said, "You're on the way, Diane. Now you'll be somebody and you'll marry somebody with money. My God, Diane, you're finally on your way."

Diane basked in the moment, but it hadn't lasted an hour. When she was on her third scotch, her mother said, "You almost threw it all away on those circus idiots. My God! It's lucky for you that I was around."

Her mother said "God" with a scorn that was breathtaking. Tonight Diane wondered how her mother had learned to use her voice that way. Her mother knew so much about tone and sound; how in the world had she learned it? She was a dress designer who was hired occasionally to be a costume designer for some big shows, but she never acted. She learned it in the Depression Diane realized. The clock made the little bing sound, two-thirty. "The Voice," Diane said aloud. "I became an actress because of Mother's voice." This was such a revelation that Diane got up and walked around the table, shaking her head throwing her arms up saying, "Her voice. All those drama lessons I had. All those voice teachers. All the work, but it was Mother who taught me about voice and I never knew it." The phone rang and she jumped. Only two people would call at two-thirty in the morning, her mother and her fiancé, Peter.

"Hello," Diane said.

"Sheila?"

"You've got the wrong number," she said and hung up. What if Mother calls? Or Peter? I can't talk to them now. She took the phone off the hook.

"Peter's impossible," Diane almost shouted. "Impossible? Why can't I be honest? He's exciting, he's brilliant, but he's cruel. He's a cruel, selfish man who gets results but drives people out of the theatre. He has this awful power. I change whenever I'm close to him. I'll never just say 'I can't marry you.' I've got no guts." But it wasn't that she lacked guts, she knew that. It was a magnetism, a power, a persuasiveness he had. "Voice! He's got Mother's voice. He's got Mother's voice!" She shouted so loud she heard a bang on the wall from the next apartment.

Diane turned out the light at four in the morning. No sooner had she gotten into bed than she heard footsteps. "No, no, no, no." She knew that it was Peter back from an opening in Boston; he'd be wanting to go to bed with her. Success or failure, it didn't matter. What mattered was passion. No, not so much passion as sex and release. "Maybe it's not he," she thought even as she heard the key inside the lock. The light snapped on in the living room, and she heard his roaring voice, "The king returns in triumph!" His voice changed when he drank. He exaggerated the words and spread them out differently. His bugle effect, she said to him once. As she got up and put on her robe, he made the sound of a bugle. She went into the kitchen where Peter waved a bottle of scotch. "The best single malt scotch in all of New York. God, I whipped those stupid buggers into shape." Peter poured an inch of scotch, and she sighed in relief. Maybe he'd just have a nightcap and they could make love and he'd go to sleep.

"It was a great success?"

"It was, lass, it was. I began with a lot of dead wood but got rid of half of the buggers and got some proper actors in there. The king returns, lass, you're a lucky woman."

She could feel his power changing the room; vibrations came from his arms, his face, his laughter and his strange, wonderful eyes. She was changing. She was drawn to his awful power.

"You look beautiful, my dear," Peter said, "but you'll look even more beautiful without clothes. I pray thee, disrobe that I may look at the lovely forest between your legs."

"Peter, please, you've been drinking."

"No, my dear, don't *please* me, instead, *please* me. I use a bit of poetry and you blush."

"It's not your language, it's your tone. You make me feel that I'm...."

"You have a beautiful body. Get your robe off or I'll take it off."

She began, "I know you think you're funny, but you're not."

"Right now," Peter said, his voice changing, "you're taking off your robe and your nightgown and we are going to bed." He poured half a glass of scotch. He was angry, "I will count to three and if your clothes are not off, I'll tear them off. Do you hear me?"

"Yes, I hear you," her voice was cold with fury. "Don't you dare speak to me that way."

"Ah, the distraught damsel." He sipped his scotch, and she realized that he'd been standing all of this time. There was such force in this man; his eyes were a blue-green that could be kind one moment, imploring the next, playful and then suddenly violent and commanding.

"Pour me a scotch," Diane said.

"You must drink up quickly, my dear, because I'm horny as the devil himself. It's time to fuck."

Diane stood still, her fists tight, her breathing shallow; she wanted him out of her apartment.

Peter put his scotch down, opened his hands wide saying, "I'm sorry, Love. For five hours I've been thinking of you and now I behave like an ass. I'm sorry." His voice was quiet and his eyes soft, "You are so beautiful. You have a wildness that I cherish, and I can't wait to see you on the London stage." He touched her gently on the cheek. Her shoulders relaxed and there was the hint of a smile.

Diane woke at six-thirty realizing she'd have to hurry to catch the train to Boston. She dressed quietly not wanting to wake Peter, went into the kitchen and wrote the note. She had gone two blocks when she turned and ran back. She ran all the way up the stairs, slipped into the kitchen and ripped up the note and wrote, *It's over, Peter. It's been over a long time. We both know it. Yours, Diane.* She noticed the time and was afraid she would miss the train.

CHAPTER 50

The train was about to leave. Her red scarf trailing behind, Diane ran broken-field running the way she had when she played football with the boys on Kirby Street in Brooklyn; she dashed in between porters and men with briefcases; two old ladies dithered so Diane ran between the ladies leaving them gaping; on she went as a deep-voiced, big-chested porter called out, "All aboard for the 7:26 to Boston," but she had some fifty yards to go and there was a bevy of Boy Scouts maybe, sixty or seventy of them blocking her way, dawdling, turning and talking, led by a scout master in his forties who looked quite unmanly in his scout shorts, but it was he who called, "Ten hut," and the Boy Scouts formed ranks so that she could dash to their left. Now she had a clean shot at the train until a huge cart filled with trunks and suitcases blocked her way; she turned right so sharply her shoe came off, and she hesitated for a millisecond deciding whether to get the shoe or the train. The thought shot through her mind, I can't go to Boston with one shoe, but the train was leaving, so she kept running towards the now chugging train where the big-chested porter stood on the train stairs shaking his head, for it looked as if she wouldn't make it. Yet his eyes bulged encouragement reminding her of when she was eleven, the only girl on a tag football team with eleven boys. She had the ball and began the run of her life down Kirby Street with Mrs. Hammershmidt hanging out the window shouting, "Go girl, go," and Danny Kennilworth came at her all teeth and arms and grin because this would be easy; she pretended to lateral the ball to Jimmy Kosowitz and Danny fell for it so she got by Danny and had only two more boys to dodge and then she would have done what no one else had done on Kirby Street against Danny Kennilworth's team. The windows were all full of faces shouting, "Go girl, go" because Danny was so stuffed with himself they couldn't stand him and here was this eleven year old girl, who said she was going to be a trapeze artist, darting down the street electrifying the neighborhood. The train's rhythm picked up and Diane had ten feet to go; it was dangerous now because the train's speed was increasing, and she had only one shoe on, and her left foot hurt because she had stepped on a pebble or some-thing sharp. In that run against Danny's team she had to outwit Saul Levinson and Johnny Sanderson who tried to force her to go between them, and she'd done just that but with a burst of speed that caught them by surprise and caused Kirby Street to erupt because she'd done it. She'd done it and the street went crazy, oranges were flying, kids were jumping, and Mr. Konlen who hadn't said a word in five years kept shouting something in another language but it clearly meant, "Hooray, girl, you've done it" and Mr. Konlen was on his feet which was amazing because he hadn't been out of that chair in years. Memory gave Diane the juice to burst forward and put her hand on the rail of the train as her other hand grabbed that of the big-chested porter, who looked as if helping her was what he'd been born for, shouting, "Jump, I've got you," and she did. Behind her she left a cheering section that was not unlike Kirby Street but different, for now she had one shoe, a torn stocking and felt so out of breath she began to panic in the arms of the porter who wrapped his left arm around her with such force he squeezed out her air. She had been unaware of the scout master running along side throwing her shoe over her head where it landed safely on the train which made the whole thing better than beating Danny Kennilworth, and when she got some breath she hugged the porter, then turned and waved at the scout master and cried tears of joy, laughter and triumph. Those two, the porter and Diane, were wise, very wise, for Diane said, "Thank you" but no more because what had happened was too great for words and somehow they knew it, and he said in a formal baritone, "May I punch your ticket?"

When she did sit down she felt she'd been on a kind of trapeze and glowed all the way to Connecticut when she remembered she'd put her small overnight bag down at Penn Station. That dampened her spirits for about five minutes after which she burst out laughing and so did the big-chested porter who was coming down the aisle. She glowed all the way to Boston, and when Ernie Marion saw her get off the train at South Station, he began to laugh and didn't know why.

CHAPTER 51

Sam, Ernie's driver, drove Diane, Ernie and Edie to Creighton Hospital. A truck turned over so they were stuck in traffic for forty minutes, and it was then Edie told her of John's death. They got to Creighton so late that visiting time would be only fifteen minutes.

Harry was sitting on the couch in the main room. After greetings and strained conversation, Harry and Diane went out onto the porch which was glassed in but chilly. They sat on a couch and Diane held Harry's hand.

"You're cold, Harry."

"How's the show?" he asked.

"It's been fine but I'm beat. I'm glad it's only two more weeks."

"I'm . . ." he just looked at her for a while and then said, "I'm so glad to see you, Diane."

She was unable to hold the tears back. "I'm so sorry you have to endure this."

"I'm running for Head Man on my corridor," he said. "Old joke."

"I'm running after you," Diane said, "I'm not marrying Peter. He's an awful ass. He's marrying himself, and I'm sure they'll be very happy together."

Harry laughed, his skinny shoulders jounced and the bone protruded through the shirt. He grew very still, "You're not getting married?"

"Not to Lord Fathead," she said.

"Jillian wants a divorce," Harry said.

"I know," Diane said hugging him crying, "I love you, Harry."

Diane kissed Harry and they went back into the main room. Visiting time was up.

Getting into Ernie's van on the drive back Diane made conversation but was barely aware of what she said. They all went to Ernie's and sat at the kitchen table talking.

"Thank you all for coming with me," Diane said.

Edie Lawrence looked tired. She looked so tired that Ernie got up, got a bottle of scotch and poured a little into her coffee.

"One is sad," Edie said.

Edie moaned and then revived herself. She shook her shoulders saying, "One is sad. He's gone through hell, and this should never have been."

Diane slept at the Lawrences'. Their sausage dog, Bones, yapped every few hours, but it wasn't Bones that kept her awake. It was Harry. She wanted to go to Creighton, put her arm through Harry's and walk out. She needed him. Deep in the night she got up and looking out the window saw a policeman standing underneath the blue globe of the police box. She watched him call in and then walk off on his beat.

She was glad her show was closing in two weeks; she needed the fresh air of Maine.

CHAPTER 52

It was June and raining. Diane sat on the couch of the Sitting Room with Harry. She wore dungarees and a bright red shirt that reminded Harry of his Aunt Harriet. "My Aunt Harriet," Harry said, "died breaking in a horse when she was seventy. She always said you have to leave to arrive."

Diane looked as if she were going to burst and then said, "We could buy that house in Maine, Harry. The orchard house."

"How would we live?" he asked.

"I'll teach drama somewhere, maybe Bates or Portland High School. You can write and we'll sell the apples."

"But you want to act."

"I love teaching, Harry, and I love you, and I want children. You can finish the book. The house is for sale for four thousand dollars. It's a steal."

"How do you know?" Harry asked. Her face shone. Her dark eyes had that gleam he loved.

"I called Higgins Inn. Jim Summers, the proprietor, told me an old woman owns the orchard house. She's in a nursing home and relying on word of mouth for the house to sell. We could do it, Harry. What do you think?"

"We could," he said. "We could. Jillian wants to sell our house. She's agreed to give me a quarter of the sale. That might mean two or three thousand dollars." He held her hand and looked over her shoulder because Elijah, his roommate, was on the far side of the room praying in a singsong voice that got so loud a nurse went over to him. Diane, on the edge of the couch, looked so excited Harry thought she'd bounce off. "I talked to Ernie," she said. "If we provide meals and beer, some of his friends will help us fix up and paint the house."

"The upstairs floor may be gone," Harry said. "The upstairs window was open, remember? And the chimney's shot."

"There's no structural damage," Diane said. "We've had it looked at."

"What do you mean? Have you been up to Maine?"

"We went up in Ernie's van. Ernie, Oak, Edie Lawrence and two of Ernie's friends."

"You all went up?"

"Yes," she laughed and squeezed his hand. "It is too good to pass up. A house with an orchard by the ocean in Maine." She blurted, "I put four hundred dollars down."

"You what?"

"I bought it," she said. "Don't be mad. Jim at Higgins Inn told us a man from New York was looking at the house. I had to, Harry. We can always sell it."

"Why would we sell it?" Harry said. "We're going to live there." They hugged on the couch, as patients drifted to and fro like dazed goldfish on a hot day. Elijah wailed. Harry had his ark.

CHAPTER 53

It was cool on the first of October when the four of them made their way from the farmhouse down the gentle slope toward the orchard. Seagulls sat on the waves far below. Oak and Harry had dug the grave the day before. Today they dressed for the occasion: Harry in a dark suit, Ernie in a sports jacket. Diane and Edie wore long black dresses, Oak wore khakis, a white shirt, a tie and a crimson sweater.

Oak was given the honor of pouring John's ashes, with slivers of bone, into the grave. A gull swept by overhead and Edie quoted George Herbert:

Who would have thought my shriveled heart
Could have recovered greenness?

She stopped because she was crying and unable to go on. Ernie said something they couldn't hear. Harry wiped his tears and said, "We start anew, John. You were the kindest of men. And the bravest. Your youth was taken and replaced with deformity, but you lived to create beautiful weavings. You honored us in the campaign. You were a kingly man."

Later, Diane whispered to Oak, "Maybe the Seventh Realm is reserved for people like John."

That afternoon they got to work on the farmhouse.

CPSIA information can be obtained at www.ICGtesting.com
Printed in the USA
LVOW061955271111

256666LV00003B/1/P